Brenda Houghton has been a jou........ and editor for more than thirty years, working on numerous magazines and newspapers including the *Guardian*, the *Observer*, the *Mail on Sunday*, the *Sunday Times* magazine and *Cosmopolitan*. Her interest in the subject of this book came about from her research for two articles about teaching children right from wrong she wrote for *She* magazine and the *Independent on Sunday*.

She is married with five children – two adopted Kenyan children from her husband's first marriage, two step-children and one daughter of her own.

THE
GOOD CHILD

How to Instil a Sense of
Right and Wrong
in Your Child

Brenda Houghton

HEADLINE

First published in 1998
by HEADLINE BOOK PUBLISHING

10 9 8 7 6 5 4 3 2 1

ISBN 0 7472 7748 6

Typeset by
Letterpart Limited, Reigate, Surrey

Printed and bound in Great Britain by
Mackays of Chatham plc, Chatham, Kent

HEADLINE BOOK PUBLISHING
A division of Hodder Headline PLC
338 Euston Road
London NW1 3BH

Contents

Foreword

This book arose from overhearing my small grandson saying, 'That's not fair.' I realised he was absolutely right and wondered where little children get this strong sense of justice from – are they born with it? I started to investigate by looking under Ethics and Morality in the baby books but found nothing. So I explored more widely and discovered that there was a lot of fascinating research being done into how children learn about morality, but most of it is written by academics for other academics. This is my attempt to bring their findings to the attention of the workers at the coalface, the parents and teachers who are trying to raise decent children. I hope it helps.

To save confusion, it is tempting in a book about parents and children to call the child 'he' and the parent 'she'. However, I did not want it to seem that only boys have moral dilemmas, so I have referred to the child as 'he' and 'she' in alternate chapters.

Acknowledgements

This book would not have been possible without the help of a host of professional people who gave up some of their precious time to answer my questions and point me in the right direction. Of course they are not responsible for the views expressed and conclusions reached, which are my own. I am particularly grateful for their kindness to: Elisabeth Boyle, probation officer, Southwark, London; Professor Nick Emler, Department of Experimental Psychology, University of Oxford; Professor John C. Gibbs, PhD., Department of Psychology, Ohio State University, Columbus, Ohio; Dr J. Mark Halstead, Reader in Moral Education, University of Plymouth; Dr Helen Haste, Reader in Psychology, University of Bath; Graham Haydon, course tutor for the Values of Education M.A. at the Institute of Education, London; James Hemming, consultant psychiatrist and broadcaster; David Ingram, Director of the Norham Foundation (Working for Personal and Social Responsibility); Mary Midgley, moral philosopher, formerly of Newcastle University; Rowan Myron-Wilson, Department of Psychology, Goldsmith's College, London; Jan Newton, Citizenship Foundation, 63 Charterhouse Street, London EC1M 6HJ; David Rowse, head of Values Education for Life, University of Central England, Birmingham; Roger Straughan, Reader in Education at the University of Reading; Dr Monica Taylor, Senior Research Officer, National Foundation for Ethical Research; David Weeks, clinical neuropsychologist at the Royal Edinburgh Hospital; Professor John Wilson, Senior Research Associate,

Department of Educational Studies, University of Oxford; John Woods, consultant psychotherapist at the Tavistock Clinic, London and Professor Derek Wright, psychologist, former Professor of Education, Leicester University.

Lastly, thank you to Daisy, Jane, Irungu, Mary and James Houghton for providing the hands-on experience of raising decent children and making the experience so rewarding.

Prologue

Imagine the maternity wing of a hospital at midnight. The mothers have finally managed to snatch some sleep, the babies twitch and dream in their cots.

One has a thatch of dark hair hanging like a soft scarf across his forehead. His neighbour is almost bald, her shapely head touched with just a shadow of downy fluff. A tiny, low-weight baby pulls faces in his sleep as if struggling to make sense of some problem. His bony neighbour opens and shuts her mouth as she dreams, ever ready for the return of the nipple.

Looking down on these tiny newcomers to our world, it is hard to imagine who will become the tinker, the tailor, the beggarman and the thief. Which one will grow up to be decent and wise – and which of these brand-new children will end up as a villain or a brute?

Every new-born baby is another chance for civilisation, an opportunity to start society anew and make it better. We now know a great deal about what makes children grow up to be good. Here is how we, the adults, can make it happen.

Chapter One

Babies and toddlers: starting in the cradle

In an ideal world, all children would be born aged twenty-one, clutching a degree. Instead they arrive helpless, speechless, messy and very demanding, and while it takes no skill or even sense to bring a child into the world, being an effective parent requires patience, imagination, tolerance, humour and love in such huge measures that it makes the survival of the human race seem a pretty amazing achievement.

Somehow most parents, even if their baby is the first one they have ever handled – and in the modern, dislocated world this is quite often the case – make a pretty good job of the physical side of things. Their babies are properly fed, decently clothed, get their vaccinations on time, have their feet measured, their eyes checked and their diet supervised.

However, there is more to raising a child than just keeping them healthy and helping them with their homework. As parents we are responsible for the growing child's moral education too, and this is much trickier. Let's start by looking at the raw material. There tend to be all sorts of ideas rattling around in the back of people's minds and many are contradictory. Some parents believe that a new-born baby is like a little blob of clay, to be moulded into shape by its parents and other adults as it grows up. Others believe the opposite: they regard their baby as an intellectual giant who arrives already determined to boss his parents about and bend them to his whims, and think they must engage in a battle of wills from day one to outwit the tiny monster.

If we look back at history, it is equally confusing. The Jesuits, for instance, favoured the idea of the baby as a blank sheet and asked only for the first seven years to fill it with all the rules. The Puritans saw the child as an antisocial savage who would only be made to recognise other people's rights by rigorous training from earliest infancy. Calvinists were convinced that the child was born full of sin. The French philosopher Rousseau argued that if you left the new-born infant entirely to its own devices for the first two years of life, the baby would just naturally grow up to be good, and Wordsworth and the Romantics rather sweetly thought that babies came from Heaven, trailing clouds of glory.

All these different and contradictory ideas about the baby matter because they affect the way parents treat their new arrival. That is important because, unlikely as it may seem, the way you handle your baby in the first couple of years will have a profound effect on his moral development.

Taking stock
So what do we have, down there in the cradle? There has been an explosion of research into the early development of children in the past twenty or thirty years and we now know that babies are not blank sheets of paper. Their brains are already set up to seize any experience offered to them to help them make sense of the world in which they find themselves, and this brain has enormous potential. One day it will be able to reason, calculate, judge and assess things for itself and quite possibly outwit its parents.

However, the baby can't reason, calculate or assess in the first weeks of life. In the early days his brain is still struggling to make sense of the flood of sensory information suddenly pouring in now that he is outside the little world of the womb. Sights, sounds, tastes, noises, touches and temperatures flood his consciousness every second and the infant magically starts to make sense of it all, day by day, week on week. The blurry world of colours and shapes that the

4

new-born sees is very soon organised into 'face' and, since all babies love company, greeted with a smile. The sharp sounds and soft whispers that he hears are sorted out and put into order as 'voice' and, if it is the mother's voice, something even a very tiny baby soon recognises and is pleased by.

As well as brains, babies also come fully equipped with characters and moods, as every parent knows. Each child arrives with a predetermined genetic inheritance. Some of this is physical – his looks, allergies, bodily strengths and weaknesses will depend on his genes – but personality has a genetic element as well. Whether a child is sociable or grumpy, serene or twitchy, cuddly or fretful, is plain to his parents from the start and, although his personality can be profoundly modified by the treatment he receives as he grows up, the broad brush strokes of character are in place from the moment of conception.

There is, however, another element that confuses our behaviour as parents: the idea of the 'good' baby. When someone remarks of a baby, 'Isn't he good', they do not mean that here is an infant philanthropist, a baby Barnardo. They mean this is a baby who sleeps through the night without a fuss, feeds enthusiastically and is not sick too often. However, this baby is not good – he is just easy. If he stays up screaming all night and throws up the mother's lovely milk, he is not bad either – he is just having a difficult start.

It would be an amazing baby who could, in its cradle, formulate an idea along the lines of: 'That is my mother and we're in a battle-of-wills situation here and I'm going to win.' For quite a long time, the baby doesn't know who or what a mother is, and it knows nothing at all about alternatives and choosing one sort of behaviour over another. The baby knows only one option: survival.

New-born babies do not have a moral character. How do we know? Because to be morally good involves choice – you cannot *be* good by accident, though you may *do* good by accident. A person can only truly be described as honest if they understand that one statement is true and another false

5

and then choose to tell the truth. You are fair if, weighing up the possibility of giving yourself the largest piece of cake, you then share it out equally. Of course, a lot of our choices are made in a flash because we have been well brought up, so we tell the truth or help others without a second thought because that is the type of person we are. However, that sort of behaviour has to be learned. It is quite a difficult, grown-up activity, and it is beyond the mental capacity of new-born babies. They are having trouble making out individual faces. They can't speak. They can't bring their little hands together at the same time to grasp their rattle effectively, and there is absolutely no way they can work out what is good behaviour and what is bad.

So, it is important to accept that while babies do have wonderful brains and can learn about the world around them at a dazzling rate, no baby has the capacity for moral choices. He is not capable of lying in his cot deciding, 'Shall I be a pest today or not?' Undoubtedly some babies are a lot more trouble than others and if you happen to have one of the tricky ones whose first weeks or months are pretty fraught, that is hard and exhausting and you can be excused for feeling fed up with your lot. None the less, your baby is not 'bad', he is just difficult to manage, and there is no justification for condemning him.

The baby will become easier – more of a 'good' baby – if you are loving and always on his side. The latest research shows that if parents are sensitive and respond quickly to their infant's needs, he is soothed and happy and will cry far less than a baby whose parents ignore him. For parents concerned about their child's future moral welfare, the news is that it is impossible to spoil a baby. In fact, loving your baby wholeheartedly is now known to be the first essential factor in the growth of a good citizen.

The unselfish gene
If you find it hard to imagine that surrounding a tiny baby with love and attention is directly linked to his future moral

behaviour, let us look at what we now know about the way that goodness develops. If we accept that babies are neither good nor bad, but just struggling to make sense of the world, does this mean that goodness arrives later like a parcel? Is it triggered by a hormone as we grow, like sexual maturity? Surprisingly, it seems that we are born already equipped with a potential for goodness. Just as a new-born baby comes complete with leg muscles and will one day stand up and walk, so he comes with the seed of a concern for the welfare of others already planted and that, too, if it is encouraged, will develop and grow.

This is not the view of human beings that has become familiar through fashionable evolutionary theory. Many recent books have argued that the reason the human race has evolved and survived successfully for millions of years is because we are essentially selfish, driven by the primitive biological need to perpetuate our genes in competition with our fellow men. To serve this end, goes the argument, our basic instinct is to grab the largest share of resources that we can get our hands on, to seize any and every chance to procreate, and to ignore anyone else's needs if they interfere with our own fundamental drive.

According to this view of human behaviour, we only desist from selfish behaviour under extreme pressure from outside, pressure that we naturally resist. It is hard, looking at the selfishness, greed and violence that rages through the world, not to wonder with a sinking heart if perhaps the strongest instinct is, indeed, the drive to put the individual first, last and foremost, and that perhaps morality is an unnatural and doomed addition to our lives.

However, many of us, when we test this theory against our own experience, find that it somehow feels wrong because we do not feel ourselves to be blindly rapacious, totally without scruple or unaffected by the needs of others. Does this mean we are just wimps, failing members of the species, doomed to die out ultimately because we are not tough enough to survive? Or is it the evolutionary theory that is wrong – perhaps it does not offer a complete answer to the complexity of human behaviour?

If we say that everyone is driven to prosper at all costs, regardless of others, we ignore one crucial fact, which is that human beings do not manage very well on their own. Darwin long ago drew attention to the fact that weak animals are never found living alone, but always in groups – and human beings are pretty feeble. We lack speed and power, the sharp teeth of the carnivore and the sharp eyes or acute hearing that warn other species of danger. Poor weak humans need a whole battery of tools to guarantee our existence. So, from the moment our ancestors first stood upright on their back legs, we have had to live together in some group – the family, tribe, nation or what you will – because that increases our chance of survival. The leopard may walk alone, but the leopard can fight his own battles; we cannot.

All the recent evidence suggests that *homo sapiens* evolved as a group-living animal and that this was the key to our survival. Alfred Adler, one of the founding fathers of psychology, explained: 'In the history of human civilisation, no way of life has emerged where the foundations were not laid communally. The whole animal kingdom demonstrates the fundamental law that species whose members are individually incapable of facing the battle for self-preservation gain additional strength through herd life.'

This need to live within a community affects our behaviour, for like every other creature that lives in groups, an individual human sometimes has to act in a way that serves the interests of the majority rather than his own desires. Every creature whose life depends on being part of a herd, a flock, a swarm or a shoal develops behaviour patterns that help it to live in peace within the group. Pecking orders or tail-sniffing prevent aggression; having one of the herd keep lookout while the rest graze keeps it safe from predators; and any creature who fails to observe the group rules is driven out.

Thus over millions of years, alongside the basic urge of the individual to survive at all costs, human beings have evolved altruistic predispositions too: the ability to be responsive to the needs and feelings of those we live among. This is the basis of the pull we feel between two opposing forces which we call good and evil. The drive to do only what is best for ourselves pushes up against our understanding that we must sometimes do what is best for everyone else. As the moral philosopher Mary Midgley explains: 'Even animals do not act only out of self-interest. The bird that feeds its young day after day, and drags its wing to decoy away an aggressor, is acting for the good of the next generation not its own. Though they are following instinct, that instinct is unselfish.'

Since living in a community gives us our best chance of support and protection, babies are born with an innate drive to form social relationships and establish contact. This sociable feeling remains throughout life – changed, coloured or circumscribed in some cases, enlarged and broadened in others – until the grown man feels linked not only to his immediate family, but also his extended family, his fellow citizens and, finally, the whole of humanity. The unselfish gene has enabled the human group to survive as long as it has. Concern for others comes naturally: all you have to do is encourage it.

Making friends and influencing babies
In order to foster that concern for others that makes a decent adult, we have to start by helping the baby to make friends with other people from his earliest days. It isn't hard, because they are born friendly.

By videoing babies and studying the results, researchers have realised that babies come already equipped with a range of social skills which enable them to attract attention from any human who passes within range. They do not just respond to our coos and chatter, they actually initiate contact. A baby lying in a crib will pull a face or wave a tiny fist, trying to catch someone's eye, and if you come close and cuddle the baby, he will make tiny adjustments in his position to imitate your posture. If you smile or stick out your tongue, the baby will struggle to smile back, or stick out his own tiny tongue. If you hold up a mirror to a baby, he will smile and make friendly gestures to the baby in the mirror. He won't realise it is his own reflection until he's about eighteen months old. Instead he thinks he sees a friend and will try to communicate with him and after four or five of these experiences, he will really enjoy the friend-in-the-mirror.

So, you don't have to teach a baby to respond to other people, because he is born with that urge, but you can do a lot to encourage the process. As the infant makes little contributions to society – a smile, a clumsy gesture, or a sucking noise indicating readiness for a feed – the sensitive mother picks up on this and reacts and this is the beginning of co-operation and social sense. If you keep a close eye on your baby and respond to his overtures promptly, he will be pleased at his success, feel encouraged to make further advances and so, with every friendly encounter, he becomes a more sociable child. If you truly love your baby you will get the very best results, because love makes us extra-sensitive to the other's feelings and quicker to respond to their moods and wishes.

However, babies love to copy you, so beware of what you show them. If you do something interesting, the baby tries to see if he can do it too, but if your behaviour is boring, or if the baby is already sure he can do it through repetition, he won't copy your actions. A baby, like the rest of us, wants stimulus and novelty, so if you show him bad behaviour and it is new to him, it will surely be copied. If your angel child suddenly does something awful, stop and see if you can trace it back to something you or someone else did in his presence recently. It might have been quite inadvertent: if, for example, you slapped your husband playfully on the wrist because of something he said, don't be surprised if your baby suddenly slaps you.

Tears and bliss

However, no baby's relationship with its parents is all plain sailing. A new-born baby does not always make contact with charming little waves and gurgles. As he lies in the cot, physically helpless, bombarded by lights and noises, conscious of hunger, cold and damp, the baby feels powerless, scared and in need of help to deal with it all. So then he cries out for help and reassurance. Now if you or I were in floods of tears and a relative or friend came by, we would expect them to rush over, ask what was wrong and do their best to comfort us. That is caring or just plain courtesy. Yet some parents feel quite cavalier about ignoring their baby's cries. Excuses range from the ludicrous, 'he needs to exercise his lungs,' to the confused, 'I don't want him to grow up spoilt and whinging.'

At the root of the failure to respond is a misunderstanding. Instead of seeing the situation from the baby's point of view, such parents see the relationship with their infant as a battleground, where they and their baby slug it out for dominance. This is nonsense. Your baby is not lying in his cot thinking to himself, 'I'm going to show who's in charge around here.' That's beyond him. All he knows is that life is getting him down and he should summon help. Crying is the way that babies are programmed to do this, and they are programmed to cry relentlessly in case help is some distance away. When I lived in Africa the newspapers occasionally carried stories about new-born babies found abandoned in pit latrines who were only discovered because someone heard their cries, and we have all heard of cases where babies have been found in the wreckage of an earthquake or car crash because rescuers heard a persistent wail.

The 'battlefield' school of thought says, 'Don't pick up a crying baby and he'll eventually stop because he'll realise no one is coming.' But Nature got there first and said, 'Keep on crying and eventually someone will appear in the haunted forest and rescue you.' Ignoring a baby never shuts it up. Worse still, leaving a sobbing baby unattended fosters the parents' self-centredness and teaches other children in the

11

family that the baby's needs are not important, and that their parents believe that misery can be left unassuaged.

The good news is that though babies are programmed to cry, they are also programmed to learn. If a baby gets speedy attention when he cries, he learns that one way of communicating – crying – has worked, so he immediately sets about experimenting with other methods of getting in touch, because he is human and loves to try something new. The best breakthrough in communication is the great gummy smile that appears after a few weeks, but parents and babies get a lot of fun out of other sorts of close-up communication too: tickling, kissing, stroking and pulling faces.

A baby who lives in this intense close harmony with its parents, wrapped in comfort and security, discovers how wonderful it feels to be among people who are loving and supportive. It is a feeling of absolute bliss, and the baby can only experience this wonderful sensation directly, at first hand; you cannot describe it to him in words. This experience is crucially important to his future moral behaviour because it is the experience of a period of bliss that leads to the development of a conscience later on.

When a baby starts out feeling loved and appreciated by the most important people in the world, he will want to hold on to that feeling. For the rest of his life, both as a growing child and as an adult, he will try to recreate that wonderful feeling of belonging and being loved. This passionate desire for other people's approval is the first brick in the foundation of the child's moral sense. So, first and foremost, a moral child needs all your love, because unless you get under his skin and form that close attachment, you will not be someone whose opinions and values are desperately important to him. Your prime task in the first years of life is to provide that love in bucketfuls.

The birth of guilt
Though it is convenient to write as if the child is being brought up by its mother and father, the baby does not care

tuppence whose love he can rely on and respond to, just as long as the love is there. Babies can be attached to lots of people – the biological parent, an adopted, foster or step-parent, grandparents, brothers and sisters, carers and neighbours – but while it does not matter who the baby interacts with, it is crucial for there to be some individual with whom he is involved in a loving relationship if he is to develop a sense of guilt. The child needs a sense of guilt if he is to grow up decent, because guilt is the starting point for our conscience.

'Guilt is laid down early by parents creating anxiety either through withdrawal of love, or just by being shocked by the child's behaviour,' explains Dr Helen Haste, a psychologist at the University of Bath who has studied children's moral development for over twenty years. 'That's important in the avoidance of sinful acts.' What happens is that as the child learns from his daily experiences that certain behaviour meets with rejection, he grows anxious about the possible withdrawal of the love he values so much and becomes afraid of seeing the adult he loves shocked by his behaviour. This blend of anxiety and fear in the infant is the first pang of guilt.

This is a crucial development because it is guilt that gives rise to that uncomfortable feeling we have in certain situations of not being a very nice person. This guilty feeling is something the child must have experienced, disliked and will therefore want to avoid in future. If he discovers how wretched it feels to be found wanting by the person he loves most, then, when he is faced with the opportunity of misbehaving as an adult, he will refuse because he wants to avoid experiencing all those miserable feelings again. The sense of guilt in the small child grows into the voice of conscience in the adult, the conviction we have that we are not someone who would do a certain thing because it would make us feel uncomfortable.

If a child does not grow up with lots of loving approval, he won't care about anybody and won't develop a conscience. Of course he will come into contact with other adults who have expectations of how he should behave, especially at school. A teacher, however, cannot get close enough to a child to create that intense emotional discomfort which will linger in the child's mind as something to be avoided. That can only come from wanting to be accepted as good by someone whose love is needed more than anything else in the world and that means the parents. Since most children learn the attachment that draws them into the moral world through their close early tie to their mother, it does put a great moral weight onto her shoulders in the early years.

What happens when things go wrong?

Sadly, some babies get precious little help in their attempts to connect with the world around them. An insensitive parent ignores or overlooks the baby's attempts to communicate because he or she is tired, or wrapped up in their own affairs, or angry about the baby's demands, and this failure to find an attachment makes the baby disheartened. No matter how long he cries, no one comes to check on him. If he gurgles and smiles, no one responds.

A child brought up in a family that is flawed, or in a bad institution, does not get the chance to learn how making a social overture can lead to a pleasant result. Any attention he receives will depend on the whim or energy of his parent, or be according to the clock in an institution, regardless of what he does. If he does attempt to make contact, the response may not be a smile but verbal or physical abuse. So he comes to believe that he is helpless, because his efforts get no results. He stops demonstrating his social skills because they are ignored and little by little, for lack of response, his sociability withers and he becomes quiet and apathetic.

Children who are neglected and ignored lie passively in their cots – not because they have been well brought up, but because they have given up. If nothing is done to give a baby the experience of being loved it will be very difficult for him in later years to make friends and feel he is a member of the community, and if the child doesn't feel he has a vested

14

interest in society, one day he will turn against it.

Does this mean that a baby unlucky enough to be born into a lousy family is doomed to grow up antisocial and wicked? Well, he will certainly run that risk, but it is not inevitable. Fortunately, life does not often run in a straight line and families are not set in stone. Many parents, for instance, find some ages more comfortable than others, so the mother who is impatient or anxious with a tiny, needy baby may find it easier to respond to the lively toddler he grows into and then there is an improvement in the parent-child relationship. If the mother has been having a difficult time and is feeling exhausted, things may improve and then she can cope better with the child. If there has been fighting at home, perhaps over finances or all the other stresses of modern life, these problems may be resolved. The mother may not feel so trapped at home if she can go out to work a bit, or a new friend may cheer up the parent. Grandparents and other relatives may appear on the scene to offer an interlude of love and affection. Later, teachers can make a contribution. Life changes all the time so children do get second chances of happiness.

A change for the better in the child's circumstances can make a dramatic difference. Reports on the tragedy of the Romanian orphanages have shown that even these desperately deprived children can begin to pick up the threads of normal life if they are given sufficient love and care. Children in this country taken out of abusive families and placed in decent foster homes can make new lives for themselves. Children are amazingly resilient. If their lives remain deprived and miserable, it will be hard for them to grow up straight, but given a chance, the infant wounds can heal.

Baby rage

It is wrong to imply that the relationship of parent and child is one-sided, with all the innocence and sweet nature on the infant's side. Babies are not angelic. As paediatrician and child psychiatrist Dr D.W. Winnicott wrote: 'A normal child pulls out all the stops. In the course of time he tries out his power to disrupt, to destroy, to frighten, to wear down, to waste, to wangle and to appropriate. Everything that takes people to the courts has its normal equivalent in infancy and early childhood.'

Babies are swept by passionate feelings of love and hate and frustration and the strength of these feelings scares them. When a baby tries to sit up and topples over, when he wants to settle down to sleep and cannot catch it, when he is hungry and nothing is available, out comes the primitive anger, fuelled by his sense that he is surrounded by an overwhelming world which he cannot cope with by himself. It is these feelings of fear and powerlessness that make him lash out. All babies have aggressive or destructive urges and will scream and bite and kick and pull their mother's hair.

From the very earliest months a baby can and should be discouraged from behaviour that is unwanted: no biting people or pulling their hair. You can do it gently and without violence. That may seem blindingly obvious, yet a large number of parents don't seem to believe it. A survey in 1994 revealed that over half the parents in Britain (and nearly three-quarters in Scotland) have actually hit a baby under twelve months old. They justified their violence with statements like, 'Well the baby was bad and had to be taught a lesson,' or 'You can't let them get away with it.' Often they had smacked the baby not because of some mess he had made but because he was crying, as if the baby's distress was indulged in solely to annoy the parent, and he could be silenced by causing him more distress.

Violence is always unacceptable – and unnecessary. Provided you have established a close and loving relationship that the baby delights in, then all that is needed is for Mum or Dad to frown, make a sad face or turn away and that will be enough to shock him into realising that he has come up against a barrier. Even a very young baby can sense that a particular deed is unwelcome and could lead to a terrible result: the loss of the mother's love. What the baby dreads most is rejection, being thrown out of Paradise. As long as you've made your baby feel loved and secure, then if he sees that what he is about to do will provoke your disapproval, that is all it will take to make him change his ways.

This is why you cannot love a child too much. You may be afraid of 'spoiling' him, but that implies damage and though you can damage a child by giving him too much food, too much excitement or too much freedom, you cannot give him too much loving attention. Babies whose parents are most responsive to them are the most obedient babies: it's as if a degree of trust has been established, and the confident baby will fall in with what Mum wants.

Drawing the line
As the baby grows into a toddler, he starts to challenge the orderly adult world more vigorously and more often. Toddlers don't agree with us about what is nice and what is nasty. They burst open our pleasant, orderly world. They are fond of squelches and messes, hate being washed and take a delight in pulling the cat's tail or their brother's hair. While you may feel you can afford to wait for them to grow out of a love of making mud pies, pulling his brother's hair has to be curbed from the beginning – but it has to be done sensitively. The network of rules you put around small children should seem like a support, not a strait-jacket.

It seems hard for some parents to get this right. If you hang about outside any nursery or playgroup as the parents turn up to collect their children you will soon see that motherhood brings out the sergeant-major in some women. You hear them yelling orders as their toddlers rush about brimming with youthful vigour: 'Stop that, put that down.' The purpose is not to protect the child, but to bask momentarily in a feeling of being in charge. Perhaps it is because many women feel powerless in their own lives that they have to boss their little children around when they have the chance.

It's nothing new. The great Swiss psychologist, Piaget, wrote sixty years ago: 'How can one fail to be struck by the psychological inanity of what goes on: the efforts which parents make to catch their children in wrong-doing instead of anticipating catastrophes and preventing the child by some little artifice or other from taking up a line of conduct which her pride is sure to make her stick to; the multiplicity of orders that are given; the pleasure taken in inflicting punishments; the pleasure taken in using authority.' One could wish that more had changed.

All of us find it a daily struggle to cope with boisterous toddlers. Professor Nick Emler, a social psychologist at Oxford University says, 'Research suggests there is a critical period between two and four when children become more mobile, can move around and get into trouble and into things they shouldn't be into, or that you don't want them to get into and one piece of research showed mothers or caretakers tell a child of this age not to do something about once every four minutes!'

You must try to be fair in drawing a distinction between protecting the infant and restricting him. A baby's nature is to reach out, crawl off, pick up and knock down as he stretches his muscles and his capability. Before popping him into a playpen ask yourself whether you are doing this for his own safety or because it makes life a lot easier for you? This doesn't mean you have to give a toddler everything he demands in order to produce a secure and happy adult. That's not true! Life is all about giving on the one hand and taking on the other and the child must learn both.

Children's play must be accommodated somehow, because play is how they learn about the world; play is, in a sense, the child's job and it is unprofitable as well as unkind to curb the toddler's natural instinct to explore. However, the adult's natural need for some peace and quiet also deserves recognition and the best way to achieve it is through low cunning and good anticipation.

A colleague of mine on the business section of a Sunday paper came in to work one day and described his frustration when he came down to breakfast and found his two-year-old daughter had picked up one of the newspapers and was refusing to let go. She had, of course, chosen the pretty pink financial paper he needed most. 'There was nothing I could do,' he said in bewilderment. 'I could of course have smashed her into the ground, but short of that I was helpless.' His wife was not sympathetic: 'She just said I shouldn't get into a battle I couldn't win!' What he should have done was be devious: as soon as he saw the baby had his paper, he could have picked up another toy, pretended it was enormous fun and she would have reached out for that, dropping the paper with no problem.

Cunning should be the watchword of the parent of toddlers. Rather than smacking a child for trying to stick his fingers in the electric socket you can buy a set of rubber plug covers and let him loose in safety. Rather than take a baby into the magical world of the supermarket and then nag at him to sit quiet and not copy you by reaching out for things, leave him at home with a relative or neighbour on a reciprocal basis, to get on with his childish affairs. There are dozens of ways of living in peace with a toddler if you put your mind to it. If you know he's going to hate leaving his toys to come out with you, hang on and have a cup of coffee until he's finished his immediate game: his attention span is only about five or ten minutes and then he'll welcome a new activity.

Temper tantrums are an inevitable part of being small and not very co-ordinated. The toddler feels angry because every obstacle he meets appears exceptionally difficult if not insurmountable. All the mother can do is contain the aggression – surround the child with things that are firm but soft, until he learns to control the destructive side of his nature. What the toddler also needs, in these angry moments, is for his parents to draw the line and teach him that certain things are not allowed. Don't worry that this will make him frustrated: it won't. What it does instead is reassure him that there is a strong and powerful person in charge of this vast, frightening world, and that there is a framework of love and strength around him, protecting him and keeping him safe.

Sometimes conflict cannot be avoided, because little children will do dreadful things, and when this happens *both* parents' response has to be consistent. It is no good mum looking cross when her baby kicks her if dad roars with laughter and tells him he's another Ian Wright in the making. You cannot have the framework in place one minute and move it aside the next. Infants who do not know what is expected of them have no idea what to do and what to avoid. Children often receive confusing or ambivalent signals from their parents and it makes them confused and ambivalent themselves. In fact, it makes them start to treat the rules with contempt. There is a great body of research to show that inconsistent discipline in childhood is one of the chief causes of delinquency later.

Sometimes one parent is strict and the other one lax, or one parent or both may swing from one extreme to the other depending on the mood they're in. If the mother yells at the child for smearing his dinner over his hair one day, and ignores it or finds it funny the next, the baby ends up not knowing what on earth to do. Eventually he will give up trying to please his parents and just do as he feels instead, and that will lead to trouble.

Winning favours
The point of discipline is to encourage the baby and toddler to enjoy behaving in a way that makes people comfortable having him around. As he learns that putting his food into his mouth instead of his hair earns goodwill, but that pinching or biting people meets with disapproval, he will choose to do the things that earn a good response because that makes him happy and in this way he learns to take account of the views of society. Roger Burton, Professor of Psychology at the State University of New York points out that it isn't too difficult to keep a sharp eye on your toddlers: 'When children are small, you can often

watch what they are doing even when they think their behaviour is hidden or disguised, and this gives you the chance to link your disapproval to their misdeeds before the child's behaviour is reinforced by too much misconduct.'

He points out that if bad behaviour is allowed to flourish disregarded for a time before punishment is introduced – for instance, if you allow a toddler to get away with murder thinking you'll start imposing a moral code later on – you're in danger of falling into a pattern of alternately rewarding and punishing the same acts and this results in behaviour that will be extremely difficult to extinguish or modify. Professor Burton adds, 'It is also important to welcome any moral responses the child makes during this early period. Lots of the time your child is doing particular things which you can praise by saying something along the lines of, "You're a good child to share, or to help, or to be so kind." '

Once your baby learns to talk, you can help to nourish the development of a moral sense by giving him the proper words to describe his own behaviour. When he's very young, the child's world is divided into two parts, good and bad, and we say things like 'No, no,' and 'Naughty' to mean 'bad' at this stage. These simple words do stop the child from performing a specific misdeed, but they do not help him to perceive that some new situation falls into the same category. Once your child is a toddler, you have to start using abstract moral terms, so he can learn to respond to different situations in the same way. For instance, if you say: 'That's stealing,' when your toddler takes his big sister's sweets and then again if he walks off with someone else's toy, he learns that stealing means taking something that isn't his. Of course it will take a long time, and many examples, before he fully understands that this particular behaviour is stealing, but labelling the crime is a real help.

Curbing the child is only one side of the coin. If bad actions are frowned upon, it is crucial for good behaviour to be rewarded. John Woods, a consultant psychotherapist at the Tavistock Institute in London, explains: 'Badly-behaved toddlers are the result of parents who punish bad behaviour but fail to offer anything positive in response to good deeds.' In this situation the infant learns a dangerous lesson: that if he wants to get his parents' attention – and every infant does – he must behave badly. It is all too easy for the harassed parent to overlook those moments when a baby gets it right, and perhaps take them for granted, but at the start, each bit of good behaviour deserves praise and approval, because that makes the baby feel terrific. He will repeat his good behaviour again and again so he can experience another glow of approval. The more you emphasise and reinforce his good deeds, the more often you will see them.

Raising a brave child

Psychiatrist and broadcaster James Hemming describes what Alfred Adler learnt from his work with children. 'We all begin our lives small and weak in a world of adult giants, so that the first message of the environment to the child is: "Overcome your weakness! Make your mark! Be someone who matters!" ' Hemming explains that this is what activates the infant, and it is fine if his experiences build courage and confidence as he explores the surrounding world and makes contact with the people in it. However, if all his efforts to be recognised as a person in his own right are greeted by misunderstanding or hurtful criticism – by lack of love in other words – the child will be driven to the conclusion that he is not as good as the others and is flawed in some dreadful and dispiriting way. Then he will retreat into a fantasy world of dreams, or a compensatory pretence of some kind.

Since none of us live in a perfect world, and since parents can only do the best they can, all children fall into grief at times and take refuge in fantasy. They may have an imaginary friend; they may dream that really they are the offspring of a king and queen, accidentally dropped into this poor-quality home, from which they will one day be rescued. We've all had these experiences, and most of us grow out of them as we develop a more realistic assessment of what we can reasonably expect from the world about us.

So from our very earliest days we pick up the idea that we have or have not got what it takes. If those around us offer us love, encouragement and understanding, we will acquire confidence in our own personal value and capacity and will set out to make the most of our abilities in life and in open relationships with other people. If, however, we are led by neglect, rejection and criticism to distrust what we are, we turn to some false way of impressing others, who we may see as a threat. Whichever lifestyle we pick up unconsciously when we are small and vulnerable, we tend to cling to for the rest of our lives.

What can be done? 'Encourage the young child,' Adler used to tell people, and 'Help the young child to come out on the useful side of life' – that is in work, friendship and love. This encouragement must start in day-to-day living, in courageous encounters with the world outside: courageous because the child is tiny and the world huge.

Encouraging your child to succeed in his little daily endeavours does not mean that you have to indulge his every whim. Infants have to learn that the adults around have wishes too and, because he wants to keep their goodwill, it pays to humour their demands. Babies are, in fact, very obedient. Research shows that at the age of one, nearly 70 per cent of a mother's commands are obeyed – a success rate you will look back at with envy when your child is older and has a mind of his own. Even more interesting, mothers who are most responsive to their children receive more obedience than those who are less responsive: good behaviour is nourished by kindness.

Small expectations
As the baby turns into a toddler, struggles onto his feet and learns to say a few words, little by little he gets an idea of himself as a separate individual. A new-born baby cannot distinguish between himself and his mother: he thinks he and you are one and the same thing, undivided. The toddler

gradually realises that he is a separate and special person, that things happened to him in the past and are happening to him now. If you ask him his name he can answer: 'John', with a laugh because the question is so easy. As he realises he is a separate person, he realises there are other separate people in the world too. If you ask, 'Where's Daddy?' he will point triumphantly in the right direction.

As he becomes aware of other people, the toddler also becomes aware of the state of mind he is in. The ability to feel other people's emotions as well as our own is known as empathy and it is a vital step in the making of a moral person. Though early child development experts insisted that children have no awareness of anyone but themselves for their first four years or so, recent research shows this is not true. There are signs of empathy even in infancy: studies show that babies will cry and show other signs of distress in response to hearing the cries of another infant (and it has to be *another* baby: if you play back a recording of his own cries, it won't have the same effect). Observations of young children have shown that spontaneous acts of caring and sharing are actually fairly common.

Professor Martin Hoffman, a child psychologist at the University of Michigan, explains how empathy grows in the toddler. For instance, one day a child cuts himself, feels the pain and cries. Later he sees another child cut himself and cry. The sight of the blood and the sound of the cry reminds the child of his own experience of pain and conjures up the unpleasant effect that was part of that experience, so he feels the other child's distress quite vividly. As the child's range of experiences increases, he comes across more and more distressful experiences with which he can empathise.

However, though the toddler can feel a genuine concern for another child, there is a long way to go before he can recognise that other people are not just separate but different from himself. A young child knows how he is feeling and believes that everyone else is having the same experiences. You can see this early confusion in action at a mother and baby group. A toddler sees another child crying and it triggers off the memory of his own distress, but the toddler can't fully understand what is going on. He can feel the other child's misery but he doesn't know yet how best to alleviate it. So he will get in a muddle in his efforts to help, which usually consist of giving the other child what he finds most comforting himself. For instance, he may hurry across to offer the unhappy child his teddy bear. What he does not understand is that what makes him feel better will not make someone else feel better. His teddy bear will not comfort another child. The toddler cannot understand this: he knows teddy helps.

Professor Hoffman says, 'I have heard of a thirteen-month-old child who brought his own mother to comfort a crying friend, even though the latter's mother was equally available; and of another child the same age who offered his beloved doll to comfort an adult who looked sad.'

So a toddler simply behaves in a way that has alleviated his own distress in the past. You cannot expect him to realise that what he's doing might be inappropriate for the other person or to tailor his response to his friend's needs. That's asking too much. None the less, these feelings of empathy are a critical step in the right direction. The desire to relieve our uncomfortable feelings by comforting or helping a person in distress is the start of altruism.

The inability of the toddler to understand that other people are not only different but may have different feelings also explains why small children can seem to hurt one other quite gleefully. It is very upsetting for a mother to see her beloved offspring make another child cry, and even laugh about it, but it happens. The consolation is that it is not due to some dreadful innate wickedness in your child, but simply because his understanding is still very limited.

Take a common situation in any nursery school. There is a little boy whose parents have taken him swimming from babyhood. He has had lots of fun splashing about and has been encouraged to enjoy getting his face wet and ducking underwater. He feels confident and happy playing with water.

25

At nursery he is drawn to the water games and starts to spray water about, soaking everyone else and bashing his hands down flat on the water to splash his small neighbour in the face, shrieking with joy. Meanwhile the neighbouring child is bawling with fright and misery because she has had no experience of having fun with water and finds it cold and scary.

The adult's instinct is to leap up and yell at the boisterous child, 'Look what you've done, you've made her cry, that isn't nice.' But this is not fair. The little boy knows that it *is* nice, it feels great – that is what his experience has been and it is all he knows. You cannot expect a toddler to understand that what amuses him may frighten someone else, because at this age he is incapable of doing that. All you can do is separate the two and let them each enjoy the water in their own way.

Since a toddler believes that everyone responds in the same way he does, it is also fruitless to ask, 'How would you feel if she did that to you?' Parents will do this, trying to make the child less self-centred, to encourage a concern for others, but you are wasting your breath with very young children. The toddler is only aware of his own feelings; he cannot yet imagine that another child might feel differently. So, although you have to be alert and ready to intervene to prevent a toddler inflicting grief on a companion, you must accept that he won't understand that he is doing anything wrong. Understanding will come in a year or two. For now you have to impose good behaviour on children by gently removing or distracting them from troublesome situations, so they learn the pattern of good behaviour while you wait for their reason and understanding to develop.

Interlude
The bag of virtues

One of the problems we face when we talk about morality is that most of us aren't very sure exactly what it is. It's not like biology or maths or history, which we had at least some experience of at school. Though there is a body of material about morality called ethics, most of us have never read it and our idea of what constitutes moral behaviour is a muddled conglomerate of what we were taught at home, school and possibly church, and of beliefs we've worked out for ourselves by thinking and arguing about moral issues such as euthanasia when they hit the headlines.

So let's clear the air a bit by looking at what morality might be. Because we humans have a passion for order, and feel driven to tidy up the world into patterns and classifications to make it less chaotic and more predictable, we have attempted throughout history to reduce morals to a simple formula such as the Ten Commandments or the Golden Rule: Do as You Would be Done By. Such formulas are often underpinned by obliging people to behave well for fear of a jealous god, or because it is their duty, or because that is the way a just society works.

Most of us accept a moral code which says that certain things, like honesty, justice and keeping your promise, are good. The problem is that teachers, parents, children and society at large all have different ideas about what else qualifies as good behaviour. There are important issues,

27

which are clearly moral problems, where decent people disagree, sometimes vehemently – for instance, over capital punishment, single parenthood or civil disobedience.

So what is virtue composed of? The dictionary definition lists moral excellence, uprightness and goodness, but that doesn't help you to decide what characteristics can be called excellent, upright or good. Probably more people today can list the seven deadly sins (pride, covetousness, lust, anger, gluttony, envy and sloth) than the four cardinal virtues (justice, prudence, temperance and fortitude) – and what about the theological virtues: faith, hope and charity?

The bag of virtues

When American psychologist Lawrence Kohlberg started investigating moral development in children, he likened the different ideas people hold about morality to a bag of virtues, a pick 'n' mix collection of goodies that people in a particular society have gathered together and put a value on. Aristotle's bag of virtues, for instance, included temperance, liberality, pride, good temper, truthfulness and justice, whereas a 1920s American code listed honesty, service and self-control. A bag dating from the 1940s put in responsibility, friendliness and moral courage and the boy scout bag incorporates concepts like loyalty, reverence, honesty, cleanliness and bravery.

What the bag shows is that the idea of morality is not some monolithic, permanent creation set in stone, but changes from time to time and place to place. We are surprised to see that Aristotle considered pride a virtue since the Christian tradition places it among the deadly sins, and where American researchers have found that in the early years of the twentieth century 'sexual regularity' (that is, married heterosexual activity) invariably topped lists of virtues, it scarcely gets a mention as a moral imperative today.

Religious figures have offered their own bags of virtue and children born into a Christian, Muslim, Jewish, Hindu or Buddhist family usually grow up with a code of behaviour based on those teachings – but something cannot be right merely because the Bible, Koran, Torah or Bhagavad Gita says so. If you base your behaviour on that, you are merely being obedient, not moral. Obedience to a given code is not morality. Morality always implies choice: we are only moral if we see that we have the option of doing good or doing harm and choose to do good. In order to make a choice, we must think for ourselves.

Research into the behaviour of believers has found no relationship between their morality and the type or the amount of religious education or participation they received or practised. In today's society, the atheist is just as likely to be good (or bad) as the believer, and we have to remember that many of the world's worst atrocities have been committed by believers, often in the name of their god.

Various collections

Religious leaders are not the only ones offering advice on morals: philosophers have their own bag of virtues. Kant's bag contained his categorical imperative, which said that when you are about to make a moral decision you should ask yourself, 'What if everybody else in the same situation were to do the same?' and go ahead only if you decide, 'Yes, I think everyone should do as I am about to do.'

Jeremy Bentham and John Stuart Mill devised Utilitarianism, which held that you could measure right and wrong by the amount of pleasure or pain a proposed course of action would produce. They argued that morality demands that we should do whatever offers the greatest good to the greatest number of people. However, pleasing people doesn't necessarily equate with virtue. What if we feel we should pursue a course of justice, or fight against a case of injustice, even when such an act would be uncomfortable or even personally dangerous? There are times when the individual must make an individual choice, when simply going along with the majority is not enough and is no excuse. How can you follow the Utilitarian principle if the greatest number of people hanker after something immoral? For instance, a lot of people take pleasure in demonstrating race prejudice against a minority, but that does not make it good.

The Romantic view of the world held that children are born innocent and pure, and people like Rousseau, or A.S. Neill, the founder of Summerhill school, stressed a rather biological model of healthy growth as the way to raise good children, claiming that to teach them the ideas and attitudes of others would interfere with the spontaneous growth of the child's virtue. The Romantics tended to put the child's happiness before its intellectual development, preferring a happy dunce to an unhappy thinker, but happiness and ignorance are not virtues and decisions made happily and ignorantly are unlikely to be moral; respect for the child's liberty must involve giving him the freedom to learn so he can choose his own eventual path.

Philosopher John Rawls suggests a more modern bag of virtues and puts in three beliefs about how morals are tied to social responsibility. First, each person has a right to certain basic liberties compatible with everyone having them. Second, any inequalities of income, status, privilege and power have to be justified in terms of the benefit to those with least income, status, privilege and power. Third, though people are unequal in a number of ways, justice requires that rewards and punishments should be distributed fairly and that those with particular advantages should use them for the benefit of those least advantaged: so the strong should help the weak, the healthy the sick, the intelligent the less intelligent and so on.

You may have found a bag of virtues bulging with social concern nudging into your own life in the form of one of the home-school contracts that many parents and schools are signing up to. The contract usually sets out what sort of behaviour is expected from both sides, with the school listing actions like 'will encourage children to be independent and responsible for their possessions', 'maintain a positive behaviour policy among all pupils', 'demonstrate that each pupil is valued as an individual' and 'provide a well ordered and caring environment' while the pupil is expected to 'try to get on with others within the school community'. Underlying these contracts is the assumption that everyone will agree with them. The problem is that the collection of virtues is often put together by a committee and too often, if one member wants self-discipline while another values spontaneity, the list includes both. The end result is an unwieldy and often contradictory collection of good intentions, and when the Royal Society of Arts did a survey of them it found 'many actual examples are either too vague to make sense, or too detailed to be of practical use.'

Picking the right mixture

Some people argue that moral education involves preaching a particular set of virtues which the community is committed to – honesty, responsibility, service, self-control and the like. The difficulty is that what the community regards as right varies. For instance, while pretty nearly everyone condemns dishonest behaviour and believes that lying, stealing or cheating are wrong, research shows that almost everyone believes it would be right to lie to spare another's feelings; a substantial number say it would be right to steal medicine if it was otherwise unobtainable in order to save someone's life; and a considerable minority believe it is alright to take towels from hotels, glasses from pubs and so on.

You can't simply divide the world into honest and dishonest people. The general agreement about the goodness of honesty and integrity hides a lot of actual disagreement over how you apply them. One person's honesty in expressing her feelings is another's insensitivity to the feelings of others. One person's integrity is another's stubbornness. Almost everyone cheats at some time in their lives, but research shows that just because a person cheats in one situation, it doesn't mean he will (or won't) in another. People's verbal approval of honesty may have nothing to do with how they act. People who cheat express just as much moral disapproval of cheating as those who don't cheat.

31

If a fairly simple concept like honesty gets complicated when you apply it to particular circumstances, other virtues are even more easily confused. Motorway protesters, for instance, think they are demonstrating virtues such as idealism, concern for the planet and courage, but their opponents believe these actions demonstrate a selfish determination to force their views on others, and contempt for the law.

Some virtues conflict with others. For instance, most communities recognise that all their members must be accorded equal rights – but just because you respect the rights of particular groups in society, such as those of people from a different culture or religion, this does not mean you have to accept that their values are equally worthy. While we must respect the rights of even someone like a serial killer, and thus grant him a fair trial, we don't have to accept his warped set of values. Respect for the right of other people to hold different moral beliefs doesn't mean you have to respect the values of the Nazis or the Ku Klux Klan, which are based on the denial of the rights of others.

Although what goes into a bag of virtues does differ from time to time and place to place, that does not mean we can't make universal moral judgements. Just because the Romans approved of leaving their unwanted babies to die on the hills outside the city and we do not, doesn't mean that infanticide was right for them but wrong for us, or that it is neither right nor wrong for everybody. We can condemn it as wrong for them and for ourselves.

What the different bags of virtues do show is that putting together a collection of rules and requirements and calling them morality is not enough. What you choose to put into your bag of virtues has to be weighed up very carefully: making moral decisions is a thought process, not a gut reaction.

Do we need a bag at all?
Though people have been drawing up moral codes throughout history, are they missing the point? Professor John Wilson

of the Department of Educational Studies in Oxford, thinks so. 'Some people, perhaps particularly older people, are emotionally attached to a very clear picture of a definite morality with a definite content. "Morality" for them means things like obeying the law, being sexually pure, loyal to one's country, respectful towards religion and so on. Moral education for them means persuading (or indoctrinating) children into adopting those values.'

Professor Wilson points out that young people react pretty strongly to this picture. 'Morality' for them means something like, 'what other people tell you to do', or worse still, 'what adults want to foist on you'. They dislike the idea of moral education because they imagine it means imposing a particular set of values.

'What both have in common is the idea that morality has a particular content,' says the professor, 'a set of given rules, perhaps laid down by some authority, but anyway somehow *theirs* and not of *our* choosing. The first group of people accept this and wish to promote it. The second resent and oppose it.' He points out that people do tend to favour moral content, that there's a deep desire to make sure that people do or don't believe in The Family, or in heterosexuality or whatever, but that these various items of content change. 'It's no good trying to get a consensus about what the content should be. Not so long ago there was a consensus that slavery and the subjection of women was perfectly OK.'

Seeing morality as a simple bag of virtues is seductive because it suggests that anyone can be a moral educator, that any adult of middle-class respectability knows what virtue is and is qualified to teach it by dint of being adult and respectable. However, being good yourself does not automatically make you a good teacher. It is tempting to try and build children's character by exhorting them to practise certain virtues, saying that if they do so happiness, fortune and a good reputation will follow in their wake, but this approach to moral education doesn't work. Appealing as the idea might seem, you cannot inject moral ideas into a child like a whooping cough vaccination because children are quite confident of their moral knowledge already. They think it is wrong to hunt foxes or whatever: they have strong views. The idea that children feel ignorant and are eager to absorb the moral wisdom of adults is one that any parent or teacher knows is nonsense.

What children need to be taught is not *what* to think but how to think about moral issues: how to resolve competing claims between individuals fairly and kindly. In this respect it can be helpful to think about what you would most want to put into your own particular bag of virtues, and to discuss it with your children. Clearly what goes in yours might not be what I would put in mine. Some parents would want to include friendliness and courage. Others may leave these out but put in self-control and stoicism. You might want to include meekness, perseverance, self-denial or self-development – and is respect for authority always a virtue or only sometimes? Is cleanliness truly next to godliness?

You can't expect your children to swallow your ideas of morality whole – they will question and struggle with every one of the virtues you hold dear – but talking to them about what you believe in gives them something to reflect on as they grow and mature and, little by little, build up a moral universe of their own.

Chapter Two
Three to five: getting into good habits

'It's not fair!' Do you ever feel with a sort of despair that children must be born knowing right from wrong as the piping clamour for justice bounces off the walls? Ask your child to go to bed before her older sister, absentmindedly win too many cards off her when playing Snap, and the plea for a better world rings out: 'It's not fair.'

Well, the child is not alone. The search for a just society has engaged moral philosophers from Plato to the present day and is undoubtedly one of our deepest intellectual quests. Nevertheless, children do not arrive in the world already furnished with a Citizen's Charter Guide to right and wrong. They have to be taught what is morally good and bad and, until they are capable of reason, adults must teach them. It's not like teaching them about dinosaurs and mathematics, where you can pick up a pen and paper or put on a video and show them what you are talking about. Morals don't have faces and children can only learn what abstract ideas like 'honest' and 'kind' mean by real-life practice and example.

So now that you have survived the exhaustion and emotional surges of baby- and toddler-hood and sailed into the smoother waters of the pre-school child, what is your next task? You have given the baby tons of love and security to get her off to a good start. What comes next on the moral agenda?

Manners versus morality

Before you start, it is helpful to sort out in your own mind
what you mean by right and good. Everyone has some idea of
what they mean by goodness: it tends to include things like
honesty, justice, forbearance, loyalty, kindness, integrity, consideration for others and the Golden Rule – do unto others as
you would they would do unto you. However, all the time we
are struggling to get some of these concepts into our children's heads, we are also trying to get them to bath themselves and eat nicely and pick up their toys and not tear strips
off the wallpaper. It is hard to keep clear in your own mind
sometimes, never mind the child's, which issues are moral
and which are social: which behaviour carries a moral
imperative and which simply makes the child more acceptable to the neighbours.

Roger Straughan, a lecturer in education at Reading University who has studied the way in which schools can teach
morality, quotes an example of the muddle children can get
into. A primary school class was asked by its teacher to write
down, 'What is the worst thing you could possibly do?' When
the teacher collected in the papers she found that some
children had written 'murder someone' while others wrote
'run in the corridors'.

Part of the code of conduct we want our children to
adopt is concerned with manners rather than morals. Manners are, to some extent, a family affair. It may be the rule
in your house that no one leaves the table until everyone has
finished eating, while the family next door may feel free to
get up from the table as soon as they please. You may
believe your way is preferable, but you cannot say that it is
morally right. Morality always has in it some element of the
general, the universal. Honesty, for instance, is expected of
your family, the family next door, people across town,
everyone in the country, and all those abroad: every society
draws a distinction between telling the truth and lying.
Whether I turn my fork over to eat my peas is my concern
and is a question of manners. Whether I tell the truth

concerns my fellow men and is a moral issue.

So it is important to remember the moral issues as you press on with all the other tasks the parent is burdened with. Of course good manners are important and help to ease our relationships with other people. None the less, while it may be hard to imagine someone who has high moral principles yet who is rude and ill-mannered, it is all too easy to think of people, some of them public figures, whose manners are exquisite and whose morals are a disgrace.

Fair's fair
Probably the best place to start teaching little children that there are rules governing how we should behave with other people is with the idea of fairness, if only because, as we have seen, children are obsessed with it. What you need is a training ground where you can show the child that there are things called rules which everyone must observe, otherwise the one who breaks the rule has an advantage and that is unfair. An easy training ground at home is with simple card games and board games.

You will have to be patient at first because, left to her own devices, a child of nursery age will not be fair. Professor Barbara Tizard of the Thomas Coram Research Unit in London points out: 'Four-year-olds are quite capable of understanding the rules of a simple game, but find it difficult to accept the constraint of taking turns, of not cheating, and winning or losing with good grace.'

Though a three- or four-year-old has usually developed sufficient intellectual capacity to understand how to play a game, she will not yet have reached the stage where she can understand the point of all the rules. As an adult, you can appreciate that unless you follow the arcane regulations of a particular game, the game is pointless: meeting the rules is the challenge. A young child, however, just sees the rules as an impediment to reaching the end result, so she will often cheat, and be outraged if mother is so careless as to let herself win. 'Fair' to a four-year-old means she gets everything.

37

So what you have to do is to encourage the child to observe the rules, take her turn and play the game fairly, and show her that if she breaks the rules and cheats the whole game is spoilt. It won't happen overnight: like all forms of learning, it takes lots of repetition and plenty of inevitable failures before the message is driven home.

At first your child will want to skip a stage in the game if she keeps failing to throw a six, or is getting a bit bored, and there is no harm in being lenient occasionally so that she continues to want to play and thus gets the practice she needs. Indeed, if you are not too competitive yourself, it can pay to let her win when she does obey the rules, as a reward for her good behaviour and to encourage her to play fair the next time. If your conscience will not let you bend the rules whatever the reason, or if you cannot bear to lose even to a four-year-old, try playing Pairs, a favourite game with small children where pairs of picture cards are spread out face down and turned over two at a time, any pair being kept. Years of experience have shown that any small child can defeat any adult at this in a humiliatingly short time, while following the rules.

Yours, mine, hers

Sharing things out equally is another aspect of fairness that little children have to learn and, again, it is not something that comes naturally. If a child is playing with one of her favourite toys and a friend comes up thinking, 'That looks nice, I think I'll play with that,' and takes it from her, uproar will ensue.

Often the child's mother is embarrassed by what she sees as her offspring's selfishness in refusing to lend her toy, and tries to prise the beloved object out of her clutches saying, 'Let Laura have it for a bit, you've been playing with it for ages. You can have it back later.' Unhappily, these wise remarks have no effect because the child has no understanding of a situation in which someone else has rights in her toy, and no concept of the future in which the toy might be returned. She is only aware of the here and now, and the feeling of loss. So you can't expect a small child to share something as personal and precious as her toy: you should aim instead to distract the newcomer with something else.

In order to teach the child to share, it's best to start by getting her to practise with something which is not as emotionally fraught as her toys, such as a packet of sweets. If you ask a child of four to share some sweets out fairly, she will make quite a good fist of doing so, though she will probably pop one or two extras on to her own pile almost instinctively. A small child's own needs are still paramount to her and it is hard for her to imagine the needs of others.

John C. Gibbs, Professor of Psychology at Ohio State University explains, 'When little children are given candy bars to distribute, to test how fair they will be, they will often allocate more for themselves and if you ask them why, they'll unabashedly say, "Because I want them," or "Because I like this kind of candy bar." In other words, she thinks, "What's fair is whatever I want." ' Pre-school children are biased in favour of themselves. Their needs or desires are so strong to them that the rights or expectations of anyone else are overlooked.

However, they are not totally selfish. Research shows that small children do enjoy sharing out things to eat with their friends, even if they don't do it brilliantly well, which is why foods like crisps and tangerines, which are small and come in lots of easy portions, are especially popular with little children. So you can help your child to start acting fairly by giving her things that she will enjoy sharing with her friends. You do need to check that she does it properly, but if you insist that she shares out the snacks equally, deals out the cards fairly, takes her turn in the game and lets her playmates do the same, you will engender a habit of playing fair and not cheating which the child can follow until she is old enough to understand why fair play matters.

Getting into the habit
In moral matters as in any other human activity, practice makes perfect. As Aristotle said, 'We become just by doing

just acts, temperate by doing temperate acts, brave by doing brave acts.' In the moral sphere you can only learn by doing and the more often your child does the right thing, the stronger the habit will be engrained.

A three- or four-year-old cannot grasp the principle of fairness by learning it off by heart and then applying it; she must discover it through practical experience. She will need to have many experiences of fair and unfair events before she can start to see that there is a pattern, and grasp that there is a moral concept called justice. However, long before she understands the ethics of a situation, your child can be encouraged to do the right thing even though she is too young to understand why she should. This helps because if children get into the habit of behaving properly it affects their long-term good behaviour.

For instance, in an experiment with kindergarten children, Erwin Staub, of the University of Massachusetts, divided them into pairs and asked them to play out a scene in which one child needed help and the other child provided the help, then he changed them about so each child played both parts. He also told the children about the positive consequences of being helpful – that adults would approve of their behaviour and that the child they helped would be grateful to them.

What he discovered was that simply playing the part of a Good Samaritan boosted the children's willingness to help on subsequent real-life occasions when their help really was needed, while acting out the role of the person in distress made the children more ready to understand and empathise with other people in distress. The children had to perform the actions, however, for the experiment to succeed. If they just had Staub's lecture without acting out the role, there was no improvement in their subsequent willingness to help others.

This shows that children must learn to do the right thing when they are young, even before they understand why such acts are thought right, and then they will carry on doing the right thing as they grow up. It also shows that you cannot rely on sermons and instructions alone to instil a sense of right and wrong in young children. Speeches simply wash over a child's head. You have to begin her moral education by ensuring that she *does* the right thing, and does it over and over. Her good habits must be both consistent and regular.

You can reinforce her good behaviour by explaining the reason why she should behave in the approved way. For instance, rather than just telling a child to give up her seat to an old man on the bus, you can explain to her that she should do so because the old person is frail and she is strong and it is only fair to stand when she can do so more easily. Then the child will associate her good behaviour with your lecture and absorb it. If, at the same time, you praise her and point out how her action is benefiting the old man and how grateful he will be, it will make her feel important and researchers have found that feeling important also encourages children to behave well.

'But for a child to feel warmly towards others, she needs plenty of experience of other people to boost her understanding,' says Roger Straughan. 'If she has seen her own mother carrying through a pregnancy, been aware of how tired she got sometimes and how she longed to sit down, she will be more understanding of the pregnant mother on the bus and more likely to offer her seat. If the only old man she has met is the bad-tempered old bloke on the corner, she will be less tempted to help old men.'

For this reason, the child's sympathy for other people will be encouraged if you bring her into contact with a wide variety of other people, and bad behaviour will be discouraged too, as her understanding grows. Just helping your child to meet lots of people, young and old, neighbours, friends and family, will foster her ability to relate to all sorts of other people and this will make her want to behave well towards them.

In other people's shoes
Empathy, the ability to identify with others, is crucial to our moral development. It is not the same as sympathy. Sympathy

41

is when you think, 'I know how I'd feel in that situation.' Empathy is when you think, 'I know how *you* feel in that situation' – which can be somewhat different.

Alfred Adler describes the feeling vividly: 'Empathy occurs in the moment when one human being speaks with another. We all know the involuntary movements people make when someone has dropped his glass! Another common example is the involuntary application of imaginary brakes by the passengers in a motor car whenever they feel they are in danger. And when a public speaker loses his thread and cannot proceed, the audience feels uncomfortable and embarrassed. This ability to act and feel as if we were someone else is universal, an inescapable characteristic of being human, inborn in us.'

By the time a child is four or five, she has become capable of understanding other people's feelings as well as her own. Professor John C. Gibbs explains how you can turn this to advantage: 'One of the most important techniques by which parents can foster a motivation to act morally is where you tell the child how she, or her transgression, hurts another person. A very young child may need an explanation like: "If you keep pushing him, he'll fall down and cry." Another might be: "Don't yell at him. He was only trying to help." Such messages can encourage the child to look at a situation from someone else's point of view.'

Of course other emotions also affect the child's response to your words: there is her desire to secure your love and approval and there may be an element of fear of your power. Both of these reinforce her willingness to listen to what you are saying, but the primary emotion is still empathy. If you say to your child, 'Don't yell at him. He was only trying to help,' it directs her attention to her friend and she then notices her friend's hurt feelings, takes her friend's perspective and feels distress for her suffering. Furthermore, because you have made her understand that she caused her friend's suffering, she may experience guilt. Both the empathy and the guilt suffuse the message that you don't hurt someone who is trying to help you, and this makes it emotionally charged and turns it into a powerful motivating force.

Doing what Mum and Dad do

As the child slowly develops the ability to see things from someone else's standpoint, it enables her to become an unselfish and considerate person. However, the single most powerful influence on her behaviour remains your own example. Children copy everything about their mothers and fathers, and there is a sex bias: studies show that boys between four and six prefer to imitate a man rather than a woman. The fathers' role and behaviour was very important to the boys, and it made no difference whether the fathers were present or absent.

Just as your children learn to walk by watching you walk and slouch if you slouch, stand straight if you stand straight, comb their hair the way you comb your hair and speak the way you speak, so they mimic everything else you do, your good behaviour and your bad. Little children start out supposing that their parents have got things right and they copy what they see. And the stress is on seeing, not listening. Young children do not think in words, they just mimic adult behaviour, so you must be very careful what example you set. If you tell your child to be considerate to other people but then, when you are out shopping, push in front of someone else, the child will copy and push other people out of her way too. If you tell her she must be kind to her brother but then make some sarcastic remark to him yourself, she will copy your sneers. You are the most important person in her universe and she is studying you every minute of the day. What you say won't make any difference. You cannot jump off the bus without paying your fare and expect to raise an honest child.

As David Ingram, a teacher with many years' experience of teaching morality to schoolchildren says, 'They see what you do, and hear what you say, and they know that what you *do* is the truth.'

'She's stolen from my purse'

What if you've led a life of blameless honesty only to discover that your beloved child shows signs of being a thief? It's a dilemma that worries a number of parents. The seeds of their concern are laid almost as soon as the baby can sit up. Babies love to rummage through their mother's handbag, helping themselves to anything that is small, shiny and capable of making a noise, like a keyring or coins. This is not a sign of the budding burglar. The baby does not recognise that 'mother' is an independent person; she thinks that she and her mother are one and the same being and that what is her mother's is hers too.

Most mothers are pretty tolerant when their baby decides it's time to turn out her bag, indeed many of us get into the habit of keeping a couple of tiny objects in the bag just to keep the child amused while we rescue the more important things from her grasp. Things only go wrong if you feel uneasy about your infant's antics and believe you have to 'cure' the thieving in its early stages to prevent it getting serious later. Stopping a baby from exploring will only cause unnecessary suffering, because left to her own devices she will simply grow out of it.

However, if a child of three or four regularly takes things from her mother's purse, father's pile of small change or the fridge, this is very upsetting because by this time she does have an understanding of ownership – this teddy is mine, this handbag is mother's – and some idea of honesty. So when a child this age starts to take things, it does look all too like a deliberate crime. Everyone is made to feel uncomfortable because the old free and easy way of leaving things all over the place has to be changed; possessions such as money or sweet things have to be guarded and the child put under constant watch.

Small children do not steal out of greed or selfishness. 'A child who steals', argued child psychiatrist Dr David Winnicott, 'is looking for her mother. She may be missing, or present but somehow absent from her or not available to her.'

Once again, we are faced with the child's devouring need to be loved and nurtured by its parents. If for some reason that love is unavailable, the child will reach out and take something else to try and fill up the void.

It is very distressing to discover that your child is stealing, and the fear that this could be the first sign of a warped personality makes it hard to react sensibly. The first, natural reaction is one of shock, dislike and rejection, but you must struggle against this response. Disapproval only makes the child feel even more cut off and neglected and the symptoms of that unhappiness – the stealing – will get worse. Winnicott argued that you have to understand that stealing by a small child is a sign of misery, not wickedness, and to meet the child's need by setting aside time to give her total attention. If you get angry, and perhaps demand a confession, you will only reinforce her feeling that she has 'lost' you.

Of course the child's feeling of abandonment is very often misplaced. You may have been extra busy, or absorbed in a new baby, or have serious financial or health problems that have preoccupied your thoughts. That doesn't mean you have stopped loving your child, but it is important to accept that she has misinterpreted your temporary neglect and is feeling abandoned and distressed. So, if you discover your child is taking things, you must respond by finding time to give her the extra attention and reassurance she needs and do so for as long as it takes to bring the stealing to a halt. This is easier said than done, of course, if you are snowed under with your own problems and tensions, and cross about her behaviour, but it will work, and restore to you the happy, honest child of before.

You must act fast, or the small child's pilfering will become the older child's delinquency. John Woods, drawing on his experience as a psychotherapist dealing with children in trouble, explains: 'If you don't respond quickly, the child will feel you don't care, and step up the level of stealing until you do respond.'

There is another pitfall you must try to avoid in these

circumstances. Worried parents often ask the child why she is taking things. It is natural enough, but it's a mistake because she doesn't know why she's doing it: she is acting out of a miserable compulsion and has no idea what is driving her. So she can't come up with an answer. If you press her, warns paediatrician David Winnicott, 'she will be full of almost unbearable guilt as a result of being misunderstood and blamed, and then she will lie.'

If your questions push your child into a position where she has to make up some silly tale in order to answer, a tale you will see at once is untrue, then you will start to worry that she is a liar as well as a thief. She does not want to be either; she is just feeling lost and forlorn. The best way to bring an end to the whole sorry business is to deal with that grief without adding extra stress.

Playing rough
Luckily most children do not give their parents anxious moments about whether they have larceny in their genes. On the other hand, they are all prone to violence, which can be disconcerting and upsetting to their loving mothers and fathers. Small children are very physical creatures. A lot of their energy goes in running and tumbling and pushing and being rumbustious and this is great fun, but sometimes the fun gets out of hand. Young children, unchecked, will push their little friends over, hit their brothers and sisters and tear their toys to pieces. How do you teach them to be less aggressive?

Once the child is able to speak, it is time to start showing her how to express her feelings in words, not blows. For instance, she may be angry because she thought it was her turn to have a go on the swing and her friend has beaten her to it. A small child's reaction is quite often to walk up and push or hit the friend. And the mother's reaction is quite often to be horrified and rush up and push or hit the child.

There is a different way. Offer the child an alternative to the physical response: a verbal one. Teach her to say something along the lines of 'I want to hit Sara,' or 'I feel like hitting her.' Saying that will act as a safety valve to release her anger and very often a child loses the need to hit out if she has that means of expressing her feelings. You can encourage your children to express their feelings honestly, but show them that they can express them in words just as effectively as in deeds. However, if the child does talk about how angry and violent she feels towards her little playmate or her baby brother, you must sympathise and understand her rage, not try to stifle it, as many parents do.

'Parents often feel the child shouldn't want to hit,' says John Woods. 'But that's a logical mistake. They feel the child shouldn't hit others and therefore that it shouldn't *want* to hit others but the two don't necessarily go together. The child *will* want to hit out, and if they can say so instead of doing it, that's an improvement. It's a simple step but one that's often overlooked, like counting to ten. It puts a brake on. And it also works for parents. The parent may want to hit a child and it is a good safety measure to build that in, to say to the child, "I feel like hitting you, I'm so angry." '

Smacks and gunfights

Admitting to anger but not acting on it is a big step along the moral road, but it is, sadly, not only children who display aggression. We all want to instil into our children a sense of respect and consideration for the feelings of other people, but it is not easy when every day they can see adults on television killing each other left, right and centre. It is not just the baddies: the goodies kill people too, and they are admired for doing so and for doing it better and having a bigger gun. This is a very powerful message for children and one that we have to struggle to counteract.

There have been decades of debate about whether watching violent television and films makes children violent themselves, but a better question is, does watching it do them any good? We know that children learn by mimicking adults and we know that visual images are particularly strong and

47

vivid, so it stands to reason that vivid images of violence will make a deep impression on children. However, the human mind can only accommodate so much intensity; when it gets overloaded, it switches off and blanks out the image. So too much exposure to vivid brutality on film leads to children becoming desensitised to those images. This doesn't mean they will go out and stab a friend; none the less, anything that makes children grow up less sensitive and subtle in their responses to other people is a cause for regret, and it makes sense to monitor the amount of violence your child watches.

Yet all the fine moral instruction in the world will not teach little children to curb their aggression if, at the same time, you behave aggressively towards them. You cannot demand non-violence of children if you regularly smack them. There is a school of thought which argues that it is all right to smack children in hot blood, but not in a cold and calculating way – but this distinction is lost on the child. Hitting children does not teach them to be self-controlled and non-violent to others. What it teaches them is that violence is sometimes acceptable, and as they observe that Mum and Dad never lash out at their friends, colleagues or neighbours, no matter how badly they behave, children learn from being smacked that it is the large and powerful who hit the small and weak. Bringing a child up to believe that might is right does not win moral Brownie points.

Smacking also makes the child lose sight of the message you might have been trying to get across. If you hit a child because of something she has done or said, her attention focuses on the blow not on the action that caused it, and the instinctive reaction is resentment and a swift shifting of blame. Philosopher Mary Midgley explains, 'The hard knocks and shocks of experience more often produce resentment than enlightenment. When knocked, most of us manage to blame someone else rather than ourselves. Who has not cursed a stupid door for being in the way when we bump into it – the ultimate idiocy!' Smacking takes the child's mind off her misdeeds and focuses it on to you as the cause of her present misery, which is the opposite of what you meant to achieve.

Parents who have been smacked themselves are likely to repeat the behaviour they have learned and smack their own children, especially when they are cross. 'Hitting isn't a good idea,' says John Woods. 'You must understand the way children think and they don't primarily think verbally. Actions always speak louder to them than words. So as a parent it is very important to try and practise what you preach. If you do lose your temper and hit the child you can redeem yourself by apologising, admit you made a mistake. Then the child can see you are not infallible and it helps her. If you can admit you've made a cock-up of something, it helps the child learn to cope with frustration. No one is perfect.'

Setting them on the straight and narrow

Bad behaviour should never be ignored, but the best way of showing your disapproval is in words, saying, 'We don't do that sort of thing,' or 'We think it's unkind to behave like that.' This way the child absorbs the message that in her family certain values are cherished and certain patterns of behaviour are expected. Because she wants to belong to the family, she will want to conform. For any child, the ultimate sanction is rejection. If she sees that her behaviour is likely to lead to her imminent exclusion from the family circle, that is usually sufficient to put a stop to it.

Other sanctions can be tailored to the circumstances. A child who is being a noisy pest can be put in her room for half an hour to sit quietly. You can refuse to allow her to watch her favourite television programme that day, or pull her out of a game if she is wrecking it for other children. Adults who spend a lot of time with small children develop all sorts of clever ways of defusing situations. One primary school teacher in London had a little girl in her reception class who persisted in kicking the other infants. One school of thought would simply say she should be smacked: another that she should be sent outside until she could behave. This teacher gave her a sympathetic ear and discovered that the little girl had been told to kick a child every day by her deeply disturbed father. While the authorities organised help for him, the teacher tackled the immediate problem by making her pupil take off her shoes at the classroom door. It is surprising how quickly you lose the urge to kick when you're only wearing cotton socks.

Children can also be diverted along the straight and narrow by having to pay for what they have done. 'It's very useful to have kids make recompense and feel the effects of what they do,' says John Woods. 'If the child destroys something belonging to someone else, she can make amends – perhaps give up her pocket money for a period. There's no harm in that.'

David Ingram adds that 'Consistency is very important, and persistence. You must see, around shops and streets, parents who cave in. And in schools you meet children to whom nobody has ever said "No" and really meant no. You hear it in the whingeing voice. I moved a girl in class the other day. I said, "Look Carol, I'm not your mother. You can do that sulky face and really it's not having any effect. And you can bite your pencil and you can look cross, but you were talking to Paula and you've been moved away from Paula so you can't talk to her so just get on with it." Oh, well, slammed doors and all this kind of thing. And I guess mother caves in. Well I know they do.'

Ingram thinks part of the problem is a hangover from the relativism of the 1960s where people said, ' "I'm really not sure what's right. I'm busy working it out myself so how can I be sure in my dealings with my children what they should do or shouldn't do?" Such parents feel disabled and can't manage to give their children clear guidance or to offer strictures. Others are busy at another level – in the Rotary Club or down at the gym. Some just can't be bothered, don't want to be there.'

You will only get good behaviour from a child through dogged persistence. A good child does not pop up over-night like a daisy. You have to make good behaviour a daily habit, which means watching, encouraging and monitoring all day, every day. It takes determination – you have to be in for the long haul. If you skip it, your infant will only be good when you are watching her and that will lead to no end of trouble.

Lending a hand

As we have seen, when children are very small, you can only instil the habit of good behaviour, you can't explain to your child why such behaviour matters because she can't yet understand. However, even at a very young age, there are ways in which you can foster her unselfish concern for other people's welfare. One of the best tactics is to give her a certain amount of responsibility. Dr Erwin Staub points to the evidence from other cultures which shows that children who are brought up in societies where they are expected to carry out certain tasks as their contribution to the family's welfare – tending animals, looking after younger children, fetching water from the well – are also more helpful in other ways than children who are born into cultures where children have few such responsibilities.

When the children have to behave in a responsible manner day after day, says Staub, 'it teaches them that this is the norm, that it is expected of people that they will do things for others, that to do so is regarded by society as an obligation, and that they can expect rewards, at least approval, for so doing, and punishment for not doing so.'

Of course we don't send our children to fetch water from the well, but you can give them some little responsibilities which indicate that they are expected to help others. Psychologist Judy Dunn, who made a study of sibling relationships, found that children who were encouraged to take a real and practical part in caring for a baby brother or sister from the first weeks of infancy were particularly interested in, and affectionate towards them, and this good relationship endured for a long time.

You can encourage a small child to make the beds with

you, to feed the cat or to fetch something for the baby. She can stand on a stool to help you in the kitchen – making pastry, spreading things on other things, stirring. All of this will foster her budding spirit of altruism, the desire to help others. Letting the child help can, of course, be a pretty hairy experience, but a child can only learn how to be responsible by being given responsibility for something and trying to cope. It is a skill and, like other skills, takes practice. However tempting it is to do the job yourself rather than watch those uncoordinated little hands struggling to accomplish it, hold off.

Also, do try to avoid prophesying disaster. Encourage the child in a positive way instead. If, for example, you warn a child who is carrying a precious cup and saucer *not* to break it, they are more likely to become fearful and do so. However, if you ask them to carry it carefully, they will be more confident and more successful. As long as you watch out that she doesn't hurt herself in the attempt, helping others helps your child to grow into a kinder person.

You will get even better results if, while she is busy doing something helpful, you explain to her why she should do it, what is expected of her and what other people will think. You can say something along the lines of: 'We have to keep Tiddles' water bowl full because she gets thirsty like us. She can't turn the tap on to get a drink, so we have to look after her, because wouldn't she feel awful if she was thirsty and there was nothing to drink? And see how grateful she is.' If you make some such commentary when your child is helping out, then she will come to associate what you say with what she is doing and this reinforces the message and makes it more likely she will want to help out in the future.

Psychiatrist James Hemming points out another pitfall: 'There is also the problem of the over-cared for child – not one who is over-loved but one who is spoilt, whose parent continually says, "I'll do that, dear," instead of encouraging her to do it for herself if she can. That child is actually at a disadvantage because she feels she's no good, she feels incompetent. If a parent loves the child but also helps her to be useful and co-operative, the child will build up her self-esteem and her capacity to live with others effectively.'

So, encouraging a toddler to help out is very important, but you must take her contribution seriously. If you laugh at her efforts, or cut her off halfway through because you have run out of patience, she will feel helpless and useless and become aggressive. You must praise her efforts and tell her how good she has been. The effect it has in encouraging the growth of altruism is worth the trouble.

Is the child to blame?

All the time you are showing your small child that her good deeds earn your approval while bad behaviour is frowned on, you have to be scrupulously fair about when the child is and is not to blame. Mia Kellmer Pringle, the distinguished child psychologist, observed: 'A toddler doesn't know at first that a dish will break if it is dropped while teddy just lands softly. He must be given time to learn these differences uneventfully, before he can be blamed for getting it wrong.' Piaget remarked of a little child pulling threads out of a bath towel, 'It has obviously no intention of doing harm. It is simply making an experiment in physics,' – but parents are liable to be cross and accuse the child of spoiling it, making their mother sad, being naughty. 'Parents,' he observed, 'are pretty unfair about the child's inevitable messes and destructiveness.'

You must be fair and accept that your child can only be scolded or punished if she refuses to do something that you know she is capable of doing, if her bad behaviour is deliberate. At this very young age, you will find that your child will accept your views on what is right and wrong without question; up to primary school age, children don't really have any sense of right and wrong in the abstract. They just have unquestioning respect for adults and believe they must obey them. Little children think that acts that are punished are wrong and acts that have good consequences are right.

They understand that the bigger, stronger people have authority and they think it is right that they should.

Most of the time, our children don't understand why they must do this or that. In the early years we load them every day with new obligations, such as not to tell lies, and the reason for these orders often remains incomprehensible to the child. At the same time, we ask them to adopt a whole set of rules about food and cleanliness which they cannot immediately see the point of. Confused, but anxious to please, children of this age are content to act in certain ways simply because mummy tells them to. David Rowse, for instance, who teaches disaffected teenagers, admits, 'I still can't throw down a piece of litter, I can't do it!' because of the training his parents gave him. It is, for parents, a blessedly easy age.

Because small children live in this world of very simple, absolute values, they have little sympathy for anyone who fails to measure up. If you ask them, for instance, how thieves should be dealt with, they will say 'chop off their hands' or something equally lurid.

You can see how little children accept what their parents tell them at face value in an experiment carried out by Professor Lawrence Kohlberg, one of the great pioneers of research into the moral development of children. Kohlberg told a group of children a story in which a boy faithfully baby-sat his baby brother but was punished by his mother; or, in an alternative version, how the boy abandoned the baby brother and was praised.

Most four-year-olds say the punished boy was bad, even though they know baby-sitting is 'good'. At five they will say his baby-sitting was good, but he must have done something bad to get punished. This blind faith in the parents is too good to last, however. By seven, about half the group can disentangle goodness from punishment, and say the child was good and there must be something foolish or bad about the mother to punish him. In other words, the pre-school child will accept your authority without question; but by seven she is beginning to judge whether you are fair or not, so watch out!

In a similar study, a group of children were told about Rocky, a bully, who successfully beat up his victim and took his toys or, alternatively, was defeated. At four to six children not only say that the 'good guys win' so Rocky must be good, even though he is behaving like a bully, but explain that you can tell who the good guys are on television because they win. Children over seven, however, are more able to separate goodness from success.

Blind obedience is necessary behaviour for small children, who must be made to respect the needs of others long before they can understand them, but it is not the basis of moral behaviour. A thing cannot be right just because a parent or some other authority says so. Eventually we have to work out for ourselves whether we accept the lessons we have learnt as a child. In the meantime, the best thing we can do for a child when she is very young is to get her into the habits of fairness, honesty, helpfulness towards others, compassion for those in distress and so on, and stand by to follow up with reasons when she is old enough for them.

Missing out
All the research evidence shows that these early years are crucial to the child's future behaviour. If she is raised in an atmosphere of love and security, shown how to behave and encouraged to help, her moral development will come on in leaps and bounds. If she is neglected, treated inconsistently so she does not know how to behave, and given no information about why she should care for others, she will become demanding, aggressive, restless and a pain to everyone around. If her needs continue to be unmet, there is a strong likelihood she will join the ranks of the bullies and delinquents.

Since children are not born only into families that will cherish and nurture them, we have to provide some means of reaching out to small children who are not getting a fair start in life. The best way of doing this is to offer them a place in a well-run nursery school where they have the care and attention they need. The Headstart programme in America, for instance, took children from some of the worst families and poorest environments and gave them first-class nursery education. Even decades later these children were still doing better than children who did not get a place on the scheme: they were more likely to go to college and get a job; less likely to turn to crime; their marriages lasted longer and they were altogether happier.

It should be the most obvious thing in the world that if we want to give our children the best start in life we should offer them the right facilities, but the message has been slow to get through in this country. We still prefer to spend State resources on boot camps and prisons than nursery education for every three-year-old who needs it. The result of this scarcity of provision can be bizarre: I once visited a terrific nursery school in Southwark, London, which was doing a great job, but it had spaces for only a handful of the local children. So it had naturally concentrated on those from difficult families – the children of disabled parents, single parents and children on the at-risk register. The result was that 'normal' parents hesitated to take up the few remaining vacancies because there was a stigma attached to getting a place at the school – it made them look failures in some sense. It is a mad world where only the dastardly or the desperate can get a decent start for their child.

There is so much evidence of how good childcare in the early years beats any other sort of approach in raising decent citizens that to fail to provide it is to fail our children: an immoral act. Of course nursery school should not be compulsory: not all parents want to send their children to school when they are very small and in the right environment little children will enjoy their freedom and thrive. But there is no freedom in neglect: the child left to run wild is not being given liberty but rather being trained to become a nuisance and, eventually, a failure, which is miserable for that person and a threat to society. For them, nursery education offers the single best chance they will ever have of escaping from the cycle of neglect and bad example and of growing up into decent adults.

Interlude
Firm parents, floppy parents

The great battleground of morality is between obligation and desire. When somebody says, 'I ought to do so and so,' we understand that she doesn't really want to do it, or would prefer to do something else, but feels she should nonetheless. What makes us fulfil our obligations is discipline: doing what you do not want to do, and not doing what you would like to do. If we are disciplined, we can control our behaviour in the interests of something we judge is more important than the immediate gratification of a desire.

So one of the valuable lessons you can teach your child is to defer pleasure now for the sake of a greater gain later: to do the homework now and play later because that way they will achieve their long-term goals; to clear up the living room now and go off to their friends later because that way they will earn the goodwill of the rest of the family.

The qualities this demands – patience, endurance, stoicism and the like – seem very old-fashioned virtues today. Today's child, wanting a telephone number, will ring directory enquiries rather than look through a phone book. If they want food, they want it *now*. Faced with something like a new piece of video equipment, they start clicking buttons in an attempt to make it work; suggest that they sit down first and read through the instruction book and you are met with disbelief: they have to be able to make it work *at once* and if they can't the fault lies in the stupid equipment, not their impatience.

Nonetheless, however alien the idea seems, it's important to find occasions where children can be taught to wait. As a child growing up in the Welsh tradition of church three times on Sunday, sitting through endless sermons, sometimes in Welsh, which I did not understand, I learnt to be pretty patient. Today such an upbringing would probably be condemned as stifling the child's enthusiasm – but I can sit in traffic jams without feeling rage.

It is part of the parent's job to do the unpopular thing and insist the child does what is necessary before she does what she wants. You can't expect her to wait for ever: a small child can only defer her pleasure for a short time where a teenager can be expected to take the longer view. However, if you insist they do their homework before they settle down to the television; ask them to baby-sit a younger child and go out with friends another night; expect them to take the video or the library books back promptly instead of putting it off and running up fines or leaving it to you; encourage them to put in the hours to learn to play a musical instrument and insist that they spend whatever time it takes to look after their own pet, then they will develop a sense of self-discipline which is not just useful, but makes them feel good about themselves. Of course, discipline is not a moral quality in itself – even a terrorist can be well disciplined; in fact he has to be – but the ability to do the necessary thing before or instead of the fancied thing is part of our moral equipment.

Parents under attack
Getting a child to take 'no' for an answer is difficult in the modern world where children are led to believe that their feelings come first. Children in our society are constantly encouraged to be self-assertive and to promote their own desires. They besiege Mum and Dad with requests and demands and many parents feel they must give in because they are afraid of their children: not of a physical attack but of the sort of emotional blackmail children use when they aren't getting their own way.

All children use emotional tactics such as temper tantrums to get what they want. Sooner or later most parents learn it is best for everyone's sake to hold the line because, over the years, children who get away with tantrums learn more subtle and more effective ways of exerting emotional pressure on their parents. Teenagers, for instance, may go on strike: they may refuse to go to school; suddenly have no activities outside the house; some even stop washing or dressing. It looks pretty serious, but it is often resolved surprisingly quickly if the parent gives in to demands they had been resisting – for a computer, a bigger bedroom, to change school. Such relief is temporary, however, and the blackmailing behaviour soon starts again with another demand.

Most parents of young children are suffering from economic as well as emotional strains. Almost every couple sees their income drop when they start to raise a family, many parents are struggling to raise their children alone, with few social supports, and some are living in real poverty. Even the better off are assailed daily by demands to keep their children supplied with expensive products, clothes, toys and outings.

At the same time the family's own credibility and authority has been diminished. Parents find themselves attacked over their shortcomings as child-rearers. They are accused of neglect or indifference because the intolerant demands of the workplace take them away from their families for damagingly long hours, and they are blamed for their children's failings by politicians bandying slogans such as 'family values'. Being a mother or father once carried automatic status: now parents are on the defensive and judged by outsiders with suspicion and little understanding. A community that truly respected children would make parenting a less demanding and more fulfilling experience.

Luckily, parents are a pretty robust lot: some sort of strength comes with the job and there are plenty of examples of parents bringing up terrific families in all sorts of circumstances. Economic deprivation alone does not stop people being good parents: during the Depression there was no

61

shortage of families who managed to raise their children to the highest standards despite their desperate circumstances, and in the inner cities today you can find plenty of families who succeed in raising decent, well-behaved youngsters. How do they do it? What are the ground rules?

Your needs, my needs

Psychologist Theodore Dix says parents have three possible goals. The first goal focuses on their children's feelings and its aim is to please them by bringing about the results the children want. This includes trying to make a child feel happy, comforting it when distressed, assuaging its pain and hunger and so on.

The second goal aims to benefit children but not necessarily to please them. It is orientated towards their learning and development and involves helping them to acquire knowledge and skills, encouraging them to develop their feelings for other people and requiring them to curb any antisocial inclinations they might have.

The third goal favours the parents. This aims to meet their needs and wishes and might include getting a child to bed on time so that Mummy can have time to read a book or watch a favourite TV programme. It is good for parents to express their own goals openly, to give children the message that there are other people in the world with needs that must be considered. A parent's assertion of her own needs may also evoke co-operation, help and a sense of service from the child and so contribute to the development of her sense of social responsibility.

If the parents concentrate on the first goal and allow the child's feelings to become paramount, they will encourage wilfulness and self-absorption in the child and slow down the development of her self-control and respect for others. Yet many parents worry that experiences such as feeling bad, not having fun, facing frustration or enduring hardship could permanently damage their child's self-esteem unless relieved at once, so they become sloppy about discipline and let the child get away with murder. However, your daughter will not wilt if you stand up to her emotional blackmail, in fact she will be reassured, because she needs to see that you are in charge.

The child also needs you to push her into achieving the second, more difficult, goal, such as how to do trigonometry or to stop hitting her little brother, even when it isn't a lot of fun. Her needs aren't always the same as her wishes.

This doesn't mean you can completely ignore her needs: if parents make the third goal, their own needs and desires, paramount, it generates an atmosphere of neglect and indifference that produces feelings of cynicism and worthlessness in the child. Indeed, some parents' lives are so filled with pressure, anxiety or self-absorption that there is little room in their minds for anything except their own goals. What is needed is to keep a balance between your needs and your child's. Of course you want to please your child and make her happy – why else do you have children? But you don't stop having needs of your own just because you've become a parent – you are entitled to have fun too! So her goals and yours have to be pursued in harmony.

When to set rules
Parents can't only do what children want; that would be short-sighted and indulgent. To encourage sharing, helping and other sociable behaviour, we have to impose rules that require children to act in ways they do not want to act. Yet nowhere is there greater confusion than over the stormy topic of discipline. The very word with its overtones of Dotheboys Hall and sadistic schoolmasters upsets some parents, while others see it as a cruel curb on the natural high spirits and spontaneity of their little darlings. However, discipline is essential if children are to fit comfortably into society and if they are to study and acquire the knowledge and skills they need for adult life.

There is a difference between discipline imposed on children from outside, and self-discipline. Self-discipline is obviously what we are aiming for as parents: we do not want children who are good only when we are supervising them, but who are good of their own accord and the evidence shows that you don't encourage self-discipline by imposing control. Giving orders, sending commands, punishing or threatening to punish doesn't influence youngsters: it only coerces or compels them.

This doesn't mean that children should be left to their own ideas of discipline, with parents simply watching on the sidelines. While there is no excuse for harsh and arbitrary regimes, it is a mistake to shrink away from any form of direct control of your children's behaviour. Parents have to exercise control when the children are young and require more direction than their own self-discipline is capable of producing. Children need the guidance of your greater wisdom even if it doesn't suit the way they feel at that moment. Take courage from the fact that you are wiser, more experienced and better trained than your child and do usually know best.

The choice is not between harshness on one hand and simply appealing to the child on the other. It is possible to combine firm discipline with reason, so you both control and communicate what you want. As Dr Benjamin Spock said recently, 'It has never been a case of "Either you punish a child physically, or you allow that child to do whatever he or she wants." There is a third way: being polite, gentle and kind to the child and demonstrating what you want from them. Children need good, firm, clear leadership.'

It may help to consider what sort of a disciplinarian you are by nature. It is hard for psychologists to research what form of discipline most parents favour since you can't actually put parents and children in a laboratory and then threaten, thump, reject or otherwise upset them in cold blood to test their responses; so researchers have been forced to rely a lot on hearsay and questionnaires. However, from large bodies of studies, experimental child psychologists have concluded that parental strategies over discipline fall into three broad categories, and they provide valuable evidence about which sort is most effective.

One: Don't do that, George!

One type of parent bases their family discipline on what psychologists call 'power-assertion', which means they use coercion and threats of punishment when their children refuse to conform to their wishes. Power assertion can involve the use of physical force, deprivation of possessions or privileges, or direct commands or threats, all backed up by severe sanctions for disobedience. Using your power can be highly effective in the short term – particularly when you are around to enforce the sanctions – and there is no harm in being bossy occasionally as a way of letting the child know that you feel strongly about a given issue, or as a means of controlling openly defiant behaviour. In fact, if you normally rely on sweet reason with your child, laying down the law sometimes can positively help.

However, relying on power as the main means of discipline produces children whose moral orientation is based on their fear of detection and punishment. Experimental evidence shows that asserting your power does not lead to the formation of long-lasting, dependable habits and beliefs because its effectiveness fades when you are absent. In fact, being too authoritarian can be counter-productive, as experiments show.

In the 'forbidden toy' experiment, one group of children was told that they would receive a mild punishment if they played with a desirable (but forbidden) toy while a second group was told they would receive a severe punishment for doing so. Then both were given two opportunities to play with it. Neither group chose to play with the forbidden toy on the first occasion, because the adult experimenter was present, but when the children returned to the lab later on, the adult was not present; the children who had been only mildly warned still refused to play with the toy, but the children who had been severely threatened were very likely to play with it. It seems that when an adult uses his power too forcefully, it actually diminishes his long-term influence over the child's attitudes and behaviour.

Research shows that the effectiveness of power-assertion is also affected by the atmosphere in the home. When power is used in a moderate way by parents who are generally warm and supportive, who set high standards and explain the reasons for their requests to the children, the children grow to be socially responsible and positive in their behaviour. However, frequent use of power, especially by hostile, cold parents, does not have good results: in a 1992 study, for example, Dutch parents who used an authoritarian pattern of discipline were found to have primary school children who were rated as pretty unhelpful by their friends.

Two: I don't love you any more

A second, more subtle and indirect disciplinary strategy used by many modern parents, particularly mothers, is known as 'the withdrawal of love', where she displays anger or disapproval in order to get the child to change what it is doing. She may show emotional coldness, turn her back on the child, refuse to speak or listen to her, express disappointment and disinterest or threaten to withdraw her love – 'I don't like you when you act like that.'

Modern parents tend to use love withdrawal a lot, and it is more effective in gaining immediate compliance from children than coercion. It will not, however, accomplish your main objective, which is to get children to adopt better attitudes and behaviour as their own. Love withdrawal leads to only limited changes in children's behaviour. It may increase the likelihood that they will put on a good show, and inhibit any tendency they might have to be discourteous or disobedient, but it does not lead them to adopt new standards of behaviour on a permanent basis.

Three: Sweet reason

The third disciplinary strategy used by parents was identified by psychologist Martin Hoffman as 'induction'. Here the parent always gives a reason to the child as to why she should do what is required of her – and no, the reason is not, 'Because I say so.' It is a genuine, convincing reason. Hoffman found that parents who offered their children an explanation of why they wanted something done were most successful at permanently changing children's attitudes and behaviour.

What seems to happen is that when you give children a reason for what you want them to do, they understand and accept the standards you are trying to communicate rather than focus on the sanctions you could use to enforce it. With this method, what is most vivid to the child is the behaviour you are trying to instil rather than the punishment for failing to comply. In fact the child may forget the sanction entirely. She may even, in time, forget it was you who promoted the behaviour because she endorses it so wholeheartedly herself. Nevertheless, your role is vital, because if you had not reasoned with her she might never have adopted such behaviour.

What induction does is to help the child to take on board the moral habits and standards that you are setting out and make them her own. Consider a typical confrontation. The child has acted in an improper way. The parent may stop the child's action or may punish her afterwards. In either case, she is unlikely to repeat the unwelcome act in the parent's presence, but will she continue to refrain from such behaviour when the parent is not around? This depends.

If the parent wants the child to think about her behaviour and do the right thing in future, she must give her a reason so the child can learn to anticipate the effect of her behaviour on others. Such reasons and explanations can take many forms, depending on the situation and the age of the child. For instance, with a very young child you could emphasise the direct effects of her actions: 'If you keep pushing him, he'll fall down and cry.' With an older child you could focus upon the fairness of her action in terms of the other's actions and intentions: 'Don't yell at him, he was only trying to help.' Or you can point to the psychological, rather than the physical effect of her behaviour: 'He feels bad because he was proud

67

of his castle and you knocked it down.'

Reasons and explanations nourish the child's concern for others and offer her information about how her behaviour can upset people. This information helps her to a better understanding of the relationship between her own actions and the physical and psychological well-being of others. However, you can't expect too much, too soon. You have to make allowances for the child's age and the limits of her understanding when you're trying to reason with her.

Getting the child's attention

Giving explanations is a good disciplinary technique because it induces a moderate level of arousal in the child's brain, which is the best level for learning – enough to catch her attention but not enough to produce high levels of anxiety or anger that would distract her from what you are saying. Being moderately aroused means the child is likely to pay attention to the information embedded in your request, and this makes your disciplinary efforts seem less arbitrary and therefore less likely to produce resistance.

Giving her a reason – 'If you take her doll she'll miss it and be sad' – also focuses the child's attention on the consequences of her behaviour for others. It builds up her capacity to empathise with another person's unhappy emotions and to feel guilty about causing harm. These feelings of empathy and concern encourage her to behave well, just as feelings of guilt produce a desire to make amends.

Adding an explanation to your request for good behaviour also means that the child plays an active role in processing the information and this effort makes it more likely that she will understand the link between her actions and their consequences. Later on, when the stored information is remembered in a similar situation, she will feel again the emotions of empathy and guilt associated with those memories and this will give her a motive for behaving well in the new situation.

Adding reasons and explanations to your requests for discipline seems to be particularly effective at promoting altruism – those acts we do to benefit others without any desire for reward. It seems to work by enlarging the child's capacity for empathy, particularly if you give reasons which point out the consequences of the child's behaviour for someone else – for instance, 'See, you made Hannah fall down.' An explanation of this sort increases the probability that the child will empathise with her victim, and higher empathy in children in turn leads to more altruistic behaviour.

If you ask a child *not* to do something, giving as a reason the harm she would do or, if it's after the event, if you encourage her to consider her victim's feelings and make amends, or if you explain how sad you feel over this bad behaviour, your words will focus her attention on other people's feelings and on the possibility of causing harm to others. Again, this will promote her ability to take another person's point of view.

However, don't think that as a parent you are completely in control of the disciplinary situation: research shows that the child's behaviour can influence the parent as well as vice versa. For instance, one group of researchers found that mothers tend to use psychological discipline, such as reasoning and dramatisation of distress, when their children are harming others, but physical punishment when the children are destroying property or for lapses in the child's self-control. Adults also offer more reasons and explanations about the consequences of children's behaviour to children who pay attention to them.

Outside, inside
Getting children to adopt their own standards as they grow up demands a gradual change of attitude on their part, from what psychologists call compliance to internalisation. Compliance is when the child changes its behaviour, for the moment, in order to conform to some outside authority, such as you or a teacher and it is what young children do. Internalisation means the child adopts these standards of

behaviour as her own, now and forever, and it is what you are aiming for.

One indication that your child has started to adopt your moral standards as her own is if she feels guilty when she has done wrong. Guilt is that feeling of discomfort or remorse we experience over violating our own standards, or causing harm, or over some untoward behaviour, and a feeling of guilt is frequently accompanied by the desire to make some form of redress. It is different from the fear of being punished by somebody else: guilt is a private affair between yourself and your personal standards when you have breached those standards. So, if your child feels guilty after some misdeed, it means she feels she has fallen short of standards she has made her own, which is a sign of her growing moral maturity.

Developing this internal motivation is critical to moral development because moral philosophers hold that only behaviour you choose to do to satisfy your own principles can truly be called moral. If a child is honest or helps merely to avoid censure, or to obtain some reward, she is compliant but she is not behaving in a moral fashion. Obedience is a virtue only until such time as the child can make up her own mind; then she must choose to be good in accordance with her own moral principles.

Compliance is necessary to start with because a child must first learn to comply with a moral standard before she can internalise. Social psychologist Mark Lepper used the 'forbidden toy' experiment to confirm that children who didn't play with the toy the first time were likely to resist temptation on the second occasion too. In other words, the fact that they had complied with instructions in the past made it more likely that they would adopt this behaviour when left to their own devices.

Rewards – in moderation
We exert discipline not only by punishing unwelcome behaviour but also by honouring good behaviour, and Lepper went on to look at what happened if children were offered rewards

rather than punishment. In this experiment three groups of children, known to be fond of Magic Markers felt pens, were asked to play with some for a while. One group was told they would win a certificate by working with the pens, which was given to them at the end of the session. Another group was told nothing, but the children were given the certificate anyway. The third group were simply asked to use the Magic Markers and weren't given any reward.

Several weeks later, all three groups were given a chance to play with the pens again, but this time not explicitly urged to do so. The third group, the ones who had not been given a certificate, showed far more interest in using the Magic Markers on this occasion than the two groups who had. In other words, the children who had had the reward of playing with the Magic Markers, but not the *extra* reward of a certificate, were most likely to repeat the original behaviour. This suggests that the most effective method of permanently improving a child's behaviour is to offer just enough of a reward to engage the child in the new behaviour, but not so much that the child finds the reward the most memorable part of the experience. If you get the balance right, the child's behaviour will be permanently transformed because she will make these standards her own.

Offering a modest reward can also boost a child's altruism. In a 1969 study, some children from six to ten were told they would receive a reward for helping children in hospital (or saw other children being told the same thing) while the other children were told nothing about a reward for helping. In addition, the mothers were asked about the degree to which they used rewards with the children.

What happened was that children who believed there would be a reward for helping assisted more often than the children who were not offered a reward. However, as in the Magic Marker experiment, these children helped less when they were given a second opportunity to assist, when rewards were not mentioned and they were left unsupervised. It seems, however, that the promise of a reward was only detrimental to those children whose mothers said they used rewards fairly often as a way of getting their children to behave. Children who are frequently rewarded at home seem to be less motivated to help when there is no reward for doing so. Rewards are good up to a point, but children should not come to depend on them.

Sing their praises quietly

As parents we have a number of rewards at our disposal but the most potent of all is praise, and like all other forms of discipline, praise is most effective when used judiciously. It can be counter-productive if it is poured out in an excessive, inconsistent or arbitrary manner. Like punishment, we should use just enough to have an effect.

The 'forbidden toy' experiment has been used to test children's reaction to praise (the award of a certificate) as well as punishment. In both cases the result was the same. Praise can encourage good behaviour just as punishment can control unwelcome behaviour, but neither is effective in the long run if they are so obtrusive that they overwhelm the message they are meant to convey. Like punishment, praise should be carefully matched to the child's actions and whenever possible you should explain the reason for your praise.

It's important, too, to remember that constant praise, like rewards, isn't a panacea that will turn every child into a little angel: you can overdo it. Parents in many traditional cultures around the world are much less likely to praise their children than we in the West. In the Third World children are expected to help their parents and, since their efforts are taken for granted, the parents do not go out of their way to praise them, though they will punish failure. And these children do not droop for lack of approval.

Children who are over-praised come to see the primary purpose of their good behaviour as earning praise and they expend their efforts in order to be applauded rather than in order to learn something or to help someone. Highly-praised children become attuned to the public relations value of their behaviour instead of its benefits for others, or their own improvement, so their efforts become hollow, are performed without conviction and are not sustained for long.

Praise should be moderate, and moderate rewards will persuade children to persist with tasks that they will find valuable only later, so it is particularly helpful to applaud their efforts when they embark on something difficult or daunting. Eventually your child may be thrilled by the sound her violin makes, but it will take a lot of praise on your part to get her through the screeches of the early lessons.

If too much praise is counter-productive, no praise at all is worse. If you don't remember to hand out praise when it is deserved, your child will stop trying to please you with good behaviour. Parents of badly-behaved children have got into a habit of only reacting punitively, coming down hard on bad behaviour but offering nothing positive for demonstrations of good behaviour, so the child continues to behave badly in order to get some attention. In a programme for parents whose small children were seriously out of control, mothers were videoed interacting at home with their children. One mother was mortified to realise that whenever her little girl was playing quietly by herself, she rushed off to try and get on with a bit of housework: so her daughter's reward for good behaviour was to be abandoned by her mother. However, when the little girl started playing up, mother hurried back to deal with it. To all intents and purposes, the child was being trained to be a nuisance. When her mother saw what she was doing, and started praising the good behaviour and refusing to react to the bad, the little girl soon learnt that being good got the best reward and her behaviour improved dramatically. The important thing is to give positive reactions to every little thing the child does right. When parents react to good behaviour, they can get much more co-operation.

Crime and punishment

Some philosophers argue that punishment is necessary because it is a symbol of censure. But does blame have to be symbolised by suffering? Traditionalists regard punishment as essential and believe a child should suffer for his crimes; progressives think that punishment is unnecessary and a sign of their own or society's failure. Punishment, however, is unavoidable in human relationships and perhaps we need to find a better word for it, to get away from the idea of harshness and suffering.

Children react in one of the two ways to punishment, both of them emotional. One way is with aggression, which lowers the child's inhibitions; the second way is with anxiety, which raises her inhibitions. The parent's attitude will affect whether the child feels aggressive or anxious.

Punishment which is aggressive and felt as unjust and humiliating will increase the child's aggressive response and lower her inhibitions, which in turn is likely to lead to more bad behaviour. However, if the child loves the parent and values the parent's good opinion, and if the parent's response to her bad behaviour is disapproval without aggression, this will provoke anxiety and increase her inhibitions, which makes her less likely to misbehave. Seeing someone else punished also inhibits a child, which is useful for teachers who can be confident that if they come down quickly and firmly on bad behaviour by the first child who demonstrates it, the rest of the class will take notice.

Severe forms of punishment appear to have many undesirable side effects as well as aggression, including chronic anxiety, deep resentment towards the person carrying out the punishment and a strong motive to avoid being found out. A 1997 survey by Dr Murray Straus of the Family Research Laboratory at the University of New Hampshire found that smacking children provokes the very behaviour it is supposed to stop, making children violent and antisocial when they grow older. Dr Straus's team studied over 800 mothers of children aged from six to nine: 10 per cent of them smacked their children three or more times a week, 14 per cent hit them twice and 20 per cent smacked their children once. The children's antisocial behaviour – whether the child cheated, told lies, bullied others, broke things deliberately and was disobedient at school – was measured then and two years later.

What Dr Straus's survey found was that the more often the child was smacked, the more likely it was to be dishonest, disobedient and a bully. The link between smacking and an increase in bad behaviour over two years was not affected by other factors such as class, the child's sex or ethnic background. Dr Straus says that since it is known that antisocial behaviour in childhood is associated with subsequent violence and crime in adults, 'society as a whole, not just children, would benefit from ending the system of violent child rearing that goes under the euphemism of spanking.'

It is the relationship between the child and the punisher which governs whether the punishment is a success. For it to work, the child must love and value the punishing parent and so come to adopt and accept the parent's attitudes towards herself. Without such a loving attachment the child may well learn to be prudent in avoiding punishment, but she is unlikely to acquire the capacity to resist misbehaving when the chances of being found out look slim.

How children feel about punishment
To see how children felt about the justice or otherwise of punishment, Piaget offered children stories which featured two different kinds. One he called 'expiatory' punishment where a child who told lies might be beaten, sent to bed or deprived of a favourite toy. In other words, the punishment had no direct link with the fault, it was simply some form of retribution.

The second sort Piaget called 'reciprocity' punishment where, for instance, a child who refuses to go and buy bread for his mother is made to go without bread at dinner; a child who persists in playing football despite being warned about the danger of breaking a window, and then breaks his own bedroom window, does not have it repaired and suffers from the cold in winter as a direct consequence of his bad behaviour. Reciprocal punishment focuses on the consequences of the naughty deed – going without bread, being left in a room minus a window pane. Or it can involve exclusion from the social group: this punishment is often resorted to by children among themselves, for instance when they refuse to go on playing with a cheat.

The stories were tested on 100 children between six and twelve years of age. The youngest children said the fairest punishment was whichever was most severe: punishment to them consisted of inflicting upon the guilty sufficient pain to make him realise the gravity of his misdeed. However, the older children said that reciprocity punishment was fairer than expiatory – doing to the transgressor something similar to what he did himself so he would appreciate the consequences of his actions. It seems that if adults want to foster a growing sense of fairness, they have to find ways of tying the punishment to the crime and making sure the child can see the link.

Another experiment shows how children start to understand psychological situations and how this affects their attitude to punishment. Piaget told groups of children a story about a mother who gave a larger piece of cake to her obedient daughter, who she liked best, than to her disobedient daughter.

At the age of six to nine, the majority of children approved of the mother's behaviour and said simply that obedience should be rewarded, disobedience punished, but among children from ten to thirteen the majority disapproved. The older ones realised it was more complicated than simple obedience or disobedience. They said it was unfair of the mother to treat her daughters differently, adding things like, 'she ought to have loved them both the same', 'you can't have people being jealous', 'she will only get naughtier and naughtier', 'she will be revenged against her sister' and 'the other one saw she wasn't loved so she didn't take any trouble to improve'.

Here you can see the evolution of understanding, with children realising that the way the parent behaves can affect the way the child behaves. The little ones accept that adults have the right to punish unwanted behaviour. The older ones have learnt to understand psychological situations and can see that some punishments are unfair because sometimes adults are unfair. They are starting to judge us according to their own moral beliefs. Children begin by attributing moral perfection to their parents and then, as they grow up, discover all our faults and imperfections.

Chapter Three
Five to seven: going out into the wide world

There is a sea-change in the child's world when he starts full-time school. Although he may have gone to a nursery or playgroup already, being thrust into the bigger environment of primary school means that he has to learn lots of new rules in school and in the playground, and he will start to discover that they don't all conform to what Mummy and Daddy taught him. For the first time, he will start to think about his behaviour and you will notice his after-school stories introduced with 'Miss says . . .' or 'Harry never has to . . .' as he seeks your reaction to the novel idea he has encountered that day. I still remember the feeling of shock that hit me when I tried to correct one of my daughter's spellings and she pointed out that Miss spelled it that way, as though God himself had spoken. I had been knocked off the pedestal of All-powerful, All-knowing Mother – and by some silly woman who couldn't even spell!

It doesn't happen overnight. At first primary school children simply fall in with the rules laid down for them at school, however absurd they may seem, just as they have been doing at home. If the rule is for the class to line up in the playground and go in when teacher gives the word, that is what they will do: they don't ask why they can't go straight to the classroom as soon as they arrive. The child's life is saturated with rules and regulations which they don't really see the point of and they will simply accept the authority not only of teachers but of older children. So if they are taught something new, such as a skipping game or marbles by the older children, they will follow the rules unquestioningly. To them, rules are there to be respected.

Mummy knows best

At five and six your child will respond to labels of good, bad, right and wrong, but he won't yet understand *why* some behaviour is labelled good and right and other deeds bad and wrong. What he does is interpret his behaviour in terms of punishment and reward, or by what is being demanded by the physically powerful people who set the rules. For a child of this age, acts are good or bad according to what the consequences would be. If he does something and is punished, he assumes the act was wrong.

You can see how young children accept adult values of crime and punishment in their response to stories told by Piaget. He began his exploration of children's moral attitudes by telling small children stories about children who were punished for clumsiness. He chose clumsiness because he noted that it played a disproportionately important part in a child's life as he comes into conflict with his surroundings. 'At every moment the child arouses the anger of those around him by breaking, soiling or spoiling some object or other. Most of the time such anger is unjustifiable but the child naturally attaches a meaning to it.'

In the experiment, children were told a pair of stories. In the first, John is called to dinner, goes into the dining room and accidentally knocks over a chair, hidden behind the door, on which there was a tray with fifteen cups, breaking them all. In the second story, Henry decides to help himself to some jam from the cupboard while his mother is out. The jar is too high and while he is trying to reach it, Henry knocks over and breaks a cup.

Piaget discovered that at five or six children can't distinguish between deliberate acts and accidents as clearly as we do: instead what matters to them is the actual result. Asked which child is most guilty and therefore deserves most punishment they said John, because he broke more cups than Henry. Even if the tester challenged them and pointed out that John didn't know the cups were there while Henry was deliberately doing something he shouldn't, the children persisted in saying that the child who did the most damage was the one who should be punished most severely. Their assessment of guilt and punishment was based purely on material damage, because at five or six children pay unquestioning respect to adult ideas and since adults tend to get cross in proportion to the amount of damage done, the child begins by adopting this way of assessing things.

However, children's ideas of what is good and bad behaviour change as they grow. American child psychologists Robert Selman and William Damon told groups of small children a story about a little girl called Holly whose father makes her promise not to climb trees – even though she is the best tree climber in the neighbourhood – because he once saw her fall off a tree. Then a friend asks Holly to climb a tree to rescue a kitten. What, the children were asked, is the right thing for Holly to do?

At four and five, children usually answered that Holly should not climb the tree because her father has told her not to. They believed he would be right to punish Holly if she did climb the tree, because he is the father and she disobeyed him. The fact that the kitten was in danger did not suggest to them that maybe the father's instruction could be disregarded. These small children have no sense of justice; they simply believe they must do as they are told.

This unquestioning obedience to what mummy and daddy want doesn't last. By seven or eight children have come to realise that the same act may have different causes and stem from different intentions. So they will say that it is wrong for Holly to climb the tree if she is simply being disobedient, but it might be right if it is to rescue a kitten. What has happened is that they have come to appreciate that a course of behaviour is not necessarily right or wrong in itself, but that acts *intending* good are generally right and those *intending* bad are wrong. When a child grasps this, he will start to distinguish between what people have the power to do and what they have the right to do, and will start to question whether, just because you can make him help with the washing up it is right for him to help. When this starts, you will need to come up with explanations instead of orders.

Learning about lies

The same progress from absolute confidence in the parents' set of rules to a more subjective approach can be seen in the ideas that primary school children have about lying. Little children are pretty confused about lying since they are not sure what a lie actually is. In their early years their heads are full of fantasies and daydreams and it is hard for them to distinguish what it is that adults would call true from what is imaginary, and harder still to understand that what is imaginary may be called a 'lie'. So the child is astonished when he pronounces something that does not conform to the strict truth and finds his words are met with reproach. He is even more confused if he uses some of the exciting new words he has just picked up in the playground and gets the same horrified response.

In his confusion, the child decides that there are things you can say and things you can't say and calls all the things you can't say 'lies' whether they are statements that do not accord with the facts or just swear words. The situation gets even more muddled since at five or six children often confuse lying with making a mistake, calling both sorts of inaccuracy 'lies'.

It is important for you to distinguish between lies and fantasy even, or especially, when your child can't. You must make it clear that fantasy is not wrong or naughty. Children do have vivid imaginations and the last thing you want to do is curb or stifle their flights of fancy. If the child is spinning you a yarn, help him to sort it out by letting him see that you know this is a story and a wonderful one. If you use the word 'story' for his creative efforts, he will start to learn the difference between fantasy and fact.

Even when children grasp the idea of a lie, they tend to rate its wickedness by its scale, regardless of the intentions of the person telling the lie, just as they thought that the child who broke fifteen cups was naughtier than the child who broke only one. In another experiment Piaget told children two stories. In one a little girl lied out of fear – she had been frightened by a dog in the street and told her mother that the dog was as big as a cow – while in the second story a little boy lies out of mischief – he tells his mother the teacher has given him good marks at school when she has not given him any marks, good or bad, and his mother is pleased and rewards him.

The experimenter found that little children would evaluate the lie according to how probable it was and said the naughtiest child was the girl, because the story of a dog as big as a cow was completely unbelievable. As there is nothing unusual about getting good marks at school and the parents would readily accept it, the boy was not so bad. In other words, little children thought the bigger the lie, the worse it was.

Alongside the problem of learning the difference between truth and falsehood, children face the difficulty of distinguishing between an involuntary error and a deliberate lie and there is some doubt about whether a child of six or seven can truly tell the difference between one and the other. The little work that has been done on the subject seems to show that the distinction is, at best, still in the process of formation at this age.

Piaget, for instance, told these two stories: in the first, a gentleman asks a boy the way on the street; the boy isn't sure of the streets, but he tries to help. However, his instructions are wrong and the gentleman gets lost. In the second story the boy does know the streets, but deliberately tells the gentleman the wrong route. However, the gentleman manages to find his way again despite this.

Children of around six say the naughtiest boy is the one who got the gentleman lost. They are still in the world where bad results mean you must be a bad child. By seven and eight they are beginning to question this and you find them starting to consider the role played by intention and motive. So now they say that the boy who gave false information for a lark deserves to be punished most. By eight to ten children can tell the difference between lies and errors. As one child explained, 'When you lie you're doing it on purpose, when you make a mistake you don't know.'

This confusion in the five- and six-year-old's mind between truth and fantasy, lies and errors, means you can't expect too much too soon: telling the truth and not telling lies are hard and complicated concepts for them to grasp. Why should you not tell lies? Ask a young child and by far the most common answer is that you mustn't tell lies because, 'you get punished' or 'Mummy doesn't like it'. If you then ask the child, 'If telling lies wasn't punished would it be naughty?' the answer comes pat: 'Oh no.' In other words, small children look upon lying as naughty because it is punished, and see lies as a fault because they are forbidden by adults, though they don't understand why.

So you have to be very careful when you reprove a child for something he has said. If you have asked a straight question and got a fantastical answer – for instance if you ask where his clean sports kit is and he says the aliens have taken it – you should explain that this is a story, like the stories he reads or watches on television and what you want to know is where has he put his clean kit. Can he remember? Then, when he comes up with the right explanation, say so: 'That's what I wanted to know.' This helps him to work out what sort of answer is required of him, and helps him to see the difference between the things he imagines and the things he does in real life.

Similarly, if you ask him a question and he gets the answer wrong – for instance if you ask him whether Richard's mother is collecting them both from swimming and he says 'yes' when the answer is 'no' – then later, when you find out the truth, you can point it out to him. 'You told me that Richard's mother was picking you up but she can't manage it today – you made a mistake.' This sort of explanation helps him to sort out in his mind the difference between a lie and an error.

It might sound impossibly difficult to pick up on your child's remarks like this, and certainly you're not going to remember to do it all the time nor have the time and energy to do so, but if you spell out these differences as often as you can, it really helps your child to get a grasp on fantasy, truth, lies and error and helps him along the path to honesty.

Double standards
One of the problems we all face is that you are trying to set standards within the home which are not observed in society at large, and telling the truth is one of the standards too often broken in public life. For instance, every small child has had the miserable experience of seeing an advertisement on television for a wonderful toy that seemed full of action and excitement and then, when he finally unwraps his present on Christmas Day, discovers it is just a few bits of boring plastic. The advertiser has lied to him.

You can use these experiences by helping him to understand his feelings, saying 'You've been told a lie about what the toy could do and it makes you feel bad. Telling lies does that, it makes people feel bad. And if you told me a lie, you wouldn't feel good.' You're saying to the child, in effect, I feel better about you if you're being honest with me. You feel better about me if you're being honest. So let's be honest because it feels better.

The relationship between the two of you is the crucial thing in such an exchange: you must give back what you are asking. If you're asking for honesty and respect, you must first give these to the child. If you are not honest yourself, you will never get honesty from him. For instance, if you say that you mustn't steal but then gloat when you buy something cheap because it fell off the back of a lorry – those weasel words for describing stolen goods – your child will absorb the message that theft is acceptable in his family. If you don't give back the wrong change in the shop, or if you hand your child a chocolate bar from the shelf as you move through the supermarket and don't declare it at the checkout, these messages, too, are absorbed by the ever-watchful child, and if you don't respect his property, he won't respect yours.

The adult world, unfortunately, does not set children a very good example. We see professional footballers pretending to have been appallingly injured in a tackle in the hope of forcing a penalty, only to leap up fully fit again moments later. In a recent survey of golfers, over half admitted to cheating and some clubs are having to install spy cameras on the links to stop their members falsifying their scores. A new problem of plagiarism has sprung up in universities because some students are down-loading highly-marked sample essays from the Internet and passing them off as their own. In a world where even the highly-paid, the middle class and the reasonably intelligent don't hesitate to stoop to cheating, it is hard for us to get the right message across to our children.

James Hemming, a consultant psychiatrist and broadcaster, recognises that these are difficult times for parents who find themselves battling against a climate of moral indifference. 'The modern child is up against the fact that society is screaming the wrong values at him or her. The values that society trumpets are the values of selfishness, and what we need is the exact opposite. If the child is encouraged and learns to like other people and to respect himself by the way he's treated, then he will grow up naturally moral. This is why the home is so important.' You have to dig in your heels and try to lean against the tide of slack morality because whether the environment surrounding a child is social or selfish will condition his whole style of life. If the rest of the world is shouting 'grab', it is up to you to offer the alternative view.

Luckily, children are on your side in the battle for higher standards. Professor Nick Emler, a social psychologist at

Oxford University says, 'One of the striking things, if one talks to children, is how reasonable they are. It's hard to understand how so many of them grow up into nasty adults. They do seem typically, more often than not, to have a sense of what's fair and what's right and what's just.'

Talking about moral dilemmas

One way of getting children to think about the sort of moral dilemmas they face when they start school – whether it is right to take someone else's pen without asking, or whether you should copy someone else's work – is to get them talking about a familiar situation and ask, 'Do you think so and so is doing the right thing? What will happen if he does that? What would you do?' Talking to your children about why they should do this or that can start as young as six or seven.

Little discussions like this will get the child thinking about what choices people have, and morality is all about making choices. If you ask your small child to weigh up the choice between helping with the washing up or playing with his toys and he chooses to help out, you know you are on the right track.

One group which has taken practical steps to encourage children to think about how to behave is the Citizenship Foundation, which was set up in 1989 by Andrew Phillips, a London lawyer. The Foundation's aim is to teach schoolchildren how to become well-informed and responsible adults, able to understand the rights and duties of citizenship and to weigh up social, moral and legal issues. It does this by presenting them with case histories and posing questions for them to answer.

Its projects are really geared to children because they are rooted in real life and deal with the sort of events every child has experienced. For instance, it developed a game for primary school children which you could easily adapt to play at home. The children are organised into groups of three: two players and a judge, and there are two piles of cards, one labelled 'Person' and one 'Item'. Examples of Person cards are an astronaut, a weightlifter, a ten-year-old boy, a rich businesswoman and a policeman. The Item cards are things like a bunch of flowers, a teddy bear, a book, a wedding ring, a £5 note and a photograph of a child.

Each child takes a card from the top of the Person pile and looks at it, then the judge takes a card from the Item set and shows it to both players. Then the two children take it in turns to give a reason why that item may be important or of particular value to the person on their card. The judge (who could be you) decides which child's reasons are most imaginative and acceptable.

The aim is to encourage imaginative and emphatic thinking to help children understand that people can place great value on things of little monetary worth. So the policeman might love the teddy bear because it used to belong to his friend, or the astronaut might value the £5 note because he had it with him in space and thinks it is lucky. This way the child sees that things sometimes have a value because of their personal and sentimental associations, regardless of what they are worth.

A game like this helps small children to realise that taking someone else's property may be emotionally upsetting as well as financially damaging. This is a particularly important lesson in infant school since there can scarcely be a schoolchild living who has not considered doing a little light shoplifting in their time, or 'borrowed' something from a friend without remembering to tell the friend. Learning that stealing can be emotionally hurtful to the victim can help to keep your child on the straight and narrow.

'Look what I can do'
Empathy is a crucial part of morality, but children first have to feel good about themselves if they are to grow up decent. Self-esteem is the starting point for moral education because if you don't feel good about yourself, then there's hardly any

motivation to think about others. If you don't feel proud of yourself, if you don't feel, 'I'm not the sort of person who does that,' about bad deeds, or 'I'm the sort of person who does that,' about good, you will never develop altruistic feelings.

Learning to do things successfully is terribly important for children. A sense of achievement makes them feel good about themselves and children who are happy are also well behaved. Unfortunately, their idea of what constitutes an achievement may not quite chime with yours – small children are likely to respect a friend who can spit farthest or fart loudest – but any success builds up their self-respect. It is one of the pleasant tasks you have as a parent to seek out some activity that your offspring can succeed at – whether it's learning to swim, making an omelette, washing the family car or whatever. Doing anything well will make him feel good about himself.

Teachers also have a very important role to play in building up a child's sense of achievement and they must try to be fair and supportive. Professor Nick Emler remarks: 'We remember for years afterwards those instances when adults have done to us things we feel are outrageously unfair. People can remember an instance when a teacher was unfair to them 30 or 40 years later.' Asking teachers to be supportive doesn't mean they have to pour out fulsome praise. Too many gold stars handed round the class will soon devalue them: a nod is often good enough.

Recognition and praise for the child's achievements are important right through childhood. You have to be grown up before you accept that a job well done is its own reward – and even adults bask in the occasional compliment. Alfred Adler was once asked at a public meeting in America what he thought were the most important things in helping a young child to become a fully developed social individual and his reply was: 'One, encourage the child. Two, help the child to come out on the useful side of life. Three, never forget the other two!'

The reverse side of boosting the little child's sense of achievement is the need to protect him from being cast down by feelings of failure. When children are small and not very efficient, one of the sensible ways of maintaining your child's self-respect is by protecting him from unnecessary competition with its inevitable risk of failure. Of course you may not be entirely guiltless yourself: some mothers have a pretty competitive streak and will remark with mock modesty how their infant seems to talk earlier or read better than the average child, seeking to justify their adoration of their offspring by suggesting he truly merits such homage. In reality, at six and seven children are still struggling to tie their shoelaces, to tell the time or to form a coherent sentence and they have quite enough to do trying to succeed in these daily endeavours without worrying about how everyone else is getting on.

Probably the silliest competition takes place at the children's birthday parties to which the schoolchild will now be invited. These are seldom the happy, unstructured events that we adults mean by the word party. I have raged inwardly at infant parties where the whole occasion was given over to endless games of musical chairs, pass the parcel, statues and the like where, of course, one child would win and all the others lose. What tension, grief and humiliation they provoke, entirely the opposite of everything we mean by celebration. Games there must be, to channel all that fearsome energy, but they should be fun. I must admit that at my own children's parties I simply cheated and stopped the music at a point that ensured every child won one game and they all went home with a prize.

Instead of competition we should be fostering co-operation, a willingness to get along with others, respect for their needs, and help if they are in difficulties. Concern and feeling for others are the basis of a moral life and pitting one child against another and making one feel useless and a failure does nothing to encourage it.

Balancing love and laziness

Much as you love your children, and essential though parental love is, love alone is not enough. Professor John Wilson of the Department of Educational Studies at Oxford explains that though a successful parent 'feels affection towards the child, shares with him, rejoices and suffers with him, cares for him, loves him in his own right and irrespective of merit, and creates a structure for him which provides security' the parent must also learn to draw the line. As well as loving your child you have to insist that he is subject to rules and discipline, that he works as well as plays, learns to treat others as equals and considers their interests, and has a sensible attitude to authority.

'These two together constitute love,' says Professor Wilson. 'If there is too much of the first, you get a 'caring' for children that permits a degree of indiscipline and laziness which is rationally indefensible. Coming back into fashion, you're now getting a passion for work, discipline and self-help which can sometimes overlook or forget about the idiosyncratic, unconditional affection and tenderness we all need. To only care, or to only discipline a child is bound to fail. We all need both.'

He argues that the best way of teaching small children to think about moral issues is to put them into situations where they have to consider other people's rights and needs. They can be simple family events like sharing food around the family dinner table or everybody taking a turn with the washing up; any family occasion where the child can see that you have to take your share of responsibility without complaining, play fair in life generally, and that it's important to be unselfish.

The child's life is getting more complicated and you can help him make sense of it if you seize every opportunity to talk through the sort of problems he is starting to face and get him to think them through. For instance, parents have to try to take the glamour and excitement out of stealing and present it for what it is at a level the child can appreciate: an everyday meanness. Another unit from the Citizenship

Foundation tells the sort of story you might find helpful. Mr and Mrs Roberts own the corner shop. He is worried that some of the children who come into his shop to buy sweets, crisps and drinks are stealing. When his wife says he should tell the police, he says he doesn't want to get these children into trouble. And furthermore, he knows that one of the children who is stealing from him gets no breakfast.

It's the sort of story even a six- or seven-year-old can understand, and you can ask the child, 'What should happen to the children who are stealing from Mr Roberts' shop, and why?' Add, 'He's always been kind to the children. Why are some of them stealing from him? Are they being kind to Mr Roberts? Is it all right to steal from a shop? If not, why not? Is stealing from a small shop different from stealing from a supermarket? Why? Or Why not?'

When they have given some thought to whether it is fair or wrong to steal, you can get them to think hard about what it means to be a thief. 'What should happen to the thieves? Why do you think this? Should they be punished? Should Mr Roberts call the police? What about the child who is hungry in the mornings and gets no pocket money, is it all right for him to steal? Why? Or Why not?'

This brings the child back to the notion of fairness, one of the basic elements in the young child's vocabulary and a very important moral principle. Even with these young children you can ask whether it is fair or unfair for all the children who are shoplifting to be blamed or punished equally, or whether the circumstances might help to excuse one of them.

The point of exercises like this is not to elicit the right answer. You are not trying to see if your child has learnt the rules of good behaviour off by heart. What you are trying to do is to get him thinking about moral dilemmas, to put his brain to work and puzzle through the implications and complications of the situation so that he can make a fair and sensible judgement. Just learning the right answer – shoplifting is bad – is not enough. It is all too easy to imagine a child being questioned in class about stealing and coming up pat with the right answer and still nicking sweets off his classmate at breaktime.

We have to give children the information they need in order to ponder over moral judgements and help them develop the skills they require to make those judgements. You must encourage the child to wrestle with these problems himself, prodded by your questions and suggestions, so that he will feel the answers are his own answers and the beliefs his own beliefs, and then he will really accept and practise them.

Out of your sight

You can get a child to obey the rules when you are watching, but if you want him to obey the rules when you are not around you have to help him to start thinking of these rules as his own beliefs and feelings – to 'internalise' them.

Nancy Eisenberg and Bridget Murphy of Arizona State University discovered that what is most helpful at getting children to develop this internal motivation is the technique you use to get co-operation. It needs to be powerful enough to persuade the child to comply, but subtle too, so that the child does not feel he is being forced into the desired behaviour. If the balance is right, the child does not feel as though he is doing the right thing because of outside pressure from you, but believes he behaved that way of his own accord. When this happens, the good behaviour will become part of his own personal behaviour pattern.

Now that your child no longer regards everything you say as gospel, to be obeyed without question, one of the best ways of helping him to adopt the behaviour you desire is to introduce at least a small amount of choice into your request. For instance, you can allow him to decide when, but not whether, to do his homework. Though we have seen that parents should be consistent, that doesn't mean you have to send a child to bed at exactly the same time every night: there can be room for a little negotiation.

Morality is all about making choices, and you can help him to develop the ability to weigh one thing against another by letting him practise making plenty of choices in his everyday life. Let him follow his personal taste in food, play, friends, hobbies, clothes and so on as far as you reasonably can. I used to stand amazed at the school gate in the morning listening to mothers describe the terrible battles they had had to get their children dressed in the morning (one of the things I liked about the school was that it had no uniform). I avoided such confrontations by simply allowing my daughter to wear whatever she wanted provided it was warm and decent. OK, so she sometimes went out looking, to me, like a perambulating jumble sale, but she was happy and she was learning to make decisions. It takes practice.

You can also get the child to think they are choosing to do the right thing of their own accord if you make a suggestion about what you want rather than giving explicit directions: 'Should we give granny a hand in the garden?' It also helps if you show him the sort of behaviour you want instead of simply dictating it, or if you offer to share the task: helping him to clear up his toys for instance.

You will get even better results if you emphasise how attractive the desired activity is and so stimulate his interest. 'Wouldn't it be fun to give Fido a bubble bath?' will get much better results than, 'It's time you gave that damn dog of yours a bath.' Finally, when the child is doing the right thing, if you make remarks that attribute his behaviour to his own motives, even when that is not obvious – for instance if you tell him that he is bathing the dog because he is a helpful child – that, too, can enhance internalisation.

A reasonable request

Once the child has started school and begun to think for himself you have to use reason whenever possible.

For instance, in a recent interview Dr Benjamin Spock referred to a study which calculated that the average American child sees 18,000 fictional murders before reaching adulthood and he argued that every time a child watches a violent programme, that child's capacity for violence increases slightly. 'Parents need to prevent children from seeing violent television programmes,' he said, 'but it is important to explain to the child exactly why these programmes are bad for them. You don't just tell a child, "I forbid you to watch violent television." You say, "There is too much violence in the world." You reason with the child. And that means the parent too. Children get to be what they are by watching their parents, so it is important for the parents not to watch violent television either – at least in front of the children – and not to be verbally abusive to their children, or their spouse, and not to swear in front of the children.'

The family ally
At least when children are small, there is often one particularly useful aid to hand to help the stressed out parent, and that is grandparents. The relationship between grandparents and grandchildren can be particularly rewarding because it carries less responsibility. Parents can't always be nice because children do have bad moods, they do behave badly at times and parents have to correct them. The children, of course, loathe it, but it is part of life.

On the other hand, grandparents can be almost continuously benign, encouraging and supportive. They have time to listen to children, which is vitally important, and to play with them, which is also necessary. They have a lifetime's experience to draw on, which makes them less inclined to make snap judgements or to be too hasty in laying blame because they know life is more complicated than it first appears. They have seen many different solutions to life's problems attempted and have a good idea which work best.

Also, if the child is angry with his parents because they have corrected him for something, the grandparents can present the parents' point of view – not to say, 'Well, you're right and they're wrong', that would be disastrous, but to say, 'Well, Mummy's very worried you know, when you behave like that, and so she told you to stop.' As a sympathetic ear and an encouraging presence, grandparents can play a wonderful supporting role.

Keeping in step with your child
Children start out by simply obeying the rules they are given, but little by little a moral sense develops. It doesn't burst out, fully-formed, overnight. You cannot say, yesterday my child was amoral, today he is moral. Morality seems to develop slowly, going through a series of stages as the child builds up a fuller understanding of how society works and what is expected of him. The broad sweep of moral development is from childish selfishness through adolescent conformity on to principled morality. The idea of moral stages means you have to think of the child as a developing person, as a thinker with a point of view; not a blank slate but an active architect busy constructing a moral view. This means you have to deal with children at their current level of understanding.

The idea that there are stages in moral development was set out most fully by Professor Lawrence Kohlberg, who studied the development of moral judgement and character in a group of the same boys over a period of fifteen years. Kohlberg reported that the earliest stage was when the child just responds to the rules. At this level of moral development, even the best children are capable of cruel behaviour because they don't really understand what lies behind the rules.

Then, as the child matures, he starts to see that there are two people involved in relationships so you are negotiating between what two people want, which may conflict. The child's appreciation of relationships grows as he becomes aware that other people's thoughts and feelings may be different from his. From about five upwards he starts to realise that people feel differently or think differently from him, because they are in a different situation. He realises that, 'Just because Peter *thinks* Billy wants to go swimming doesn't mean Billy *does* want to go swimming.' He also realises that the same act may have different causes and stem from different intentions, and that some of these intentions may be considered 'good' and others 'bad'.

The next stage, which Kohlberg called the 'conventional' stage, comes in early adolescence when children become aware of the expectations and rules of the community, which is made up of their family, their school and of society at large, and are keen not only to conform to the social order but to uphold it and support it. At this stage, good behaviour is seen as acts that please or help others and win their approval. For the first time the judgement, 'he means well' becomes important: being nice earns approval and right behaviour means doing one's duty, showing respect for authority and maintaining the given social order for its own sake. A child at the conventional stage views human relations as a sort of market place where the right action satisfies one's needs and occasionally the needs of others. At this level he will be capable of showing some fairness and reciprocity, but always in a pragmatic way. Reciprocity means, 'You scratch my back and I'll scratch yours.'

The third stage comes in the late teens and twenties when the child starts to understand the more abstract idea of 'society'. Now he accepts that there are certain moral principles which are valid irrespective of the authority of the groups who hold them, or his own identification with these groups. He sees that there is a social contract, and right action is now defined in terms of the rights and standards that have been agreed on by the whole of society. By the late teens, the youngster knows that personal opinions can vary from one individual to another and there is an emphasis on formal procedures such as the law for regulating competing claims among different groups in society.

You may not agree with Kohlberg's analysis in detail, and many of his followers have since criticised or adapted it, but seeing moral development as a series of stages that a child passes through does help you to meet him at his current level of understanding, where you won't expect more than he can deliver and where your efforts will have most chance of success.

For instance, with the primary school child, still attached to his belief that he should obey the rules however baffling they are, you can get results simply by saying something like, 'Geoffrey, this is a chance for you to do as you're told.' At the tit-for-tat fairness stage of the older child you can say, 'I did a favour for you yesterday, now I'm asking a favour of you.' To the teenager, obsessed with, 'What will people think of me?' something along the lines of, 'I'm disappointed by your behaviour, you can do better than that,' will be most effective.

You have to do more, however, than just work out what moral stage your child is at. In order to boost their moral development you have to challenge their present level of moral decision-making with more demanding reasoning in order to nudge them along to the next level. For instance, you can challenge a small child to see that fairness is a better reason for co-operating than fear of punishment. It's very tempting to play by the rules of authority and tell small children that they have to behave because the Bible or mummy says so, because 'Nice girls don't do that sort of thing,' or 'Big boys don't cry.' However, it is better to put them gently but firmly on the track of the right reasons and to explain why this particular behaviour is wrong.

Roger Straughan, who teaches student teachers at the University of Reading, explains that, 'Children should be taught as soon as possible that rules are not proven facts, but moral judgements that can be supported, discussed, challenged and perhaps revised. So any moral rules that young children are expected to obey should be provisional, and you must accept that the children should not simply learn to obey them, but seek the justification for them.

'Of course letting children think for themselves and work out their own conclusions and make their own decisions is time-consuming, and can be boring or irritating for the adults, and much slower than just telling them what to do. But they must work things out for themselves if they are to develop into moral agents.'

Interlude
Raising a bully

When I was a little girl at infant school, I bounced home one day and told my mother what a wonderful playtime we had had, standing in a circle round a strange new girl shouting 'snotty nose' at her because her nose was dripping.

My mother nearly fainted away. How had she raised such a monster? She asked where the little girl had come from – perhaps she had been bombed out of her house (this was during the war) and all her things had been lost, including her handkerchiefs? Maybe she had even lost her mummy and daddy? How would I feel if a whole gang of strange children picked on me? In five minutes my mother had me full of concern for the little girl, and appalled to think what I had done, to realise I had to call myself a bully.

I wasn't quite so keen on my mother's idea of redress: she produced a pretty new handkerchief and said I was to take it to school next day and give it to the victim. What would my friends think? I was hugely relieved when I got to school the following morning to find that the girl was not there and, indeed, never came back, but it left me feeling less smug about myself, and I still cringe at what we did and wish that I could have apologised.

My behaviour wasn't unusual, however, and certainly not due to any failure by my sainted parents to explain about kindness and cruelty. All small children can be cruel because they are pretty egocentric and simply don't have sufficient experience of the world to understand in every circumstance what causes hurt or how it feels. Young children are not yet able to think about other people – it takes a mum to sit down and say, 'Can you imagine how that child feels?'

Rowan Myron-Wilson has been studying children and parents for her doctorate at Goldsmith's College in London, to establish to what extent the parent is responsible for producing a bully. It is not an easy task. You can't just walk into a school, ask them to nominate the school bullies and then accost the parents to ask them how they feel about the nomination.

'I don't think I've come across any parent who's stood up and said, "Yes, my child is a bully," ' says Rowan. 'Whereas if I just approach them saying I'm doing a general study, they always assume their child is the normal one.'

Rowan went into seven local schools and tested all the children. She measured the degree of attachment between the parent and child and carried out an in-depth interview with the parent about the family, asking them what they thought about discipline, how they treated their child and how they saw themselves as parents. She also asked the children about parental style and looked at how both parent and child saw the power relations within the family. She assessed bully status by peer nomination: the children said who had been doing what to whom in the class and pupils then got a score for how much bullying behaviour they were showing to their schoolmates.

Rowan was particularly interested in parental attitudes to bullying because they have been strangely neglected. Although a lot of important work has been done on bullying in recent years, most of the research has concentrated on schools, not families. 'And though parents may be brought in, it's to look at what can be done, not at the root causes of the behaviour, which I think is remarkably stupid,' says Rowan. She points out that psychologists have seen again and again in the last twenty years how two things, attachment theory and parental style, affect children's behaviour including their relationships with other children, yet nobody has taken that knowledge and asked whether they also affect bullying.

The importance of attachment

The most important thing in every child's life is to have a consistent attachment figure says Rowan. 'It doesn't matter if it's mother or father, aunt or uncle or grandma, as long as there's somebody throughout at least the first seven to ten years of life to be a consistent role model to say, this is how life should be run, this is the good, this is the bad and these are the boundaries between what you can do and what you can't do.

'A child can get by without being very happy. It sounds awful, but children don't need to be loved and wonderfully happy to survive and become a decent adult as long as they have that kind of foundation, an understanding of good and bad.

'Attachment theory has moved on since the early days and what we have now is what's called an Internal Working Model. This is the idea that through all the interactions with Mum right from the very beginning, an infant develops an internal working model on which it bases all other relationships. So if, for example, there's an insecure mother who is not quite sure what she's doing or is suffering from post-natal depression or whatever and is not interacting well with the child – if there is a dysfunctional model, the child learns that dysfunctional model. And when it goes out into the world at large all its other relationships will be based on that dysfunctional model. And very often they go on to make their own insecure marriages, raise their own insecure children and the cycle continues.'

Where earlier childcare experts such as John Bowlby suggested that the mother was the essential figure and should be available to the child more or less 24 hours a day, the latest research suggests that an Internal Working Model can be created by any attachment figure. Also, although huge separations will affect it – if the attachment figure disappears for three months, say – shorter absences such as a parent going out to work are no problem. In fact some studies show that parents who work part-time are actually getting better results than those who stay at home. Even children in very dysfunctional families can form a strong attachment to someone other than their parents, such as a grandparent. The trouble here is that it is in the very nature of the relationship for it to be short-lived since grandparents die. To lose someone for the first time can be a dreadful experience for a child and bereavement can dislocate a child dramatically.

The parents of bullies
What Rowan found, though so far her results are preliminary, was that the more negatively a child sees its parents and the higher the parent scored on the neglect and punitive scales, the more likely the child is to be a bully. Also, she found that children who were only insecurely attached to a parent are much more likely to be involved in bullying. 'Secure children seem to be able to just keep out of it – they've got their friends or they can go home and tell Mum and they just seem to avoid the situation.'

Insecure children sometimes block off their feelings of insecurity by becoming very cold and distant. In the past such behaviour was thought to go hand in hand with bullying, but Rowan found such children were more likely to be victims, 'because they are distant and mostly passive and unable to cope with the aggression'. Other insecure children become ambivalent and Rowan found the bullies tended to be on this side. 'When a parent has become inconsistent so the kid doesn't know where it is you find them acting out tantrums and thrashing about and this is more likely to lead on to bullying behaviour.'

The Goldsmith research contradicts a common view that over-protective parents raise bullies because their children expect to be favoured and pampered all the time. Rowan and Professor Peter K. Smith looked at the link between parental style and bullying and found that the children of over-protective parents were more likely to be victims than bullies.

They identified four styles of parenting: authoritarian, where a parent is very strict and controlling but does not give much loving care to the child; authoritative, where a parent is high both in control and parental warmth; permissive-indulgent, where a parent is high in warmth but low in control; and permissive-indifferent, where the parent is low in both loving care and supervision. The Goldsmith research shows that the three aspects of parenting most liable to lead to bullying are lack of warmth, punitive and inconsistent discipline and a failure to monitor and supervise children's activities.

On the question of warmth, the study reveals that the more negative a parent is, the more likely a child is to be aggressive and a bully. 'I found that a bully's parents were much more likely to score high on neglect and punitiveness.' Unexpectedly, they found that high levels of parental warmth were also linked to bullying, but they feel that possibly these parents come under the permissive-indulgent heading, being carelessly warm and affectionate to the child but failing to set boundaries or keep the child under control. This type of over-indulgent parenting can unintentionally encourage aggressive behaviour as the child has no boundaries against which to measure his or her wrongdoing. On the other hand, says Rowan, 'Children are not stupid and may simply be trying to portray their parents as warmer than they really are.'

The second factor in the making of a bully is parents who fall down on discipline. Rowan explains: 'I don't think it does a child any good at all to be allowed to run wild, because then they don't learn where to stop and they go out and do what they like. They react badly to other kids because they don't know how they should be reacting. On the other hand, if the parenting is too rigid and conforming the child might rebel against it and take it out on a classmate.' High on the list of destructive parental habits is inconsistency – one day slamming their hand on the table saying, 'You can't do that,' and the next day, when they're very depressed or there's something wrong with them, not being fussed about what the child does. The result of these shifting boundaries is that the child never knows what to expect or what sort of behaviour will meet with approval.

Bullies themselves reported more troubled relationships with their parents than ordinary children. They scored their parents lowest on proper supervision and warmth and highest for both over-protection and neglect, which suggests they came from families where discipline and supervision were inconsistent and not tempered by warm affection. There is clearly a link between family structure and bulling: the higher the child scored on the bully scale, the more likely they were to see their family as fragmented and themselves as powerful. Bullies also had bad relations with their brothers and sisters, often seeing them as more powerful than themselves and expressing ambivalent feelings about them.

The Goldsmith research is backed up by the findings of a 1993 study of Australian adolescents where bullies reported poorer family functioning, more so for boys than for girls. They also reported poor relationships and more negative attitudes with their fathers than non-bullies and, for boys only, with their mothers too. A Cambridge study at the same time noted that fathers who had been bullies themselves at school tended to have children who bullied. They also found a link between violent parenting and bullying: over a third of the fathers convicted for violent offences had children who bullied.

Altogether it is clear that although schools can take many important steps to eliminate bullying, to be totally effective they need to work with the bully's family to tackle the root causes if they hope to change the child's long-term behaviour.

Can a child have a change of heart?
An experienced teacher can sometimes tell when a child walks into school at five that it has problems, but how those problems manifest themselves can be affected by circumstances. A child's upbringing depends on many intertwined

factors and the first years of child rearing can be very hard for parents when they have to face many sudden life changes, including whether they're working or not, whether their marriage is happy or not and whether they have family or friendship networks to support them. If any one of these sub-systems breaks down, young parents can find it very difficult to manage.

'I've seen a young girl who was a paragon of virtue almost. Her parents have just got divorced and now she's the worst bully in the class,' reports Rowan. 'So there are life events that can change a child. And a child can be changed for the good, too, if they form some kind of attachment relationship with someone else, whether it's Auntie Lou or the woman across the road, who can show them the boundaries and that it's not OK to hit Joey just because he annoyed them.'

At Goldsmith's they are looking into whether the children's fathers live with them or if they are living with a stepfather, to see if it matters. They don't know the answers yet, but they have found that it can be devastating if the parents break up and the children are left with a mother who they don't really get on with because Daddy always looked after them properly and was the real attachment figure, and Mum is the insecure one.

Home and family
Is there a kind of osmosis between parent and child? If a child grows up seeing punishment – dad bullying mum, brother bullying workmates – does that child think, *that's the way to do it, that's the way to get what I want?*

'I find the worst of the children I've come across have parents with the biggest problems,' says Rowan. 'Usually when I meet the parent, their mother or father or one of their relatives always seems to be an alcoholic. It always seems to be there somewhere. Or there's abuse or some awful trauma. It's messed the parent up and in turn they've not been able to pass on a normal model of family attachment to their child.'

When we are getting hot under the collar about a child's

nasty bullying behaviour, it's important to remember that no baby can choose which family takes it home from the maternity hospital: it could be Fred and Rosemary West. Erin Pizzey has pointed out that a child in a violent home is effectively suffering a life sentence. A murderer may serve only twelve years in gaol, but a child in a cold or brutal home is trapped there for sixteen years or more, learning nothing but grief and misery.

Research also shows that bullying has nothing to do with class: it occurs right across the board. The fact that they were upper class did not stop the boys at Gordonstoun from making Prince Charles's life a misery. 'Kids can be cruel,' says Rowan. 'It doesn't really matter what really sets you apart, if you're the odd one out, you're more likely to be the target. Whether it's the fact that everybody is moderately rich and you're dead poor, or the other way round, whether there a disability, facial scarring, having the wrong trainers or being Prince Charles: it's the difference that counts.'

Brainy bullies
The Goldsmith research challenges the popular stereotype that bullies are pretty stupid and lacking in social graces since it found that much successful bullying involved skilful manipulation of people and situations. Contrary to expectations, the bully group scored better than any other group on stories designed to assess their understanding of other minds.

Bullies are usually divided into three categories: the *bully*, who is active, takes the initiative and is leaderlike; the *assistant*, who is also active but more a follower than a leader; and the *reinforcer*, who incites the bully and provides an audience. Active bullies scored better in their manipulative skills than either assistants or reinforcers. The research suggests that ringleader bullies use their high social skills to organise the others into gangs, and to carry out indirect bullying.

The bullies' social sophistication was not matched by their emotional understanding: there is a gap between thoughts and feelings which produces a cold, effective bully. 'We have shown that some bullies know very well how others are thinking and are very manipulative,' says Rowan. 'They have mental ability but lack empathy. I think you see that kind of bullying in schools. There are bullies who can be reached by the sort of interventions you see in schools – you can sit them down and say, "Do you realise how much it hurt him?" and this will work. But there are some kids who really do have what is called "a cold cognition" – they understand but they don't care.'

Such bullies do not collapse at the first sign of resistance. I come from a generation which was taught that all bullies were cowards at heart and that if you just faced up to them they would cringe and slink away. It was a reassuring view, but wrong. In fact many bullies are extremely tough and just trample over opposition, and grow up to become highly-regarded captains of industry or politicians.

Nor are they all male. Girls are every bit as likely to bully as boys, but girls' bullying is generally less easy to see. 'Boys' bullying is likely to be much more physical,' says Rowan, 'more hot and passionate, the "give them a good kick and walk off" variety. Girls' bullying tends to be much more indirect, sending someone to Coventry or spreading rumours, saying to someone, "you're a slut, a whore", really nasty things that teachers don't tend to see. This sort of bullying is clever because it's hard to pinpoint and the bully finds it easy to shrug it off because there's nothing to show. It is not as obvious as being hit in the eye. If tackled, the bully will deny anything happened and it's very hard to prove. The victim doesn't tend to stand up and cry – she will feel unhappy but she won't let anyone see her misery.'

What schools can do
Changing the bully's behaviour is a lengthy, time-consuming process with quite a high likelihood of failure. One of the most effective ways of stamping out bullying is through peer pressure. Children can be helped to outlaw bullying among

themselves after long discussions, role-plays, drawing up and signing contracts and understanding what is and what is not acceptable behaviour between individuals and groups.

This can only happen at school and there needs to be an atmosphere throughout the school that bullying is completely unacceptable. You need a whole-school policy where if a teacher or dinner lady sees someone bullying in the play-ground they go up to them and say, 'You just don't do that.'

Confronting bullying head on often involves explaining to children that it is sometimes right and even necessary to tell tales. It is odd how powerful the prohibition on tale-telling is, considering the ban so much more often benefits the law-breaker than the good citizen, which is why villains prize silence so highly. If children are to put an end to school bullying, they have to be shown how to hold out against the silence of the peer group and encouraged to think of them-selves like the stalwart heroes of a Victorian novel, facing up to the evil-doers.

Of course you have to give pupils a good reason why they should report bad behaviour and not just keep quiet like their friends, and this means you give them an explanation – that there is always a pay-off, so if they don't tell on their friends a child will suffer. The situation has to be real.

David Ingram is working on a Just Community school project where the children themselves help to set the stand-ards. 'It's open to question all the time: you come back to questions of school uniform endlessly! But our school council actually commissioned research on bullying. They said they'd like the pupils to be actively involved and came up with a scheme called "Bullywatch". What they said was, "At the moment it's dealt with by the senior teachers and we feel safe with them because they have the power to combat the bullies that we're afraid of. But teachers don't know how much bullying goes on. We can see what's happening in the places the teachers will never see." '

All pupils need to know that their school has a policy on bullying and that there is someone they can turn to if they're in trouble. For instance, I visited an excellent secondary school in Castle Cary in Somerset where there were colour photographs on the noticeboards of the bully monitors for each year, so every pupil knew which child they could turn to for help, and the monitors were trained how to respond. David Ingram says that children at his school asked for three or four bullywatch monitors in each class so there was always a pupil you could go to and there were enough of them to resist the pressures of the bullies. 'That's why the model for moral education in the classroom that I would advocate is one that offers the opportunity for action, where the children actually have to make a decision which they will implement.

'For instance, I arrived for a meeting of our school council on Wednesday lunch time to find one of the girls in tears. She said, "So and so picked me up, carried me bodily into the boys' toilets, put me in a cubicle and held the door to." And she was distressed by this. And it turned out it was a boy who was on the school council. I got quite angry and asked him to leave, because I didn't think he could take part in a discussion on bullying at that time.

'We then asked the others to discuss what should happen and finally they decided he should be invited back to the council but reminded what their responsibilities were in the school. And the difficulty was to get him to accept that what he was doing was bullying where he saw it as horseplay. All the younger pupils saw it as bullying, but the older ones saw it as, "well he was laughing", "it was all right", "it was just a bit of fun".'

Rowan Myron-Wilson believes that part of the reason bullies get away with it can be put down to British reserve. 'My mother was a teacher and she was always the one who'd say, "Hey, stop that," and I'd be thinking, "Oh no, shut up mother." But you need someone to be constantly saying in the school, "don't push in the queue, don't hit that child". And it needs everyone to say that – just because you're in the town centre and not in school, it's still not acceptable.'

Though we all, as citizens, have a responsibility to challenge bullying behaviour wherever we see it, and not to look the other way as passive bystanders, in the end parents are the key factor. Rowan Myron-Wilson concludes: 'The school is fighting against the tide, especially if the child is going home to a successful bully family. If the father is a successful manager who bullies his staff, bullies everybody, the child is not going to retain anything of what he learnt at school about how roughness towards other children hurts them because he goes home and sees Dad doing that constantly. And Dad is a much stronger influence on that child. Children are like wet cement, everything that lands on them makes an impression. Everything that happens to a child is imprinted on its mind somewhere.'

Chapter Four
Eight to ten: doing the best they can

By the time they get to the top end of junior school, most children can apply basic moral principles to everyday situations. Professor John Wilson describes what they are like: 'I had working with me a psychologist and a sociologist and we went round asking children what they thought was right and wrong and, particularly, why they were so. And we came across some perfectly ordinary kids, not frightfully clever or middle class or anything, who would say, "Stealing's wrong." We asked them why, expecting to hear, "Well Mummy said so", or "It's in the Bible". Not a bit of it. I remember one kid saying "Don't be daft. How would you like it if your things were stolen?" In other words, it just doesn't work out for any of us if we don't have some principle about not taking property, and children soon understand this.'

Children learn these basic principles by living through first-hand situations which you then give a moral name to. It has to be that way round, from the practical to the theoretical. They don't grasp the idea of fairness by learning it first and then applying it, but by living through lots of examples of fair and unfair treatment at home, at school and in the playground, and learning to understand these events in moral terms. A principle means nothing to a child unless it is derived from her own experience.

By the time they are nine or ten, children have acquired principles such as fairness and co-operation and can apply

111

these principles to a range of situations. However, American psychologist William Damon points out that though a child of this age does have deeply held and frequently expressed moral principles, these concepts are still fairly new to her and she doesn't yet see morality as one of the features that makes her what she is; they are not part of her sense of identity.

'Ask a child, "What are you like?"' Damon says, 'and they'll describe their bodies, where they live, their clothes, their activities – "I'm short", "I'm athletic", "I'm smart", "My friends like me to play games with them". They might also include expressions of mood – "I feel cranky in the mornings sometimes" – or add comments about activities. "I don't know much about fixing bicycles", "I'm always anxious to do a good job". But they don't mention morality. And the wishes, hopes and aspirations of childhood almost always focus on material or action opportunities. Children usually wish for more money, a new car or a special outing.'

Damon also found at this age that moral principles, though understood, did not yet have a very strong hold. If children were put into a real-life situation where they had the chance to further their self-interest, most of them would hedge on their moral principles and promote their self-interest. For example, he and an associate asked children, in groups of four, to make bracelets for them and then rewarded them with ten bars of chocolate. The children had to decide how to split the chocolate fairly among themselves. They ranged from four years old to ten and the researchers found that at all ages the pull of self-interest was powerful. All the children tended to demand more chocolate for themselves with one exception: a group who were given a hypothetical version of the task where they were given cardboard chocolate rather than the real thing. On this occasion the children were happy to offer more chocolate to others than to themselves!

The experimenters did find that brighter children often chose solutions based on merit – 'Give Janey more chocolate because Janey made most bracelets and worked hardest' – but these children only did so under one condition – when they themselves were Janey, thus being in a position to benefit from the claim. So the high moral principle of giving most to the most deserving was, in the hands of the older children, only used in the service of self-interest.

It is not a very encouraging result; nevertheless the researchers discovered that there were signs of moral reasoning developing in older children. Where younger children's solutions were often blatantly self-interested – they might grab seven bars of chocolate for themselves 'because I want all these' – older children constructed solutions with precision and some balance. They still awarded themselves more chocolate on merit, but in a carefully chosen extra proportion.

Morality and self-interest interact in various ways as children make real-life decisions, but they are uncoordinated during the childhood years and you cannot predict whether they will be fair or selfish on any particular occasion. So you can expect to see a split in younger children between what they say you should do and what they actually do, and not be dismayed by it. It is just a stage they are going through and they will grow out of it. It is not until ten and upwards that they become aware of the dilemma that the interests of the self are often incompatible with the demands of justice, that you cannot share out the chocolate equally and still keep most of it for yourself, and that the goal of helping someone in need may conflict with the goal of gaining approval, or wanting to succeed in a given task.

You can try out the following dilemma on your own child to see whether she is more likely to choose self-interest or justice. A little girl is told by her mother to be home by teatime without fail, but on the way home she sees an old lady struggling with heavy shopping. Ask your child, should she help the old lady and get home late? At eight a child is likely to say that the little girl should get home by teatime as her mother asked. By ten, the child is usually able to suppress her self-interest in getting home on time, and therefore avoiding blame or punishment, in favour of her moral judgement which tells her she should help the old lady. None the less, children are more likely to choose altruism over self-interest if the competing goals can both be satisfied by one act – helping someone in need *and* gaining approval.

Hot air and good deeds

One reason for the gap between what children say is right and what they actually do is that for all of us, talk is easier than action, and particularly in the realm of moral behaviour. It is easier to preach generosity to a child than actually to make a donation to charity, especially if you are feeling hard-up. If you've ever been involved in fund-raising, even if it was only a sponsored swim at your daughter's school, you'll have discovered that there are always more pledges made than honoured.

One revealing examination of the gap between words and deeds and how it affects children's attitudes was carried out by American psychologist James H. Bryan. In the experiment, children of eight to eleven were introduced to an adult who addressed them on the subject of charity and then, on leaving the hall, might or might not put some money in the charity box. Then, as they left the lecture hall, the children were given the chance of putting money in the charity box (the researchers made sure all the children had some spare cash before the experiment began).

The first group of children were introduced to a man who preached to them about the need for charity and, as he went out, put money into the collection box. The second group was addressed by someone who told them that greed was natural and who gave nothing. The third adult again spoke in favour of charity, but he did not put any money in the box. The fourth advocated greed, but none the less made a donation as he left. Then the children were left to make their own contributions.

The findings were crystal clear: if the group of children saw the adult make a donation, they were far more likely to make a donation themselves. Whether or not there was a lecture encouraging them to be generous didn't affect their behaviour. They were more likely to copy the sinner who did give to charity than the saint who did not. So just preaching isn't good enough. It is the action of the role-model that has most effect. All the collecting for charity that teachers do won't work if they simply tell the children things like, 'you should give', 'it's good to give', 'others will like you if you give'. These fall on deaf ears. What will have an effect is if they see their teacher (or their parent in a family situation) being generous, and the effect will be even stronger if the adult reinforces the action with praise and reasons: 'It's good to give to the homeless because they're cold and miserable and have no families to take care of them.'

From obedience to co-operation

A child's idea of morality shifts at about seven years of age from the infant's view, which is governed by obedience and respect for adults, to a more mature attitude based on co-operation and mutual respect. You can monitor this slow but sure growth of your child's moral reasoning by observing their attitude to lying. A small child will say 'lying is naughty' because she knows you will disapprove and punish her. By nine or ten children will argue that lies are wrong even if they are not punished, 'because it's a lie all the same'. So the rules have become independent of punishment; the child has taken the rule and elevated it to the position of a universal law. And by ten or twelve they will explain that lying is wrong because truthfulness is necessary to hold society together: in other words, they have grasped that lying is antisocial.

The changeover from obedience to willing co-operation occurs when the child tries to please you rather than to obey. This can only happen if there is mutual respect between her and you and for it to occur you need to place yourself on her level and give her a feeling of equality. The best way to do this is to talk to the child about your own obligations and admit your own deficiencies. If you are willing to draw attention to your needs and difficulties, even your own blunders, and point out their consequences, you will create an atmosphere of mutual help and understanding. She needs to know that you are struggling and trying your best too, and if she sees other people as well as her parents – her brothers and sisters or playmates – also doing their best to provide each other with mutual help and sympathy, then her earlier unquestioning obedience will be replaced by mature co-operation.

What you need to do is practise empathy yourself – try to put yourself in your child's shoes and see what you're asking her to do from her point of view. Are you making unreasonable demands? Are you giving her the chance to say what she thinks is the right thing to do? Are you really listening as she struggles to make sense of her behaviour and that of the others around her? It's all too tempting to put words into a child's mouth rather than listen to what they have to say, but they will never develop a moral sense if they are not encouraged to question and think about what they are doing.

You can assist her moral growth if you ask her questions about moral dilemmas in order to clarify what she thinks and check that she understands, but you must do this gently: if you seem to criticise or challenge her, present her with complicated alternative considerations, or simply hand out information, you're not helping her. She will feel any challenge you make is a hostile one, while any information you hand out is simply seen as lecturing and greeted with boredom. A supportive atmosphere is much more successful than a heavy-handed confrontation.

Giving tit-for-tat
From eight upwards, children become more and more concerned with fair play and equal treatment. If you start issuing contradictory commands and aren't consistent about discipline, the child will begin to feel you are being unjust and this can lead to revolt. The only punishments accepted as really legitimate now are those based upon fair play. So if, to quote a common example, a teacher punishes the whole class

because one or two children have misbehaved and he can't identify them, the pupils will feel outraged and say it isn't fair. In conflicts between punishment and equality, equality rules.

As the child grows less and less to respect adult punishment unquestioningly, she also begins to show signs of a retributive type of conduct herself. For instance, if a child hits her she now starts to believe you can hit back rather than telling Mummy or Daddy. It is a matter of tit-for-tat or reciprocity – Charlotte thinks she has the right to hit me, she therefore gives me the right to do the same to her. John won the game by cheating so we'll take back the marbles he has won. When a child starts behaving in this way it is a sign that she understands there is a balance in people's behaviour and that most people will give back what they receive.

This, however, is reciprocity at the blow-for-blow level. Children have to move through this stage in order to understand there will always be a relationship or balance between people which they must learn to take into account, but it helps if you can encourage them to think about reciprocity in a more generous way than simply, 'I'll scratch her back if she'll scratch mine.' Then the idea of crude equality is replaced by the concept, 'Do as you would be done by.' Once she grows familiar with this idea, she will start to put generosity and forgiveness above revenge.

Learning the words for morality

The way you react to the things she does gives your child the idea of what you mean by morality. For instance, when we say, 'that's stealing' or 'that's cheating', we're not simply describing the act in the way that we describe a flower as 'pretty', but expressing our disapproval and the child picks up on this and learns to have negative feelings towards behaviour such as stealing, cheating, cruelty or whatever.

First, however, she has to learn the names of these sorts of behaviour. She may well say 'stealing is wrong', but that won't get her very far unless she understands what 'stealing'

117

is. She probably has a pretty clear idea by now of what some sorts of stealing are – when someone makes off with her bike or her toy for instance – but she may not think that borrowing a friend's favourite video and 'forgetting' to return it is stealing.

You need to teach children the correct words for moral behaviour. If, for example, when she sneaks an extra £100 from the bank when playing Monopoly, you say, 'that's cheating', and again, when she copies someone else's homework, you explain, 'that's really cheating', then when she finds herself confronted by a similar situation in future she will say to herself, 'hang on, that would be cheating', because she will have grasped the concept. This may sound rather heavy-handed and self-conscious, but children do need to learn the words that label all these different kinds of dishonest behaviour.

Research shows that the words honest and dishonest, which are more abstract than stealing, lying and cheating, are not used very often in real life. Investigators found that children around the age of nine begin to understand the concept of 'dishonesty' but had never heard that word actually used to describe unacceptable behaviour when they were being punished: they were just told that they were bad, a cheat and so on. In fact children don't even talk about 'stealing' among themselves: they use much more direct language – 'she took my doll', 'he's got my pen'. The concept of honesty and dishonesty is an intellectual one and children have to be taught that it covers many different kinds of moral behaviour before they can include lying, stealing and cheating under that one heading. Here schools can help by having children play-act situations where an abstract moral term such as 'honesty' is actually said out loud, to increase the likelihood that the child will use that word herself when she's interpreting a real-life situation.

Even so, learning the appropriate words will have little direct impact on the child's immediate behaviour. In order to get children to do the right thing you have to think about motivation. No one behaves in a moral fashion unless they want to. For instance, a girl may know very well that she should go home on time and not worry her parents, but still fail to do so because she's having a good time with her friends and she wants to stay on doing that more than she wants to avoid upsetting her parents.

When we want to do something, we feel attracted towards it because we see it as desirable in some way. So, if we want our children to act morally, we must make moral behaviour seem as desirable as possible so that they will want to do the right thing. With small children, rewards and punishments act as pretty powerful moral incentives and sanctions. They can make your daughter, for instance, decide that she does want to look after her baby brother because that brings a reward from you of cash or gratitude, while abandoning him and going off with her friends is punished – but this leaves her stuck at the non-moral level of wondering, 'What am I going to get out of that?' To make it attractive you have to add a reason to the request, such as that she's looking after her little brother because he is small and helpless and will be miserable unless someone kind and capable like her takes care of him. Then she understands why such behaviour is considered good and is drawn to it.

When feeling bad is good

One contentious argument put forward by psychologists researching moral behaviour in children is that for a child to take moral action it has to have been aroused by some bad experience, such as being shouted at for eating all the crisps. The idea is that the child learns the required moral response (in this case the need to have fair shares) because she realises it avoids the uncomfortable feelings of anxiety that were evoked by her parents' angry reaction to her greed.

Since we know we can shape behaviour so well with positive reinforcement, do we really need to make our children feel bad? Professor Roger Burton of the State University of New York says we do, because behaviour shaped through positive reinforcement remains flexible and therefore unreliable. The problem is that in moral situations, the immediate rewards usually lie with the immoral options – such as lying, cheating, stealing, ignoring others' rights, being selfish, not going to the aid of someone in distress and so on. The positive reinforcement for ethical conduct tends to be delayed and modest, or else there's no reinforcement because the moral choice is only what is expected of us. Even when reinforcement for moral behaviour does come it is often rather faint, in the form of seeing, hearing about or reading of someone else who was honoured for some moral action.

So how are we to ensure that people do not choose immoral behaviour to achieve material rewards, success, fame or power? Professor Burton argues that negative feelings will maintain moral behaviour when positive reinforcement is weak. In an experiment, Professor Burton discovered that this negative effect could be achieved indirectly, by having a class of children watch a video of a child being severely reprimanded for breaking the rules of a game, when the terms 'honesty' or 'dishonesty' were used. Through this means the concept of honesty was suffused with the anxiety-arousing overtones that were needed in order for the children to accept it.

Since you probably don't want to go around showing your children upsetting videos, what this means for parents in practical terms is that you mustn't allow a child to get away with unethical conduct because that will only reinforce her behaviour. For example, if you allow your daughter to eat her sister's sweets every time she takes some, to keep the fancy pencil she has shoplifted, or to retain some money from a wallet she has found in the street (all possible scenarios in early childhood) she is getting a strong and immediate reinforcement for her bad behaviour which will set her off on the wrong track. You must be strict and condemn wrongdoing at once. It's a mistake to be soft-hearted and overlook the offence this time with the lame intention of doing something about it 'when she's a bit older'. You have to make the child feel uncomfortably aware of your disapproval as soon as she does anything wrong if you want to influence her behaviour – without, of course, condemning the child. It is enough to say, 'It's wrong to keep teasing your brother like that, you know it upsets him.' You don't have to add, 'And you're a horrible little bully.'

The teacher's dilemma

We don't learn moral behaviour by witnessing wrongdoing – we condemn behaviour as wrong because it violates the moral code we already possess. If, for instance, you were brought up in that Mediterranean village where they threw a donkey off the church tower every year during the village festival, you could accept the event quite happily, but if you were brought up to think that hurling donkeys to their death is wicked, then seeing it would fill you with horror. We cannot leave children to draw their own conclusions from the world they see around them as they grow up. They need guidance from a more experienced adult, and the chance to discuss their reactions.

One dilemma teachers often face is that children in the same class come from families with widely differing moral standards. One teacher in Salford, Lancashire, described the difficulty: 'We have a problem in the local area with children taking motor cars and we lead on from that to the whole idea of stealing. Many of our kids think that provided you can get away with it, it's almost acceptable: the big thing is not to get caught. The absolute "I shall not steal" seems to have disappeared. They'll throw back at you something like, "Well my dad brings back stuff from work," and "Don't *you* take envelopes from the office?" '

Dr Mark Halstead, a moral philosopher at Plymouth University, believes you can counter this by looking for the morals they do have. 'I lived and taught in an inner city school in Bradford for twelve years and have some experience of life at this raw and rough end. I found that people who will accept something off the back of a lorry and so on will

121

nonetheless have their own moral standards and virtues and very often there's huge helpfulness and friendliness and love and care among such families, even if they have less respect for property than we middle classes would like.

'So you get the children to think through the virtues that they do have and lead them gently on from these to think about other virtues. The awareness has to come from the child, you can't impose morals on the child and say, "You must behave like this." Well, you can, and you can beat them every day – some people think that's the way to do it, but it's not. You can't make people good by caning them. You have to draw it out of them.

'And I think that, firstly, by praising the good qualities that you do see in the child and, secondly, by encouraging reflection on these things, those children will be put on the path of growing towards moral maturity and will start to think about other issues as well. If you encourage empathy, that will begin to help them put themselves in the shoes of the other person and, for instance, if they know of someone who has had something stolen from them, to ask themselves how must they feel about it.'

Even when the child can understand a particular situation, it doesn't mean she will do the right thing. For that to happen she must realise that the situation is one that calls for a moral response and the best way to ensure that children actually use their knowledge to make a judgement about a situation is to encourage them to start talking things over inside their heads, because moral discussion doesn't have to be confined to the classroom.

You can start to encourage the child to conduct a sort of interior dialogue asking questions about the situation she faces – 'What should I do?' 'What will the consequences be for me – and for the other person concerned?' 'If I do this, what will happen?' 'If I don't do it, what will follow?' This is the sort of questioning Socrates used to teach the youths of Athens and is still the best way to start children thinking about what is the right and wrong thing to do. If they can get into the habit of mulling over moral issues in their heads they will grow more and more capable of making the right choices.

Teachers can help by making time for class discussions. Pat Parker, an Essex teacher, says, 'One thing that surprises us is how sort of cut and dried children are, they see things very much in black and white. They are not so inclined to make excuses as adults are, it's all "cut off their heads". So we try to encourage them to explore attitudes: "Yes I do feel that way about X" "No, I don't like people doing Y". Sometimes we give them a story, say, about the teacher leaving the room, an incident happening and the child who responded to the incident but wasn't responsible for it being blamed. We ask the children to see it from three points of view – that of the teacher, of the child who is being blamed and of the child who really did wrong. It helps them to develop skills and make reasoned decisions.'

Another lesson children need to learn is that moral principles are universal and must apply to everyone, even to children who really irritate them. Young children are all too likely to believe that if they don't like someone in their class, that leaves them free to be horrid to that child, even if the child in question is quite innocent. You can explain how this is wrong by pointing out how a doctor, for instance, cannot decide whether or not to give a patient the treatment she needs purely on the basis of whether he likes that patient or not; he must treat her fairly and in her best interests regardless. In the same way, a moral child must treat other children fairly regardless of how likeable they may or may not be.

Seeing yourself as others see you

As she approaches ten, the child becomes capable of reflecting on her thoughts and feelings and can also appreciate that other people can view her just as she can view them. For the first time she starts to appreciate that her judgements and actions are open to scrutiny by others and that she must anticipate their reactions and any potential conflicts, and try to resolve them by making judgements that take other people's views into account.

In other words, by the time they reach ten children are able to see the world from another person's point of view and this makes them more rounded and sympathetic. For instance, if an adult gets a small child to give him a bar of chocolate in exchange for a penny, young children will accept this as fair as long as child and adult agree to it. However, an older child can step outside and see from a third-party point of view that the trade is unfair because the adult is taking advantage of the little one. The ten-year-old has learnt to take a broader perspective.

You can encourage your child's understanding of other people's point of view by seeing she has lots of contact with the wider community of friends and neighbours. It also helps her to understand others if you get into the habit of discussing friends and neighbours whom she knows with the child, explaining that there are lots of different lifestyles and attitudes.

Teachers can also help children to see the world from a wider perspective. English teachers, especially, can discuss fictional characters. It's easy for an eight-year-old to enjoy Charles Kingsley's *The Water Babies* and meet kind-hearted Mrs Doasyouwouldbedoneby, who rewarded children for good behaviour. Once they have worked out that this extraordinary name means 'You should treat other people the way you would like to be treated yourself', their moral development will be well under way. Teachers of geography and social studies can illustrate different lifestyles around the world, to enlarge the children's understanding of diversity and show, for instance, how international trade may benefit or exploit people according to how it is handled.

Nobody's perfect
Some people find the whole idea of behaving in a moral fashion daunting and rigorous, but it's not really all that difficult to try and behave well. 'You just have to get a few

principles straight,' says Professor Wilson of Oxford. 'The Golden Rule is entirely straightforward, you just have to get it into your head. Societies all round the world disapprove of murder and theft and approve of things like keeping your word. They're not necessarily sophisticated people but they manage to come up with these concepts and hold them fast, so we're not asking something very difficult of people.

'It's just that we all get led astray by various unconscious pressures – wanting to be big boys or wanting to prove oneself, or to preserve one's self-respect, or be popular in the peer group. We all do other things instead of the right thing – that's what happens.'

David Rowse, who teaches disaffected youngsters, agrees that no one is perfect and all we can reasonably expect of children is that they try. He asks, 'Who, hand on heart, going back to their early years, hasn't been naughty? I must have been the biggest bane of the neighbourhood with the gang I used to go around with. Lots of little boys throw things at the cat and still grow up to be quite decent. You can't expect too much too soon. Children aren't going to be paragons of virtue, because adults aren't. These are things that we aspire to. There's no harm in setting out an ideal as long as you realise that it's something to aim at. Life is such that it is incredibly difficult to meet one's ideals on every occasion, but it's quite virtuous to have a go.'

Growing and understanding

For children to develop a moral slant to their lives, they must be able to grasp the moral outlines of a situation. This may be a very straightforward business in the Old Testament where every situation appears cut and dried, but everyday life is a more ambiguous business and children have to tease out their moral obligations.

Dr Keller of Berlin University devised this experiment to test children between seven and thirteen to see how their moral feelings and attitudes were developing. The children were told this story: Jack has promised to see his best friend

Peter (girls were given a story with girls' names) on a given day, but he is tempted to accept an invitation to a film from another child, Ben, which will conflict with the scheduled visit to Peter.

The children in the experiment were told that the friendship between Jack and Peter is long-standing and close and that they meet on the same day every week – the day of the proposed film trip. Peter wants to play records and talk some things over with Jack (there is a hint he may be experiencing some trouble). Ben, the other boy, is new to the neighbourhood and has not yet made any friends. He is offering Jack a film, hot dogs and soft drinks. Jack and Ben seem to like each other, but Peter doesn't like the newcomer. The children were asked, what should Jack choose to do?

At seven and eight years of age, children have no awareness of the idea that Jack has an obligation to Peter. They choose purely from a self-centred perspective – which arrangement would offer most fun? They are aware of the consequences of ditching their friend to go to the film – they know Peter will feel bad – but they don't think these feelings are caused by a broken obligation, but by the frustration of Peter's hedonistic wants: they say he is feeling bad because he isn't going to the film, is being bored at home. This doesn't make the child acting the part of Jack feel bad – he feels good because he's going to the movie. These young children have no awareness of the violation of a moral principle, so they don't see any need to justify their decision. They don't think the decision to go to the cinema is a problem.

By nine or ten the children can see that Jack's reasons for visiting Peter are not purely selfish – 'we have fun together' – but arise from the friendship itself: 'liking the friend, liking being with him, the fact of being friends'. They start to be aware of negative consequences and wish to avoid them – they'll say things like, 'I don't want to leave the friend out.' So now they are starting to weigh up choices. The consequences for Peter if Jack goes to the cinema – that he'd feel sad, or hurt, or is looking forward to the visit (they understand the feeling of expectation) – are taken into account. Or they think Peter may be angry with Jack – may hit him, or not play with him any more.

So now the child understands that there is a problem and will choose one of two solutions: he will either try to conceal his action from Peter, or he will see the need for an act of restitution – taking Peter to a film next time they meet.

By eleven and twelve, children appreciate that the friendship is an important element in the situation. At this age they understand the expectations and obligations of a friendship; they also understand that by giving a promise, an obligation is created. The context is also a factor: Peter not only wants Jack to come but expects him to come, so not living up to this obligation is seen as a betrayal and one does not want to betray or cheat one's best friend to whom one has made a promise. The betrayal of a friend is seen in a moral way – it makes Peter feel hurt, left out, disappointed. He will feel anger or sadness over the betrayal and his disapproval may lead to the breaking of the friendship. These older children no longer suggest that their self-centred needs are sufficient reason to ditch a friend.

Altruistic motives, however, may persuade them to take into account the special neediness of Ben, the new child: some children said Jack had an obligation to help Ben because he is lonely and has not yet made friends. You can see here the beginning of self-evaluation. The child putting himself in Jack's shoes feels bad about cheating Peter because he understands about violating obligations and responsibilities. He is also starting to be aware of the moral principle of truthfulness as an obligation not to lie to one's friend about one's intentions or actions, so telling lies will lead to feelings of guilt. Though the child playing Jack may still lie, the guilt the child feels shows that he is aware of the obligation to tell the truth.

By eleven and twelve friendship is seen as implying trust, reliance and a special concern for each other's needs and feelings. The fact that Peter says he wants to talk suggests to older children that he has special needs that are emotionally significant for Jack and put a special obligation on him. The older child sees the promise to meet on the same day each week as an obligation that cannot be changed arbitrarily. In other words, by the time they reach eleven or twelve, children are referring to the rules of fairness and to personal ideals of the way that good, loyal and trustworthy friends should act towards each other. The concept of trust also arises – Peter would not trust Jack any more if he let him down – and consequences – children realise that Jack would feel guilt and shame, and will talk of a guilty conscience.

The main feeling in these older children's minds is the idea that a promise is morally binding. There is also a growing awareness of the need for communication about any change of plan – Jack could negotiate a new arrangement with Peter, attempts could be made to reassure him. But a new form of lying also emerges: the children will say, 'Peter would have done the same', or 'anyone would have done the same', in an attempt to deny responsibility for the action. However, because of the child's awareness of the moral inadequacy of such behaviour, rather intense feelings of guilt and shame may arise and even take the form of psychosomatic reactions such as tummy ache.

By thirteen the children are weighing up priorities: if Peter really needs Jack then Jack must go to him, but if the situation is not that urgent, Peter should accept that Jack visits him later. The legitimacy of Peter's needs is weighed against the legitimacy of Jack's and there is an assumption of mutual understanding for each other's claims and obligations that can be negotiated – friends must take each other's needs into account as well as their obligations towards each other. So now Peter is seen to have a moral obligation to take Jack's situation into account. This is the beginning of a concept of autonomy, where people are seen to have complex needs and to be embedded in multiple relationships.

Overall, Dr Keller's experiment shows that as children grow up there is an increasing awareness of the psychological aspect of situations, an understanding that other people's feelings have to be taken into account. The milestone seems to be at around eleven when they start to think, 'How will I appear to others?' Now the moral rules are no longer external, something other people impose on you, but have become part of the child's definition of herself. This seems to be the point at which the child starts to see that the rules that she should obey should also apply to everyone else.

Interlude
Teacher, teacher

As people look around the modern world and see what seems to be a frightening decline in everyday morality, there has been a growing clamour for schools to play a bigger part in teaching moral education. It's clear that the Church will never again be able to fulfil this role now that the number of regular churchgoers has fallen to fewer than three people in every hundred, and in casting around for a substitute, school seems to offer the best alternative. This is why the School Curriculum and Assessment Authority (SCAA), the body set up by the government to decide what should be taught in our schools, is conducting a wide-ranging investigation into how the study of morals could or should be handled within the education system.

Dr Mark Halstead, a philosopher from the education department of the University of Plymouth who has been taking part in the SCAA research project, explains that although everyone accepts that parents are the most important source of moral education, 'schools act as a sort of safety net. If the children aren't getting adequate guidance and moral education at home, the schools can pick up some of the things.' He adds that children will learn from wherever they happen to be and as they happen to be in school six hours a day they're bound to be influenced by the school. 'They're particularly influenced, I think, by the atmosphere of the school and the example they're set by teachers rather

131

than by the things they are taught directly.'

Jan Newton of the Citizenship Foundation, which designs course material that teachers can use to raise moral, social and legal issues in the classroom, makes the point that schools have a special advantage: 'Children come from very different homes and some from homes with very limited notions of what constitutes moral standards or social responsibility, and school seems to be the one place where you can bring them all together and where they can learn about community- and society-based behaviour.'

Don't expect cheers from the staff room

However, teachers are not rushing to welcome the chance to teach children about morality. 'Parents are copping out,' they say. 'They want schools to do a job which they ought to be doing themselves.' The real problem, however, is that teachers themselves are deeply unsure about morality and don't know how on earth they can teach it to others. It's rather like asking people to teach mathematics when they're not sure whether two and two equals four or something else.

Mark Halstead found from his research with SCAA and the questions he puts to his own students that most teachers and student teachers are very lacking in confidence about teaching morals, partly because they're not given any guidance on their teacher training courses, and partly because somewhere along the line the vast majority of students arriving at university have picked up a kind of moral relativism.

'If you ask them if there is anything that they think is totally, always wrong,' says Dr Halstead, 'the majority of students will say, "No, it depends on the society in which you're brought up and the values of that particular society." And it's hard, I find, to break that. I'm very interested in the processes by which this is picked up: I'm sure that schools don't teach it directly, but it's very, very widespread.

'My suspicion is that it may be a woolly understanding of tolerance by society at large that is producing this sort of misguided moral relativism. To me, tolerance means deciding not to interfere with behaviour of which you don't approve. Now if you don't approve of behaviour it implies that you're starting with clear-cut standards from which a judgement is being made. Whereas in the popular mind it seems that tolerance of diversity means that anything goes really, it's other people's business to decide how they're going to behave.'

In an attempt to see how far his students would go with this moral cop-out – would they go so far as to say that bullying, for instance, is sometimes acceptable? – Halstead reports, 'Well, I've pushed them and even on cannibalism you'll find some will still take the relativist stand! I think there are probably one or two things, like rape or physical bullying that they would, if pushed, disapprove of but they may still say, "But that's because of the standards in my society." '

Professor John Wilson of the Department of Educational Studies at the University of Oxford has met with exactly the same reluctance by student teachers to agree that any list of virtues is good in itself.

'But if you ask the teachers to write down what, if anything, they honestly believe reason requires from any serious moral thinker, it nearly always turns out that the lists they make are more or less identical both with one another's and with the one I originally put forward. This is no surprise: items such as honesty, fairness, sympathy, keeping one's word et cetera are pretty obvious and don't demand an immense intellectual talent to discern. It's just that teachers have an intense dislike of being *told*, or any suggestion of authority.' Professor Wilson thinks that perhaps this is an argument for putting teachers on the spot and getting them to face up to moral questions themselves rather than just reacting to pressure from other people.

George Carey, the Archbishop of Canterbury, writing in *The Times*, observed that modern society has become morally reticent, even inarticulate. 'The main culprit is the popular cultural assumption that to try to define something as good and right in an absolute sense is an unwarranted and potentially oppressive incursion into a domain which should be purely private. According to this view, what is right is simply a matter of individual opinion.'

However, the archbishop goes on to argue: 'There have to be some absolutes, which may be high ideals which people can only aspire to, but if you haven't got those, then how on earth have you got a yardstick? How do you know you're not crossing the line, going beyond the pale or whatever? And in my experience the vast majority of people, even if they say morality is a purely private affair, actually have strong beliefs about some things that are absolutely good and others that are absolutely evil. Without values such as trust, honesty, consideration for other people, love of justice and peace, there can be no individual liberty.'

Dr Halstead argues that teachers cannot justify keeping out of the debate and not talking to children about moral issues because they're cropping up all the time. In school, on the news, in programmes on television, in the stories they read, every area of a child's life has its moral issues and moral controversies and if teachers are truly trying to educate children they can't avoid dealing with them.

Baroness Mary Warnock, moral philosopher and former headmistress, has no doubt how teachers should act. She says firmly: 'It has always been a teacher's job to inculcate tradition and values. That is not a new task. If you go into teaching you have got to be prepared to take this responsibility to display and insist on certain values.'

However, if teachers are going to be asked to offer some form of moral education, they first have to be shown how to do it. Dr Monica Taylor, editor of *The Journal of Moral Education* and another member of the SCAA forum, says one problem they found was that they could not discover how much time is being given in teacher training to developing the students' understanding of the moral and spiritual dimensions of teaching: 'Apparently it can be just one lecture or one seminar in the whole of the course unless they specialise in moral education.'

She adds, 'I think that teachers saying, "Oh we can't recommend one thing or another" is an abrogation of their responsibility. I put it as strongly as that. And I think it's also a form of dishonesty, because it's impossible for a teacher to be a kind of neutral chairperson. It isn't just what they say, it's what they do. They reveal their moral attitude in the whole way they operate, observing rules and being firm and fair and I think from having observed classes over the years that a lot of teachers don't really understand that.'

Teachers, of course, are only reflecting the fact that the whole issue of moral values has become something of a grey area because we have all seen our expectations and practices change in quite major ways in recent years. Where divorce, for instance, was once an embarrassment now it is commonplace. Where an illegitimate child was once a figure of shame, we came to understand that there were no illegitimate children, only illegitimate parents and soon this, too, was rejected, so now thousands of children are born to parents who are not married and no one feels any the worse.

In this climate of rapid change, we naturally feel more uncertainty about morality and what we can actually agree on – but that doesn't mean there is nothing we can agree on. Schools can agree not only about particular values in the abstract but also on how they interpret them in their school and what that means in specific instances. First, however, the teachers have to be reassured that they can do the job, and shown how to do it.

David Ingram, director of the charitable Norham Foundation which aims to further personal and social responsibility, recalls: 'I asked teachers whether they felt comfortable doing PSE [Personal and Social Education] and a lot said no because, they said, their initial training and their subject specialism didn't equip them for that kind of work. English teachers felt most comfortable; religious education teachers were no more comfortable than history, geography or science teachers.

'And when I asked what the difficulties were, they said they didn't have the pedagogic techniques for handling discussions. They wanted to be given *content*, a body of material to teach, and instead they were being asked to manage a *process*, of questioning and reflection. Secondly they said, "We are being asked to stand for values which society at large doesn't stand for and we're members of that society and we're like them." And thirdly they said, "We also have those kinds of problems in our own personal lives. If I'm asked to talk about marriage and my marriage is breaking up, I'm being asked to be a humbug or to say things that I don't experience." '

How to put morals on the curriculum

Professor John Wilson of Oxford University points out that it is a symptom of our uncertainty about moral education that we use so many different titles for it. 'Currently in many secondary schools it is called PSE. In the USA it is called Value Education. Earlier it was called character building, life skills, learning to live, citizenship, religious education, socialist values – the list goes on.'

There is also wide variation in how often it is taught and by whom. Dr Monica Taylor found that some schools operate a system where PSE is specially timetabled and may be taught by a team of specialists, who quite often have some training or who at least attempt to work to some kind of scheme which they've devised as a team. Other schools may just include it in the tutor period, which can range from ten minutes' registration time to a whole period.

At present PSE is often taught not by specialist teachers but by other subject or form teachers as an adjunct to their other work. What often happens then is that if, for instance, PSE is being taken by one of the English teachers, and another member of the English department is suddenly taken ill, the Head is likely to look at the timetable, see that Mr X is 'only' teaching PSE and pull him away to take the 'serious' subject. One of my daughters achieved only two PSE lessons out of a possible eleven for this sort of reason.

'It is possible to timetable it,' argues Dr Taylor. 'Schools will say there is no space, but it depends on the will and the leadership of the Head. If the Head thinks it's important, it happens. But I've only encountered one or two schools where there's been some really formal and systematic approach, dealing with the issues from a philosophical, psychological and sociological standpoint.'

Observers find that even when teachers do approach controversial social issues, they often duck the moral aspect. David Ingram believes, 'They shy away from the moral dimension. We have a PSE programme but it doesn't adequately deal with values. Every form tutor deals with PSE, but they'll teach about drugs as information and show a film or do some handouts. Accidents in the Home they like, but the values dimension really scares them.'

So PSE, or whatever it is called, blooms or fades unpredictably from school to school. Dr Taylor explains what she has seen happen all too easily: 'Particular teachers or particular schools key into a certain way of doing something for a little while and so Citizenship can be the fashion or you might get Philosophy for Children or Circle Time or whatever. One of the problems is that it is very much left up to one teacher. If she is seen to be enthusiastic they say, "Oh, Miss X is doing so and so", and leave it all to her. And if she leaves the school and moves on, the course may disappear.'

Should morals be an exam subject?

One way to avoid all these difficulties would be to give PSE a statutory basis and make it part of the National Curriculum. Dr Halstead sets out the options: 'It depends on whether the thing is turned into an academic subject with examinations and, therefore, with status or whether it stays at the level of guidance offered by the form teacher – non-examined work and therefore work which the children don't take very seriously.

'Currently there's a big divide in most secondary schools between the pastoral side and the academic side and everyone, students and staff, sees the academic side as serious work. The pastoral side is a bit of a joke to both sides unless they're in need of some very definite help. If a pupil has got in trouble with the police, or drugs, or they need some help or support or guidance, fine. Otherwise it's a low-status thing.'

Of course if moral education is put on to the National Curriculum and becomes a compulsory examination subject, every child will have to take it and room would then be made available for it on the timetable because it would be important. This poses other problems. If Morals becomes an academic subject, there is a danger that children will pick up the 'right' answers by rote rather than discovering how to make moral decisions for themselves. It is all too easy to imagine a situation where a teenager gets grade A on the multiple choice paper and still goes out joyriding that evening. Also, what happens if large numbers of children fail the exams – would that make them immoral? More importantly, what would happen to the less academic children? Would they drop Morals if it proved too hard and therefore receive no moral guidance? Do you have to be clever to study how to be good?

If morality is put on to the curriculum, schools will take it seriously, courses will be written and children will study it; but some children will fail, some will swot up just enough to pass the exams without really developing a moral character and some will cheat. If it is not put on to the curriculum, the pupils could learn about moral issues through class discussion and by questioning their teachers and each other and this might well be the best way. Only there is no guarantee that schools will bother to make time available for it.

And who's going to teach it?
Everyone concerned with moral education knows that the sooner you begin, the more successful you will be. It is far

easier to bring up a child to have a moral sense than to try to introduce one in a disaffected teenager or adult. This means that moral education should start in some form in primary school, and there is talk of making moral education a compulsory component in the training of all primary teachers, which isn't the case at the moment.

Any training will have to be reasonable and manageable: one reason the GCSE was such a nightmare when it was first introduced was that the specialists who drew up each particular course, in history, biology, maths and so on, each wanted their own subject to be as complete and comprehensive as possible. So the syllabuses they drew up were impossibly wide-ranging and caused havoc until they were drastically pruned. If primary school teachers are to add morals to the syllabus, they need simple courses in how to make it easy and accessible to every child.

Dr Halstead is one of those convinced that moral development must start in primary school, explaining: 'Primary children are often very idealistic and have a very strong moral sense. Think of the number of primary school children who've become vegetarian these days, and they're desperately concerned about the environment; they have very often a very strong sense of morality. But teachers don't have any training to know how to cope with this, or how to develop it, which seems such a shame.'

He also believes that all children should get at least a couple of years of moral education under their belts at secondary school, too – the whole school, not just the academically gifted. 'There should be a chance within the school for children to discuss moral issues and discuss how to cope when you're faced with a challenging moral situation. On what basis do you make your decision? And the fact of making a decision is important, rather than just letting things happen: children must be encouraged to think things through in that way.'

He doesn't think this necessarily means that secondary schools should have specialist PSE teachers; rather he believes all teachers should consider the moral aspects of their subject and encourage children to think about them. 'I've always thought that English teaching was very largely about moral education, because the children are being projected imaginatively into situations where they can see the need for moral decisions to be made. Certainly Shakespeare and others more accessible to the children, perhaps, such as John Steinbeck, can do this.'

David Ingram is another who believes that the opportunity for discussing moral issues can occur naturally in any lesson, but he is not convinced that teachers welcome it. 'The difficulty was that Sir Keith Joseph forbade schools to deal with those implicit moral dilemmas because, he said, 'You're there to teach science not the implications of science.' And Paul Hirst, who was then Professor of Education at Cambridge, argued that what you need is a trained moral philosopher who could deal with those questions, not a scientist.

'I challenged him, because it wasn't as if the science teachers had a button on the desk labelled Moral Issue and the teacher could just press the button and a moral philosopher would pop up! It should be part of the training and education of the scientist that he is aware of the moral dimension of what he does. They are clever, adult people and who better to discuss it with the child than the teacher of the subject?'

What schools could do

If teachers are to embark on moral education, how should they go about it? Derek Wright, former Professor of Psychology at Leicester University, says: 'Many people believe that moral education is a one-way process. Teachers prescribe to students how they ought and ought not to behave, with or without giving their reasons. They then indicate their approval and disapproval through rewards and punishments. This doesn't work because it induces conforming behaviour in students through the appeal to self-interest, the desire for approval and the fear of punishment. The whole point about moral action is that it is not motivated by self-interest.

'And there are bound to be occasions when the teacher's prescriptions do not ring true to the pupil's moral sense and may, indeed, be in direct conflict with it. To persuade or coerce students into behaviour which does not coincide with what they think is right is certainly to confuse them and possibly to corrupt them, morally. There are times when integrity requires disobedience of authority. This is as true for children as it is for adults.'

The alternative to this sort of brainwashing is serious thought helped by serious discussion, and discussions of this kind can be carried on in schools from quite an early age, but it involves treating the children's views with respect. It probably won't do the children any harm if their teachers do present them with a particular moral stance, such as a Christian version of morality, because they won't necessarily accept it. They will develop their own ideas as they mature, or when they're presented with a more objective approach which encourages them to think things through for themselves and develop their own values.

We don't all make the same moral decisions because our values are not the same: they are different because each of us has been influenced by different important people and by a different cultural environment. The point of teachers discussing moral dilemmas with pupils is to make them aware of these different values. For instance, one child may think in terms of avoiding punishment, another would be cornered with the welfare of other people, a third might see the issue in terms of certain rules, a fourth just want to get as much out of the situation for himself as he could. Children need to be encouraged to recognise that others have different values and to think which values they accept and hold themselves. As long as moral issues are brought to the forefront of children's thinking by some means or other, it will help them to mature morally. Of course they will mature in different ways according to their personality, their home experiences and a lot of other influences outside the school, but at least they will be thinking about moral issues and not just drifting along regardless.

Dr Mark Halstead believes: 'It's best to give children a stable and secure basic understanding, from which some of them will eventually grow to make their own decisions about moral issues. But even if they're not able to develop to that level of moral autonomy, at least they would have a solid foundation. It doesn't matter in the end if they drop Geography, but I think it's absolutely vital that all children have a solid foundation in Morals.'

Chapter Five
Eleven to thirteen: hearing different voices

By the time they turn eleven and enter secondary school our children are becoming increasingly independent. They can get out and about on their own, have homework to do, friends to go and see and a horde of things to occupy their time. They think they know everything and they do know lots of things you don't, like how to dial call-back on the telephone and how many Sumerian tigers are left in the wild. Their world no longer revolves inward around the home, but starts to focus on the world outside the family circle, and as they become more sensitive to the world around them, they are also becoming more and more moral creatures.

Feeling someone else's pain
As the child grows up, he starts to realise he is a person with a history and identity all his own and by eleven he understands that others as well as himself also have their own personal identity. Now he understands that other people react to situations with feelings of pleasure and pain just as he does and also that these feelings are shaped by their experiences of life, which may not be the sort of experiences he has had himself.

This makes the eleven-year-old much more responsive than a younger child. For instance, if a small child sees another child crying he will react to her distress by feeling sorry for her, but the eleven-year-old can also imagine a friend's experience of distress even when it is not directly in front of his eyes – if his friend is in hospital, for instance, or if a friend's parent has died. So the older child is sensitive not only to transitory distress in a specific situation, but also to what he imagines to be someone's general condition. A secondary school child can envisage what would constitute a friend's overall standard of happiness and well-being and, if the friend's life seems to be falling below that standard, will feel a sympathetic distress for him, which is at a more mature level than the simple sharing of visible misery.

As the child continues to grow intellectually, he will gradually acquire the capacity to comprehend the plight not only of an individual, but of an entire group or class of people such as the poor, the politically oppressed, the socially outcast, victims of war or famine or the chronically sick. Although his own experience of distress will be different from these others, as he grows up he will develop the mature ability to generalise from one experience of distress to another. We don't actually have to have suffered in that particular way ourselves to feel sympathetic towards people in a tragic situation.

Another sign of a growing child's moral maturity is that he stops seeing dilemmas from an objective point of view – Mummy says this is naughty – and becomes more subjective, taking intentions into account. Piaget discovered that when he told twelve-year-olds the two stories about lying we saw in Chapter Three (the little girl who said the frightening dog was as big as a cow, and the little boy who falsely said his teacher had praised his work) – the boy's intention to deceive out of mischief was now described as being more naughty than the girl's simple lie. They also took the opposite view about the size of the lie to that of younger children, who thought that the bigger and more improbable the lie, the worse it was. The older children argued instead that since the story of the dog as big as a cow was unlikely and you could

144

see straightaway that the girl is not trying to deceive but was exaggerating or making a mistake, the lie is not serious. The boy's falsehood, which was quite plausible, is naughtier because of this: for older children the more convincing the lie, the worse it is.

Around this time, too, children start to consider that justice is not a rigid, invariable thing but something that can and should be tempered by considerations of fair treatment. Asked to judge on simple childhood dilemmas, children of eleven and upward say it isn't fair to apply the same punishment to everyone; you should take into account the extenuating circumstances. For instance, they will almost invariably argue that you should make allowances for the mistakes of little children and not come down hard on them.

The way that children grow more sympathetic and understanding is a reassuring sign that morality comes naturally to us. James Hemming, psychologist and broadcaster says, 'I would put the emphasis on morality being a normal human state. If children are encouraged, and socialised at the same time, then morality is just the rules of the game of life. You can't run a society if everybody's lying, everybody's stealing, everybody's violent, that's obvious: these are intrusions on society.

'And most people are extremely moral. We couldn't run society for ten minutes if people weren't reliable. If the trains didn't run when the timetable said they would, if when you rang your bank manager about your account he told you a lot of lies, the world wouldn't function. We take for granted a certain level of morality and we're outraged if it isn't lived up to: if we ring up a friend and ask a question we expect to be told the truth, don't we? The people who drift into Marks and Spencer don't usually steal goods and consequently Marks and Spencer are able to have many fewer employees than they would need if everybody went in to steal. We are moral and society is moral. And all we have to do with children is to bring these values home to them by the quality of their lives.'

Goodbye to the simple life

Dr Helen Haste, a psychologist at the University of Bath who has researched moral development in children for over twenty years points out, 'Almost everyone knows the difference between right and wrong: they know the rules. But how do you make them see that the rules apply to them? There is also a difference between avoiding sin, and socially acceptable behaviour and moral independence. Guilt inhibits the way we behave and helps us to avoid sin. But acceptable behaviour and the ability to make our own moral decisions doesn't depend on guilt but on reason, judgement and commitment.

'Unfortunately, right-wing politicians are enthusiastic about avoiding sin because they've got this very old-fashioned idea that you're stopping children doing naughty things. But you can't make them do good things by haranguing them, by punishing them and preaching absolute values which you say everyone must know. If you preach absolute values, you only have to have one teacher falling off the "Ideal" pedestal and the whole system falls into disrepute. Absolute values is a very low stage of moral reasoning. It's what children hold when they're very young. Five-year-olds have absolute values: they'll say "chop their hands off" when people steal, they have wonderfully lurid accounts of how we should deal with criminals, but they grow out of it.'

Absolute moral truths and universal principles have a poor reputation as a stimulus to good behaviour. Under the flag of universal truth every manner of violence and destruction has been let loose in the world by one zealot or another: churches destroyed, disbelievers burned at the stake, armies let loose on each other, people slaughtered.

'Absolute values are a wonderfully simple, clear-cut view of the world and it seems as though some people want to foster a permanent ten-year-old mentality about moral development,' says Dr Haste. 'But when you talk about recognising and dealing with moral conflict, grey areas, personal responsibility and how to make decisions as well as how to fit into the system, then you are talking about a much more difficult, much more problematic affair. It isn't neat and tidy at all.'

In this complicated world, what you can do is encourage children to do good things by giving them a strong sense of identity – so they think, 'I'm not the kind of person who does that' – by respecting them, by giving them a strong role in the community, a sense of involvement and responsibility. You do that by creating the kind of environment where children can feel that they belong. You have to explain to your child that in order to be morally sophisticated, he will have to base his dealings with other people on tolerance and find some way of constructing workable social arrangements.

You can also help him by not demanding or expecting absolute moral perfection. One major tension in our moral lives is that we all fail. There is always a gap between what we do and what we ought to do. Of course if we reduce morality to a few simple rules, like not stealing and not bearing false witness, we can probably manage to keep them, but as soon as you endeavour to love your neighbour as yourself you realise that morality is more complicated than just observing a few rules.

When we fail in some moral endeavour, our usual human response is either shame or guilt, or to blame someone else. It helps children to cope with their inevitable lapses if parents and teachers can admit their own failings. Children need to see that adults are governed by the moral law, not the originators of it. Children won't grow into moral maturity unless they inhabit a world where they are not subject to a system of commands requiring unquestioning obedience, but are enmeshed in a system of social relationships where everyone does their best to observe the same obligations out of respect for one another. They learn about social relationships by having them, by growing up within society and thinking about it, and by working out what helps and what doesn't. This practical morality has to come first; then they can start to formulate ideas about theoretical morality as they get older.

147

Children as teachers

Though you can't indoctrinate children with good behaviour directly – would that it were so simple – Erwin Staub of the University of Massachusetts discovered that they can be taught good behaviour indirectly. Direct moral instruction with its 'oughts' and 'ought nots' tends to provoke resistance in children because it seems to curb their freedom. Staub discovered that you could get impressive results if, instead of children being the target of instruction, the position was reversed and the children became the teacher.

In an experiment, children were asked to learn a certain amount of moral material so that they could then teach it to other children. There were a number of consequences. The first was that, as teachers, the children became involved in what they had to teach and thought about it more. Being a teacher also made them feel important, because teaching others was seen as a privilege and an indication of trust, so the whole experience was rewarding. Also, when children taught other children moral behaviour or values, the content of what they were teaching came to be accepted and valued by them as their own views.

You could try this out at home by asking an older child to teach his younger brother or sister the morals of a particular piece of behaviour, using the sort of dilemma children come across in real life. For instance, should a child tell the truth when he has broken something of yours but could easily get away with denying any responsibility for the damage he's caused? Should a child hand over to the rightful owner a Walkman he has found and could pocket without risk? Should you tell the checkout girl the correct price for an item when you could save money by lying? Explain that not telling the truth is lying, not handing over the Walkman is stealing and not telling the checkout girl the right price is cheating, and then ask him to explain these ideas to his little brother or sister.

Or you could ask him to spell out why a childish trick such as knocking on doors and running away is bad. You could ask: 'Do you feel that all grown-ups are huge and powerful and it feels good to cut them down to size with a trick?' 'If not, who are the exceptions?' 'What would be the position if an old or crippled person lives in the house who has a painful struggle to reach the door?' 'What if the occupant has been mugged or burgled in the past and, when there's a knock on the door and no one is there, becomes frightened that the mugger or burglar is watching again?' Once you've let the older child talk through the situation and seen it from everyone's point of view and realised what is the caring, co-operative thing to do, you can ask them to teach this lesson to their little brother or sister as a way of reinforcing the message.

How do we learn to think?

Though you can't ram your moral opinions down your children's throats (or rather you can, but they'll only throw them up again), if you tell your children what you believe in, it gives them something to think about – grist for their moral mill. They do need to learn to think, and think for themselves. How do we do that? Not with a big stick, nor a cold shoulder.

American psychologists Hoffman and Saltzstein studied eleven- and twelve-year-olds and found that parents who threw their weight around had a poor effect on their children's moral judgement. Parents who used their power, saying things like, 'shut your mouth', 'do what I say if you know what's good for you', tended to have children with what the psychologists called an external conscience: that is, they were more concerned with not getting caught than with the rightness or wrongness of what they were doing.

Parents who used a lot of emotional blackmail (typically, shaming or threats of the withdrawal of love) saying things like, 'you're acting like a baby', and 'I don't want to speak to you', also had a detrimental effect on their children's moral behaviour. Their children tended to have a rigid and rather heartless conventional conscience and would say, for example, that it would be wrong to tell a lie even if it was to protect a friend from persecution, or to steal medicine even to save your dying wife.

However, parents who used reason with their children and focused on the other person, asking, 'How did so-and-so feel when you did that?', tended to have children who were able to weigh up all the extenuating circumstances and who would make moral judgements according to the spirit rather than the letter of the law.

Other research by Dr Holstein in San Francisco confirms that the styles of reasoning that parents use has a big effect on their children's moral development. She studied twelve- and thirteen-year-old youngsters in a professional community. The children were tested to discover the level of their moral development and then the parents were questioned about what went on in family discussions.

What emerged was that the children who got the highest scores in moral development were those whose parents had most encouraged them to talk about moral dilemmas, irrespective of the children's IQ. She also found that parents whose own moral reasoning was highly developed were likely to take their child's opinions seriously when they had family discussions about how to solve hypothetical moral dilemmas and these teenagers got about 40 per cent of the discussion time with their parents. However, parents whose moral reasoning was at a conventional level behaved differently: they were likely to explain to their child that they were right and to expect the child to conform to their judgement; and adolescents in these families got only 20 per cent or less of the discussion time. It's clear that we have to get away from the idea of morality being all about content, a bag of virtues, and lay it open to discussion if we want our children to take it seriously.

'I remember about the only time my father really got cross with me,' says Professor John Wilson of the Department of Educational Studies at Oxford. 'He said, "Why are you doing that, John?" and I said, "Well *you* do that," and he said,

"That's a reason, you think that's a reason, that I do it? I might be quite wrong." I was supposed to make up my own mind. I think the idea of making children think for themselves requires a firm tradition of behaviour in the family, from parents and others, so they can see what decent behaviour is like. Then they can criticise it and make up their own minds if they don't like bits of it.'

Getting father in on the act

All the evidence shows that even more important than whether parents respect children, set them a good example, pass on proper values, teach them to think, give them responsibility or a consistent code of behaviour, more crucial than all other influences on moral development is love. From the very first work by Piaget into children's development onwards, the research shows that parental warmth and nurturing are consistently and positively linked to children's moral development and that lack of parental love is a crucial factor in the making of a delinquent.

Work carried out in the 1970s, for instance, shows that you can predict what stage of moral development a thirteen-year-old has reached by checking his mother's level of moral reasoning: if she is highly principled, the child is very likely to be highly principled too. Fathers, however, are a less reliable indicator, since principled fathers sometimes have morally immature children. Why is this? The researchers compared successful fathers (principled fathers who had principled children) with unsuccessful ones (principled fathers who had unprincipled children). When the adolescents were asked to rate how often their fathers showed them affection or played with them, it emerged that the successful fathers were much warmer and much more involved with their youngsters than the unsuccessful ones. Moral reasoning grows best when it is nurtured by love, and it flourishes best of all if the father demonstrates his love as well as the mother.

British philosopher Richard Peters has argued that the chief business of moral education is getting people to care. A father who cares for his children – who cooks, cleans up, takes them to the doctor, attends the school open day and sits through the school concert without falling asleep – is demonstrating to his child that he thinks other people, their needs and their feelings, are important. The child is learning that human relationships and all that they demand from us must be taken seriously.

Discipline – the balancing act

Though parental love is paramount, it is not enough on its own. You do have to control your children's behaviour until they get it right every time themselves, and in order to do this effectively you have to tread a delicate line between strictness and indulgence.

John C. Gibbs, Professor of Psychology at Ohio State University, and Julia Krevans, set up a study to investigate the relationship between the sort of discipline parents used with their children and how moral and altruistic the children were by testing children aged from eleven to fourteen, and their mothers, plus a teacher chosen by the child because he or she knew them well. While the parents answered a questionnaire about how they disciplined their children, the children were tested to assess their empathy and the teachers gave their rating of the child's moral level.

The mothers were shown three types of discipline and asked which sort they and other members of the family used most often and how frequently they used it. One type of discipline was 'disappointment' and a typical disappointment statement from a parent was, 'I would tell him I never expected to hear that sort of thing from him.' The second sort of discipline was 'other-orientated' where the parent said things like, 'I'd point out how his friend must feel.' And the third type was 'power assertion' where a parent's typical statement might be, 'I'd tell him that he'll be punished for what he's done,' or the withdrawal of love: 'I'd ignore him for a while.'

The study found that the most successful parents were

those who used expressions of disappointment as a way of getting their child to improve his behaviour. Their children showed high levels of altruistic behaviour in their tests and were rated highly by their teachers. It seems that when the mother says she is disappointed, it has two results. First it cultivates the child's empathy, because it makes him focus on someone else's hurt feelings – his mother's. Second, if the mother says she is disappointed in the child's behaviour (not, it must be stressed, with the child), it also tells him that she has confidence in his capacity for better behaviour and this gives him a good opinion of his own potential so he starts to believe he can do better. The parent's expression of disappointment not only cultivates the child's empathy, but fosters his idea of himself as a caring person, and this fits in with all the other findings which show that when you enhance a child's self-esteem, it improves their behaviour.

Parents versus teachers

By the time he is eleven, a child's moral education is being increasingly taken out of his parents' hands as he spends more and more time in school and comes under the influence of his teachers, and the school may not take exactly the same line as the parents. There is a tension between parents and teachers and it is inescapable because the parents are committed to their particular child and are training him and forming moral habits according to their views of morality and of the world. The teacher's task, however, is to run an even-handed institution where that child is just one of 400 or 800, so he isn't the sole focus.

David Ingram, a teacher who has specialised in moral education, says that there is a sort of conflict between home and school because, 'School is where what Jessica's mother and father have taught her is open to critical assessment. And Jessica herself must learn to think about and re-examine what she's been trained is the right way to deal with X and Y. The teacher is the person who helps Jessica to become a person in her own right, to get an external perspective on the life that she's been trained in by her parents. And in that sense the teacher is the enemy of the parent. There is no way that a school can reflect all the differences in interpretation, social relations and so on, quite apart from the actual cultural and religious differences, of all the parents.'

Simon Newell, head of a school in Shrewsbury, sees another possible conflict between parental attitudes and school. 'If you're talking about how willing children are to be open to new ideas, then a great deal depends on the equipment they are bringing with them from the parents. Some, obviously, come from homes where there is black and white and they're told, "this is right, that's wrong and you'll get a clip around the earhole". And I feel parents are more likely to treat boys that way, and more likely to reason and explain to girls.'

Moral education concerns deep underlying habits of action and feeling, habits which are closely linked with tribal loyalties. Parents and close relatives inevitably determine the shape of these, for right or wrong, and though this original pattern can be changed later, it can only be done with enormous difficulty. Children start by supposing their parents have got things right. So if a teacher attacks something like truancy, or shoplifting or travelling without a bus ticket, the attack will fail because it looks like a criticism of the parents who taught them this behaviour.

Talking in the classroom

The alternative to making a direct attack on children's mistaken views is to engage them in serious discussion, and that means treating the children's views with respect. Moral philosopher Mary Midgley describes a successful American approach. 'Matt Lipmann has been doing philosophy with children from an early age. He was originally a teacher of logic at Stanford University and after a time he decided he was getting nowhere because he was getting students too late; they hadn't got into the habit of thinking. They could do logic – they could be trained to do tricks – but they weren't going to use it to think systematically about anything that mattered.

'The technique he developed with children is that you read them a story and then you ask them what questions do they want to ask about this story? It's a matter of having them talk about the story and then bringing the talk towards the big issues. It has enormous advantages over any style of handing it out, because alienated teenagers aren't going to take in what anybody hands out. That's their trouble. You haven't got their ear at all.'

Dr Monica Taylor, who has been researching how British schools teach moral education for the Schools Curriculum Assessment Authority says, 'There are now several groups who've been quite active in philosophy, not studying Descartes and Aristotle but applying philosophy to issues that young people encounter. It's getting them to think and also usually to get the discipline of sharing ideas between one another. It has formal rules and procedures and it is quite interesting to see how quickly children latch on to the procedures and then what kinds of ideas they produce and how they discuss them.'

A number of schools have introduced something called Circle Time, which involves teachers sitting in a circle with children and getting them to talk about what is important to them and giving them an opportunity to express their personal views, to say what makes them happy or sad. Teachers acknowledge that this raises issues about privacy because of the danger that the child might reveal things about their home life that their parents would prefer to keep quiet, but it does help to make children more aware of other people and more sensitive to their feelings.

These supervised classroom discussions bring other welcome spin-offs. The child learns to take criticism, to pay attention to what he is saying, to be tactful and tolerant of his classmates, not to take criticism too personally or become too angry, to stick to the point, not to interrupt, not to mind making a fool of himself and so on. Above all, he learns that when he is having this sort of discussion, his views and feelings must be governed by reason no matter how passionately he feels.

155

However, Professor John Wilson adds a proviso to teachers who might be attempting this approach: 'We are unlikely to learn these lessons unless our learning is rewarded. In the family, the child learns with loving parents – the child's reward is his pleasure in sharing something the parents have to offer, wanting to imitate them and enjoy what they enjoy. So those leading a classroom discussion have to generate something like the trust and security of a family discussion.'

Dr Helen Haste points out that Lawrence Kohlberg set an early example. 'First he had children engaging in debate and discussion in the classroom and considering other people's point of view from the cognitive point of view, not the emotional sense. And he found that confronting children with the limitations of their view through debate and reasoning was quite successful at moving them on to the next moral stage.

'But he also examined the whole approach of the school and found there was no point in trying to teach moral development if the whole institution is, in fact, operating at a low level – do wrong, get caught, get punished, avoid getting caught if you can. If the school has this attitude there is no point in expecting the children to move on. So he tried to get the children involved in decisions on how to run their own community – he called it the Just Community School. You can create an environment throughout the school where moral reasoning is fostered and a progression to more complex reasoning takes place.'

David Ingram, Director of the Norham Foundation, worked with Kohlberg setting up a Just Community School in the Bronx, New York. Kohlberg took 100 children who were persistent truants and invited them back to school on a restricted curriculum; the remainder of the time would be spent working out their social relations.

'To start with they were disorderly and they shouted a lot and it was very difficult,' recalls Ingram. 'But within a couple of years they'd created the kind of community where they'd experienced trust – these were children who came from quite deprived backgrounds in many ways – and who knew about social experiences from their own experience of regulating themselves in the school. It was quite dramatic.'

Ingram applies what he learnt in the Bronx to the school where he now teaches. 'What we're doing in this school is having a weekly meeting where the children have to struggle with real issues. And at the end of the day, they'll have been heard and they'll understand the nature of the opposition. It's an on-going thing: they make a case, they submit it and get an answer, even if it's a refusal. Then they continue to push. They get an insight into how decisions are made, and the problems and the processes involved.

'This is why I like Circle Time discussion. Instead of the teacher taking over the situation, say bullying or whatever, it becomes an issue for the group to discuss. But it needs to be handled very carefully so that the child who's a victim doesn't become more of a victim and the child who is seen as the perpetrator of the incident isn't branded in some kind of way. How we do things here is with some kindness and support for one another.'

This sort of discussion time is very popular with children as there is now so much going on in their lives that they want to explore and talk through their problems with some qualified adults. Head teacher Simon Newall finds that, 'Children are very keen to talk about moral issues, though if you present them with abstract questions about morality they're going to switch off very quickly. But if the dilemmas are real, rooted in real events, they are generally very interested.

'They do have cut and dried answers, and what the teacher has to do is to try and challenge them and get them to think that there is more than one way of tackling things, and one might be more moral than another. Potentially these children are just as responsive as previous generations. They're just as capable of appreciating the issues and understanding the judgements, of thinking and acting in an unselfish way as when I was a child, when children didn't even discuss moral issues.'

Why teachers must stand firm

Schools can take a firm and fair line on moral behaviour, but a great deal depends on the moral leadership of the Head and what particular rules, injunctions and sanctions he or she is prepared to put in place because it is the head teacher, above all, who sets the tone of the micro environment of the school. One problem is that there has been a general decline in respect for authority – not that authority automatically has to be respected, it should prove itself worthy of respect – but it has swung very much the other way. Children come to school not respecting the teachers either as teachers or even as human beings because slinging mud at teachers has become a brutal spectator sport in recent years, with the many good, innovative and dedicated teachers being treated as contemptuously by politicians, parents and even princes as the genuinely substandard ones.

Some teachers have hacked away at their own authority, too, through weakness or from a confused wish to be chums with the children. As my youngest daughter remarked of a teacher who wanted the class to call him by his first name, 'I've got friends thank you. What I want here is a teacher.' Professor John Wilson believes that part of the diminishing status of teachers is their own fault. 'Many adults today are afraid of exercising authority,' he points out. 'It is one thing to encourage, cajole, support or even bribe children into obedience, quite another to say something like, "Look, you have got to do this, and without caring whether you like me or respect me as a person I am going to make life sufficiently unpleasant for you to make sure you do actually do it."

'It takes nerve and self-confidence to take such a line and in modern liberal and pluralist societies there are not many such adults left, especially not in schools. It is, of course, an unpleasant line to have to take, but any parent who needs to stop his son bullying a little sister, or any teacher who needs to make absolutely sure that the weak pupils are not done down by the strong in school, knows such a line has sometimes to be taken. For many people, however, this is the sticking point: to apply fear as a motive, particularly fear of punishment, seems to them morally intolerable and (for themselves) psychologically out of the question.'

Professor Wilson believes this fear of violence and domination is destructive if it affects the interaction between those in authority and the children in their charge. Today, for instance, teachers are encouraged not to confront disruptive or disobedient pupils but to try and defuse any potential conflict instead by some form of evasive action – cajolery, humour, smoothing things over. So the pupil challenges the teacher's authority and the challenge is evaded instead of being met head on. The psychological results of this corrupt the child because he needs to learn that he must live in a world where there are rules and other people with their own interests. The present aim is to avoid trouble at all costs, but at some point the teacher must bring it home to the pupil that there are certain limits which he cannot be allowed to go beyond.

The just community
Evidence of how the moral climate of the school can affect its pupils' judgement and behaviour was revealed when Ann Higgins, Clark Power and Lawrence Kohlberg tested high school students by posing a variety of moral dilemmas. Some of the students were attending 'alternative' schools where staff and students settled the rules and issues in a weekly community meeting based on one-person, one-vote. The other students went to 'regular' high schools where the rules were simply set out for the pupils. The aim of the experiment was to see if the atmosphere of the school had any effect on the way the students thought and behaved.

The first dilemma put to the pupils was about caring: Harry needs to be driven to an early Saturday morning interview for the college he has applied for. His tutor has agreed to take him but at the last minute the tutor's car breaks down. He goes to Harry's hall of residence and asks his classmates and his teacher if they can help. They mostly don't like Harry, think he shows off, and refuse. One boy, Billy, could drive him to the interview, but he hardly knows Harry. Should he give up his Saturday morning lie-in when Harry's friends won't help him? Should Billy volunteer to drive Harry? Why? Or why not?

The second dilemma concerned stealing: Mary arrives in the history class but the teacher is not there. She decides to chat to friends in the hall outside until the teacher comes. She opens her bag to get out a letter to show to her friends and then goes to meet her friends, leaving the bag open. Tom looks in, sees a banknote and thinks about taking it. What would someone like Tom do in this situation? Why? Should Mary have been so trusting, or more careful?

The third dilemma brought up the idea of restitution: Tom takes the money. Mary notices it has gone and tells her teacher. The teacher asks the person who stole the money to return it, but no one does. If no one owns up, what should the teacher do? Why? Would there be a general feeling or expectation in your school that everyone should chip in to reimburse Mary? Are people supposed to chip in? Would you expect all the members of your school to chip in? Why?

Betsy explains why people in her alternative school should expect Billy to give Harry a lift: 'Because you have a responsibility to the kids in this school, even if you don't like them all that much . . . you are supposed to think of them as part of the school and part of the community so you should do it.' Later she adds: 'It is our school, it is not a school that all these separate people go to that don't care about each other.' 'Anyone who is in this school knows they should help out – there is a general feeling and everyone knows that.'

In other words, Betsy sees herself as a member of a community and she speaks from the point of view of the group when she says, 'We think we should do X.'

Rob, on the other hand, said he did not consider his regular high school a community. 'Too many people hold grudges against each other because maybe they look different or act different. Or some kids come to school to be with their friends, to get stoned, and some kids come to do work. Most people think of themselves really.' He adds, 'A lot of kids mess up the school, like write on the walls. There is no need for that, there is paper to write on.'

So Rob finds no shared belief in helping each other out in his school: he thinks it would be a good thing to have, but does not believe it exists. 'Everyone knows that it is good to help someone out. But people just don't care about anybody else.' He adds that if he wanted to help, 'I would wait till after class. I would keep it quiet so nobody might know about it, and then I could help the kid. Then nobody would say anything to me, because they would not know about it.'

In other words, he is aware of a peer group who would disapprove of his helping out, thinking it uncool to associate with an unpopular student like Harry, whereas Betsy thinks the school would be very mad at Billy if he didn't give Harry a lift.

The answers to the second dilemma – should you steal from Mary's bag? – were more clear cut, with most children seeing only one option whatever the school environment. Jay is typical when he says he wouldn't take the money, though it's a big temptation. 'I respect people's property because I expect them to respect mine. And it's against the law. You can't take it just because you want it as otherwise we would have a pretty sick society with no laws and with chaos.'

The students found it hard to decide what to do if they found themselves facing the third dilemma: was restitution an obligation or not? Should the other children chip in to make up Mary's loss?

'Yes,' says Betsy, 'because if everyone gets away with stealing and no one cares here, then it just can't be a good place. If people think everything is everyone else's tough luck and it is too bad that happened, then this place would not be a very caring place.' She values the community: 'You have to do what the majority wants to do or else we would have no school and it would be very unorganised and nothing would go right.'

'No,' says Rob, 'because the class didn't steal the money, just one person did.' Asked: 'If there was an agreement to chip in, would most students do so willingly?' he replies, 'No, not willingly.' Should the school have an agreement that everyone should chip in in situations like this? 'Nope.'

Jake, who went to a regular high school like Rob, was also unwilling to help because it was Mary's fault, or lack of responsibility, leaving her bag open. 'She was too trusting. And why should I pay for what somebody else did? Why should other students?' Jake says there is little sense of community in his school so they don't go out of their way to help each other: 'Nobody really takes pride in the school except a few who are good students or very good athletes.' Would he try to find out who was the thief? 'No, I wouldn't go out of my way. It's Mary's responsibility.'

What the experiment showed was that the responses of the students varied according to the sort of school they attended. In the alternative schools, most students reported that they themselves would make the community-minded, altruistic choice and act on it and 80 per cent of them believed most of their fellow students would do the same. The picture was quite different in the regular schools: though the majority also said they themselves would make the altruistic choice, only 40 per cent felt their fellow students would follow suit. They clearly saw their fellow students as different from themselves and in some sense as less responsible, and this seems to be the result of a school environment which provided few opportunities for discussing and creating shared rules of behaviour. There was a lack of collective and agreed patterns of behaviour, and little valuing of the schools as communities.

It is clear from all this that a school with a positive moral atmosphere provides the sort of environment in which students feel it makes sense to think in terms of responsibility and to act morally towards their peers and teachers. Schools which gave their pupils lots of opportunities to discuss how they wanted the school to be run and what its standards should be had the highest sense of collective altruism based on a strong sense of community. If we want children to take rules and standards seriously, we first have to give them the opportunity to get involved in making the rules and setting the standards themselves.

Interlude
Rude boys and vandals

We must expect teenagers to be tempestuous. A sea of shining, obedient faces would be worrying because it would suggest a lack of energy, a failure of the desire to change the world which youngsters should be overflowing with. But seriously alienated teenagers are another matter. We have all seen alarming incidents of young people who are unmanaged or unmanageable, beyond anybody's sphere of influence. Some children cannot or will not be controlled: they disrupt a train ride, a family outing or a whole neighbourhood regardless of every threat or plea hurled at them. When we see teenagers mugging, joyriding, stealing, defacing our world with graffiti and litter and abusing themselves and others we have to ask what went wrong. Could it have been prevented? What must parents do to be sure they don't raise a little horror?

None of us is perfect
We can start by admitting that no one is morally perfect. All the experiments show that it is much easier for us to take the high moral ground when we are pronouncing on what other people should do than when we are deciding what to do ourselves in a tricky situation. We are not morally consistent either: we all find it easier to pursue some moral goals than others. I might be quick to offer someone a seat on the bus, but slow to brake to let another car pull out in front of me. You might organise a collection for someone at work who's

been robbed, but walk past a man slumped on the pavement without pausing to see if he is drunk or had a heart attack. Some people find it easy to be helpful to people in physical need, but not to those with mental problems. Others are only concerned about people of a certain kind: perhaps people they think of as similar to themselves, from the same ethnic group or class perhaps.

We all have a tendency to divide the world into them and us, differentiating between an in-group and an out-group. In one revealing experiment, volunteers were given an art test based on the work of the painters Klee and Kandinsky, and afterwards some were told that they clearly preferred Klee and others that they preferred Kandinsky. Later, when they were given resources to hand out, those who'd been told they preferred Klee were more generous to people they thought also preferred Klee, while those who'd been told they preferred Kandinsky favoured those who liked Kandinsky.

In other words, we can't help favouring the in-group and discriminating against the out-group even when the grouping is as tenuous as this. This tendency to favour the people you identify with and reject those you don't means that teenagers will behave badly if they feel alienated or outcast from the rest of us.

Baby rage

Which comes first? Are teenagers outcast because they behave badly, or do we make them outcasts and are we therefore responsible for their aggression? What makes some individuals act aggressively towards everyone else?

Well, we are all aggressive when we are little. A baby and toddler finds the world hugely frustrating – he is constantly picked up, put down, fed, ignored, played with and put away at the whim of others. As he grows he can see lovely shining things his hands cannot yet grasp, great new places to explore which his legs cannot propel him towards yet and a whole world of fascinating objects he is not supposed to suck, tug or even touch. All babies resent the power their parents have, as well as appreciating their strength and comfort, and they show their resentment in aggression, whether it is the baby pulling your hair or a toddler having a major tantrum.

One of the signs of growing maturity is that we learn to control our aggression and to realise that there are very few occasions when it is really an appropriate response. For some youngsters, however, this understanding never arrives. They remain stuck at the infantile, lash-out-at-anyone level and when they do so with an adolescent's strength, they become dangerous and scary.

What triggers aggression?

So what makes a person who is nearly grown up behave in a childishly aggressive way? Psychologists have identified two chief causes: the first is being frustrated in the pursuit of accomplishing one's goals, the second is an attack on one's self, or extensions of ourselves such as our family or property. The frustration or attack does not have to be a real event: a person can feel aggressive just by anticipating that his goals, including his hopes for the future, are going to be frustrated, or just by the expectation or threat of an attack on his self-esteem.

Frustration or threats can also leave a youngster feeling a failure, because he feels unable to protect himself and his family or friends, or because he feels unable to live up to society's expectations. Although they may seem full of bluster and Dutch courage, most delinquents are hiding huge self-doubt and anxiety under their swaggering exterior. However, before these young men lash out at other people, there is something else they need.

Aggressive people need to make other people their scape-goats, to differentiate in some way so that another group appears inferior and worthy of blame. As the Klee and Kandinsky experiment showed, we all tend to favour some people and reject others. Whites have scapegoated Blacks, Christians and Muslims scapegoat each other, workers blame the bosses, women blame men. Accusing a group or an individual of causing your problems, difficulties and misfortunes represents both an added incitement to aggression and a handy way of selecting your victims. Tests on aggressive young men in laboratories show that when these individuals are insulted, frustrated or threatened in some way, they enjoy contemplating the suffering of those who inflicted the distress or harm on them.

Scapegoating is particularly handy for youngsters who feel they are failing because it relieves them of the responsibility for their failures. If someone else can be blamed and seen to be harming you intentionally, your failure is no longer your fault. Scapegoating also unites teenagers into gangs by creating solidarity within the in-group facing the harm-doers, the common enemy.

The early failures

How is it that some youngsters feel threatened and believe the world is against them, or feel like failures, when they are only just starting out in life? What does a child need in order to grow up feeling strong and capable? The first thing, though this isn't fair, is to avoid being born into a wrecked environment. Most juvenile offenders have grown up in the places they trash, they don't taxi in from the smart suburbs. Parents bringing up families in poverty on clapped out high-rise estates where the shops and banks have put up the shutters and departed, the school buildings are grotty and in need of several facelifts and the local play area has been vandalised, have a hard time keeping their children out of trouble. That isn't to say they can't do it: many parents are quietly heroic and raise thoughtful, caring children in abominable circumstances; and some children are born into opulent homes in the most desirable neighbourhoods and still turn out to be dishonest, mean and dangerous.

However, the feelings that lead to aggression – powerlessness and outside threat – are more likely to be found in children who are growing up in an environment which offers no chance to live normally. For instance, I visited a council estate outside Glasgow, housing 10,000 people, which happens to be home to the highest percentage of teenagers in Scotland, and it had been built with no social facilities at all. There was no park or playground, no pub or local shops; you could not buy even a loaf of bread, a bottle of milk or a packet of fish and chips without catching a bus to somewhere else. There was no launderette, post office, video shop, nothing. There had been a football pitch, but they discovered coal underneath and it was incorporated into the local mine. For the youngsters, facing massive local unemployment, there was nothing at all to do with all their youthful energy and many had turned to drugs and under-age drinking.

It isn't just inner cities and council estates that fail to cater for the ordinary needs of growing youngsters. In many country towns and villages today, the local shops have shut and bus services to distant town centres with their cinemas and dances have been severed. So a generation grows up that is shown, in magazines and on television, the wealth of fun the young are supposed to be having and with access to none of it themselves. If we just show them the picture and offer them nothing in reality, we cannot complain if young people become bored, troublesome and destructive.

The feelings of being threatened and helpless which foster aggression can give rise to a sense of injustice and even moral outrage if the helpless youngster sees that others are clearly not suffering from the same conditions. Then the victim is likely to commit some act of violence to redress this real or imagined imbalance, whether it's smashing up the school where other pupils are doing better than him, or running a nail down the side of a Porsche.

Violence not only fulfils an emotional need for the perpetrator, it also enables him to think he has achieved the economic or social gains that are due to him. If the youngster has been feeling frustrated or threatened for a long time, or indeed for most of his life, he will respond even more intensely to what he sees as his unfair situation and will go out looking for someone or something to vent his aggression on.

Youngsters who mistrust other people and expect the worst from them often respond to actions that are not actually doing them any harm with some act of self-defence, in what might be called pre-retaliation. Aggressive delinquents are highly mistrustful and tend to perceive other people's actions as an attack on themselves even when they are perfectly innocent. Some of them learn to enjoy seeing other people's suffering. The American psychologist Hartman showed groups of aggressive delinquents a film in which a boxer was severely beaten in the course of a match. He found that they behaved more aggressively after they had watched the film, whereas delinquents who were not aggressive felt sad after watching the boxer's suffering. Seeing other people suffering made violent youngsters even more violent.

Raising a gentle child

So what can we do to ensure we don't raise a violent child? It's not a question of moral rules: all children can tell the difference between right and wrong, at least in theory. They don't stand outside a pensioner's flat trying to remember whether they're supposed to sing carols or chuck a brick through the window: they know the answer. However, they are vulnerable and impressionable – they are children after all, not adults – and many of them are not being taught the right lessons.

If feeling frustrated or threatened makes youngsters react aggressively, then they should be taught how to handle these emotions, since they are bound to crop up in their lives. Parents can show them how to resolve frustration by being persistent and patient in their attempts to achieve a goal, and how to resolve conflict peacefully through discussion and compromise. To reduce the numbers of aggressive delinquents, we must foster a sense of competence in young people, to give them the feeling that they have the ability to achieve their goals and also make sure they have plenty of opportunities to do so. Self-esteem and self-confidence are the best antidote to violence.

Some children, however, because of the nature of their experience, never learn non-confrontational ways of resolving conflict or constructive means of regulating their everyday behaviour: all they are taught is to get what they want by hitting and grabbing.

Professor Donald West of the Institute of Criminology at Cambridge University has followed over 400 boys as they grew up and found that the factors most likely to lead youngsters into criminal violence were criminal parents, poverty, lots of siblings in the home and inattentive parenting. Children who scored badly on intelligence tests were also more likely to become criminals. West said such children could be spotted early on: 'They appear scruffy, they are not so well socialised and they are not responsive to discipline. They don't get on with other children and are too aggressive and irritable.'

In order to function well, you must believe that you are a capable person, but for many children this is unrealistic. They don't feel they can do anything at all about the world they find themselves in. They feel trapped in inner city, ethnic or class problems. They genuinely are not strong, capable people and it would be unfair to expect them to be without a great deal of support and help.

The feeling of alienation that young delinquents suffer from comes out of a sense of: 'Well, what the hell does it matter? No one cares.' And it's true, they don't. Some youngsters come from dreadful families who really don't care and who do terrible damage to their children and we have to remember this when people talk thoughtlessly about family values as if everyone was brought up with a fair ration.

Watch that child!
Teenage criminals are not born with a brick in their hands. Something happens to them between the pram and puberty to turn them into tearaways. What starts it off and keeps it going? Psychiatrists who have studied parents' behaviour in depth to see what effect it has on the aggression levels of their

children have found that one of the key factors is supervision.

Part of the parents' job is to organise the home and supervise the child. This means setting limits on what the child has access to, being aware of his whereabouts, activities and social contacts, talking to him, listening to him, requiring the child to be accountable and spending time with him. The evidence shows that if you manage and monitor your children effectively, you can prevent aggressive and antisocial behaviour developing because you will spot and control any hint of aggression as it arises.

Studies show that parents of delinquent children are much less effective at managing their child's behaviour than parents of good children. If you don't bother to keep a close eye on what he does, where he is or ought to be, and who he is supposed to be with, he will find opportunities to pick up aggressive behaviour by hanging out with outcast and aggressive friends. Erratic monitoring and poor supervision within the family are two of the factors most likely to lead to delinquency because the children grow resentful of any attempts by their parents to be involved in their activities and the likelihood of aggressive behaviour increases.

Parents who can't or won't impose any discipline on their children unwittingly encourage aggression because it puts too much control and responsibility upon children when they are not ready for it and this makes them feel inadequate. This is why children of permissive parents, who receive very mild tellings off or no punishments at all, are likely to exhibit aggressive or even criminal behaviour. Whether the permissiveness is well-meaning and based on some idea of democracy, or is neglectful and really a way of ducking the responsibilities of child rearing, floppy parenting leads to delinquency and aggression. In addition, over-indulgent parenting is often combined with poor monitoring and management, which again is very likely to result in delinquency, especially among boys. If the parents are ineffectual, the children will almost certainly get involved with the wrong crowd and this then leads them into mischief and worse.

Quick, firm responses are always a great help in controlling bad behaviour in adolescents. For instance, a headmistress I know woke up one morning deciding she had had enough of the graffiti in her school. She marched in and announced to the whole school that in future the staff would be conducting spot checks on children's bags: anyone found with indelible markers would be sent home immediately and suspended. The graffiti problem simply disappeared. She admitted privately that such firm action would not have been possible a couple of years earlier, when her staffroom contained a small group of militants who would have claimed the searches were an infringement of the pupils' liberty, but they had gone and she was able to take control, and a firm and decisive Head will always have a well-run school.

Unreliable parents

If poor supervision is one factor linked to aggression in children, inconsistent discipline is another. Over and over again, inconsistency has been associated with aggressive behaviour, conduct problems and criminal behaviour – and it is usually mother versus father. If a parent's attitude to punishment is unreliable and spasmodic – carried out mainly when the parent has had enough rather than whenever the child does something wrong – it increases the child's subsequent resistance. It seems that children don't take inconsistent punishment seriously.

It takes a little skill to handle discipline well and some parents make a botched job of it. They may threaten and scold the child frequently, but fail to follow through with punishment; or they confront the child with anger rather than with a more appropriate response. They may nag, complaining about almost anything the child does or says; or they don't make themselves clear when they are giving the child instructions and then blame him when he gets it wrong. All these ineffectual methods strengthen a child's bad behaviour.

Some parents' behaviour actually encourages aggression. The process often begins when the child acts in a rude and rejecting manner and, in an attempt to discipline him, the parents react in similar fashion instead of responding in a constructive, adult way. This escalates the interchange and the cycle continues until one or other (and it is usually the parent) gives in. Thus the child's bad behaviour is reinforced, and he learns that his parent's threats are nothing to be feared. In many families the rude child dominates the family and the parents have little control over him.

Other children grow up aggressive because their mothers keep on attributing bad intentions and dispositions to them and blame them for every little thing that goes wrong. The mother starts off reacting in a rejecting, antagonistic manner and the child begins to behave in a way that matches her assumptions. Parents who tell a child he is bad, whether their attitude is the result of his bad behaviour or the cause of it, encourage his aggression.

Brutal parents

If weak and inconsistent discipline breeds aggression, heavy-handed punishment does not curb it, because what the youngster sees is the parent demonstrating hostility and he interprets aggression as an acceptable approach to dealing with others. Studies show that in response to harsh discipline, children become more aggressive in their behaviour towards their peers, and this is true of children of different ages and from all sorts of backgrounds.

There is a close relation between extreme levels of punishment, particularly if it is physical and at the level of abuse, and very aggressive behaviour: the more severe the physical discipline is, the worse the outcome is likely to be. This shows the futility of those who demand that young delinquents should be given short sharp shocks to improve their behaviour: most of these youngsters will have had a daily lifetime of hard knocks and physical abuse – and it has not made them decent, it has made them delinquent.

We have to look at what works. Moderate forms of punishment can reduce the incidence of aggressive behaviour if they are delivered in a warm, nurturing context by a loving parent. If you use reason and explanation and respect the child as an individual with a mind of his own, then being firm and sensible will curb his natural aggression.

Troubled parents

It's not just the way they are treated, but what they observe going on around them in the home that influences a child's capacity for violence. Children who are witnesses to verbal or physical violence between their parents will grow up showing aggressive, antisocial behaviour, though it seems to affect boys more than girls. If the level of parental conflict increases, the seriousness of aggression-related problems in the child increases as well. The parents' conflicts affect the children both directly, by offering them a role-model of violence, and indirectly through the style of parenting they use, since parents in a bad marriage usually provide less warmth and control to their children, which again leads to aggression.

Witnessing violence at home is not the only trigger for aggression: seeing misery can also have an effect. Children need to feel that adults are reliable and trustworthy, not vulnerable and helpless like themselves. A young child needs to feel there is one person who is truly capable of looking after him: if he sees that person frequently troubled and distraught, abandoned or betrayed by a partner, or weeping over unpayable bills, the world becomes a frightening place against which he is obliged to be as well-defended, tough and aggressive as he can.

Children unfortunate enough to be born into families where criminal behaviour and drug abuse are rife have little option but to grow up aggressive, not only because they naturally model themselves on their antisocial parents, but because such parents are generally quick to use physical punishment on their children, which teaches them violence.

A 1991 study also found that antisocial mothers were not very involved with their children, failing to supervise them

175

and never sharing their activities, and this breakdown in parenting was directly linked to children's antisocial behaviour, poor peer relationships, low academic skills and low self-esteem. A child has to identify with the important adults in its life, and if those adults present a corrupt model the child becomes very disturbed. There are lots of children whose parents are simply lousy people.

Testosterone rules OK?

Not all aggression in teenage boys, however, can be put down to parents failing in some way. John Woods, a consultant psychotherapist, points out that: 'Much acting out is the result of acting out a fantasy or instinct which can't be acted out in any other form so comes out as aggression. A very common example is when boys commit burglaries or break into cars as a way of acting out their sexual impulse, which they can't express in any other way.

'Growing up can eventually give them other ways of expressing that, first through having a relationship with a girl and eventually through sex. It's often like that. If the teenager can be provided with some way of expressing themselves – which may not be the direct, instinctive gratification, but even putting things into words, getting angry with their parents, feeling resentful, even if irrationally – that often reduces the danger of them taking some destructive action.'

Groups of teenage boys are intimidating. It's a primitive reaction and in a sense it is biological, instinctive, because these young males would have been the fighters in any earlier society. Society has always had a problem of what to do with its aggressive young men and a foreign war used to be a convenient solution. Now we have almost the first generation of young men with no war left to fight (Ulster is a defensive operation so they don't find it attractive) and you can't just stick a hypodermic in and suck the testosterone out of them.

John Woods says: 'We should look on antisocial behaviour as a demand, a sign that the child has been frustrated in its nurture in some way. If you see antisocial behaviour as a sign of deprivation and try to respond, to meet its needs, you will get results. If you punish, you deepen the deprivation, though it depends on how you punish: the short, sharp shock is a mistake but it's very useful to have the children make some sort of recompense. Adventurous pursuits help, and we should make social provision so they have things to do, otherwise they'll go joyriding.'

Woods adds, 'You must remember that children are dominated by pleasure, so you should always provide a pleasurable alternative to the bad deeds they are contemplating. If you let them do what they want, they will watch television all day, so you must set limits. But if it becomes more pleasant for a child to co-operate and join the others instead of fighting, they will go in the direction you want. They want to belong and fear rejection so teenagers will accept the rules of their own peers, the football club or whatever, wearing the same clothes and identifying with the group. We must give them a sense of belonging to society or we have no leverage in the sanction of rejection.'

There are many ways in which young people can be given a lesson in social cohesion: team games offer useful experiences, so does taking part in the school play or playing in the orchestra or steel band. These group efforts teach youngsters that they have to be reliable and turn up regularly if they want to be included, and that if they drop out or make trouble they spoil it for everyone else in the group as well as themselves. Schoolfriends can be brilliant teachers because they are far less patient than adults with someone who is messing about and ruining things.

However, the group the youngster joins has to be a decent one. 'Boot camps for young trouble makers don't work because adversity welds the group together,' says Woods. 'It's like in the trenches where the men were dependent on the group for survival and became very close: the same thing happens in gaol. And they also see those who supply them with dope as true friends, so there is no point in making them part of a tightly-knitted group which will offer them the wrong values.'

177

Is it all in the genes?

Recently scientists have begun to explore whether aggression might be inherited since it often seems to run in families. Is the desire to act violently dictated by our genes, or by the way we are brought up? Professor Hans Brunner has been studying the men of an extended Dutch family who have a long history of criminal behaviour and has found they all had the same gene defect. He admits that people who say that behaviour is nothing to do with biology and only to do with environmental factors or upbringing are not happy with his results, but even if he is right and a gene is partly to blame, it seems reasonable to suppose that the fact that consecutive generations were brought up in a criminal and dysfunctional family must also have affected the children's behaviour.

Dr Malcolm Carruthers, a hormone specialist, puts the explosive behaviour of young men down to their high levels of hormones, which peak in the late teens. He singles out testosterone and noradrenalin. The typical boy, having no legitimate outlet for his testosterone-driven aggression, finds some antisocial stimulus – which usually involves danger and stress since both of these produce noradrenalin, a hormone that hits the feel-good areas of the brain which also respond to drugs. So the habitual football hooligan, joyrider or ramraider is seeking a hormone boost which will make him feel good.

'Biologically we are still in the Stone Age,' says Dr Carruthers. 'These "fight or flee" urges and male competitive drives are very strong: the only answer is to channel them into something positive.' This is why projects such as those which involve setting up workshops where young joyriders can strip down and race old bangers, though it seems like rewarding poor behaviour, can actually deflect young hooligans from their wicked ways into something less destructive to the rest of us.

Sir Michael Rutter, a child psychiatrist who acknowledges that genes and environmental factors both play a part in children's behaviour says, 'Genes do not lead people directly to commit criminal acts. There may be a propensity to aggression or antisocial behaviour, but whether or not the individual actually commits some criminal act will also be dependent on environmental factors.' The Commission on Children and Violence which was set up after the murder of James Bulger in Liverpool in 1993 argues that there was no truth in the suggestion that some children were bound by their genetic inheritance to grow up wicked. 'That an individual child becomes violent is never inevitable,' reported the Commission. 'Families can and often do provide the security and love necessary to protect children, even high-risk children, from becoming violent.'

Whatever genes a child inherits, the risks they pose can be held in check by raising him in the right environment, which means offering better parenting.

In our hands
Children are not just the property of their parents. It is no use complaining about the bad behaviour of modern children if you turn a blind eye to every example of it. Children are a collective responsibility and need to be shown promptly that adult boundaries are firmly in place.

I remember watching a group of children, aged about thirteen, getting on to my tube train with their teacher. One lad sat down next to me and lit up a cigarette – this was when smoking was permitted in some carriages, but not the one we were in. I looked over to his teacher, hoping he would respond, just in time to see him turn his head away and pretend not to have noticed. He obviously preferred not to deal with the situation.

I turned to the boy and said politely, 'Excuse me, this is a non-smoking compartment. If you want to smoke, you should hop off at the next stop and get in the next carriage.' (I didn't think this was the moment to challenge under-age smoking, but did feel I should challenge bad public behaviour.) There was a moment's silence while everyone in the carriage waited for the response. The boy said nothing but just took a long drag on his cigarette. So I reached over, took it out of his mouth and trod it out on the floor. There was an even longer silence and then nothing, that was the end of it. The boy didn't say a word, he didn't leave the carriage and life went on.

Recounting the story to a friend she pointed out that he could have thumped me or even pulled out a knife, but violent thugs are actually few and far between and I saw in that boy's eyes something I've seen in other teenagers' – a glint of relief that some adult, somewhere, is taking control. Most youngsters are sweet-natured, given half a chance, and we do them a disservice to quake at their misdeeds and let them get away with them.

There used to be plenty of people prepared to represent society's belief that there were rules and they should be obeyed. The truant officer, the policeman and the woman who knew your mother made up a squad of figures who stopped wayward children doing naughty things. Though they were seen as interfering old killjoys, to be outwitted by any child worth his or her salt, they were a symbol none the less of standards that were widely held, and we have abandoned them at our peril.

Chapter Six
Early teens: talking about my reputation

Two main changes take place when children turn into adolescents. First, they grow sensitive to the expectations and opinions of other people, so 'reputation' becomes their prime concern, including their moral reputation. Second, they realise that they are now expected to assume responsibility for the welfare of others, particularly people close to them, and that in order to do this they have to live up to the expectations of the community. So in this respect, too, they must try to improve their reputation. Teenagers are starting to see themselves in terms of their social activity and how they behave with others and this focus on interaction has moral implications because attitudes such as being helpful, generous, open or suspicious in our dealings with others are all moral characteristics.

Alongside the new concern with reputation, the other big development is that adolescent morality has a strong ideological flavour. Teenagers will suddenly announce that they are Buddhists, eco-warriors or at the very least a vegetarian. Ideological morality blooms most vigorously during the teenage years and you will find them defining themselves according to their beliefs – 'I am a pacifist.' In adolescence, the child's ideas of who she is and her ideas of morality are knitted together: it is a critical advance.

Making virtue sexy
Since teenagers are obsessed with appearances and the

impression they make, one way you can boost their virtue is by making it seem desirable. Moral philosopher Mary Midgley suggests appealing to their wish to be brave and heroic. She explains that: 'Vice is, above all, easy. Virtue takes effort, willpower. You fall into sin, you have to gear yourself up to virtue. Faced with imminent danger, it's very easy to be afraid – you never hear anyone say he had to screw himself up to feel afraid. But if you decide not to be a coward but to summon up your courage and face the danger, that takes resolution, strength, effort and will. So you can appeal to a boy's natural wish to be strong and powerful by pointing out that virtue is the activity that demands their strength and power – vice is for wimps.'

Taking on real responsibility
The average person seeing a bunch of teenage boys approaching in the street feels a flicker of unease: so much energy and unruliness is intimidating. Young people today do have both time and vigour at their disposal, which the devil can find work for. In the past young boys and girls from working families entered apprenticeships, household service or farm work at fourteen years of age. The indentures they had to sign often included a ban on drinking, card-playing and visiting brothels and public houses, and the working hours were exhausting, sapping youthful energy. If there were fewer gangs of young people roving the streets till all hours fifty years ago, it was because they were worn out.

Today the picture is dramatically different. Young people are encouraged to stay on into further education until eighteen or more, which gives them time on their hands, and there is no sign of the work that youngsters used to move into; unemployment is up to 50 per cent higher among sixteen- to 26-year-olds than among older groups, which leaves them feeling unwanted and alienated from the adult community. One sad proof of this is that the suicide rate among under 25-year-olds has risen by 30 per cent in the past decade, and drug and alcohol abuse among the young is also growing. In this environment, what can we do to help them on to the right path?

Young teenagers are, in a way, on the sidelines of life because they lack the real responsibilities that would foster moral maturity: excluded from full-time work or providing for their own needs, what they have instead is a lengthy adolescence devoted chiefly to their own studies, hobbies and pleasures. However, children can only become responsible if they are given responsibility: without this they will remain self-centred. We don't do teenagers any favours, and we hold back their moral development, if we shield them from responsible involvement in the lives of others whether it is baby-sitting a younger brother, cleaning up their own messes or getting a Saturday or holiday job.

Both parents and schools need to find ways of encouraging teenagers to offer service to others as a way of nourishing the seeds of citizenship. Many schools have started to provide opportunities for pupils to do meaningful and responsible work – helping younger children with their writing, multiplication tables or in the playground, for instance. Schools, parents and organisations like the Scouts or the Duke of Edinburgh award scheme can encourage adolescents to take up voluntary work, so you can find teenagers helping old people, working with young or handi-capped children, cleaning up beaches and so on. And there is a wealth of evidence to show that taking part in such activities does help the moral progression of the youngsters who put in the time.

Children also need to learn that acting responsibly means taking responsibility for your bad actions as well as your good. Professor Wilson recalls: 'We had some Russian visitors to our schools who were appalled by the fact that if the kids broke a window then along came a glazier at £30 an hour and mended it. They thought the kids should jolly well do it themselves. And they should cook their own food instead of having it done for them in chromium-plated kitchens. They thought children should take responsibility for the institution they were in, otherwise it's totally unreal to them. And I think that's quite right.'

The power of the peer group

There is, inevitably, a degree of conflict between the child and the adult, no matter how thoughtful and gentle parents try to be. Professor John Wilson of the Department of Educational Studies at Oxford explains how it develops: 'The young child is essentially powerless and needs to be looked after, fed, taught and told how to behave. And so he feels ambivalent: on the one hand he wants the psychological and material security, on the other he resents the parental domination. And as the child grows up the need for security diminishes and the need for independence from adult power grows stronger.

'So there is a fear of domination or aggression in any conflict with the parent, but there is also separation anxiety. The young child lives in a world which sometimes seems a world of isolation and slavery; he is alone, powerless, surrounded by adults larger and better equipped than he is, where his only allies as he gets older are other children, the peer group. Hence, the immense power of the peer group whether in the form of street-gangs or any other. They represent the only defence against the powerful adults.'

If teenagers see their parents as an unfair barrier to their freedom, they see impersonal adult authority – whether it is policemen or park-keepers, ticket inspectors or doormen – as particularly intolerable because here the authority is divorced from the idea of adults who are also caring and sharing parents: the child is brought up sharply against impersonal notions like laws and penalties.

The way to resolve the conflict is by giving teenagers the ability to love and care for other people, which sounds rather sentimental but actually means giving them the imagination to see the world from other points of view, to sympathise with other people's difficulties and to want to do something to help. You can point out that ticket inspectors might seem bossy, but then again if there were no inspectors and large numbers of travellers got away with not paying their fare there would be no money to finance the public transport system and everyone would have to walk. So they should sympathise with the inspector doing his job. They must learn to think, to have reasons for their chosen course of action.

Some children are born into families where they have never been exposed to love or co-operation, far less to reason or moral principles. 'A lot of children don't get the chance to start to think because no one has ever shown them how,' says Professor Wilson. 'They're what I call morally autistic, locked up in their own world. It's not their fault. The ones that turn out wrong are the ones that have never been encouraged or enabled to share anything. Like any other sort of education, if you do morals with them, they'll latch on to it.'

A little respect

As young teenagers struggle, not always charmingly, to win more and more freedom and independence, one thing that helps to maintain good relationships between them and you is mutual respect. A survey of Swedish adolescents, for instance, found that they rejected paternal authority if they thought it stemmed from their parents' desire to dominate or exploit them, but they were willing to accept it when it seemed to be based on a reasonable concern for their welfare – in other words, when the parents showed them respect.

The best way to foster mutual respect is to adopt a fair approach to discipline, which is where most conflict arises. This means that when you have a confrontation over what they want to do and what you think is appropriate, you don't yell orders. What you need to do is to sit down with the child, talk through the different ways of improving the situation that occur to both of you, decide which approach to adopt and then both commit yourselves to making the necessary changes.

For instance, if she wants to go to a mid-week disco and you have refused and are faced with a teenager flinging herself about in a sulk, you can sit down and talk it through. You can say you think she should miss the disco and go to bed at the usual time because of school next day. She might argue that the disco only happens once, she really needs a little treat and she will do her homework before she goes. You might offer to let her go if she agrees to come home at a sensible time, and you can ask her if she understands why you worry about her getting over-tired. You may offer to make an exception in this case if she catches up on her sleep the very next day. She may suggest that midnight is absolutely sensible, and offer to do the catching up at the weekend.

In the end, what you actually decide is not as important as the business of discussing the dilemma and reaching a compromise. Your teenager doesn't enjoy living in an atmosphere of hostility and recrimination any more than you do: if you can ask her for suggestions of how you can resolve your conflicts, state your own concerns and fears clearly and explain what you think it is reasonable to expect, you will be surprised how helpful and accommodating she can be.

American psychologist Thomas Lickona explains that this process works, firstly, by requiring the youngster to think morally – she has to stop putting herself at the centre of every issue and consider the needs of others as well as her own. Secondly, it sets her a good example by showing that both of you must respect each other's rights and feelings, and by demonstrating that reason rather than power can be used to resolve conflicts. Thirdly, talking through conflicts as they arise teaches your child responsibility by making her an active partner in the business of finding a solution.

A positive relationship between parents and children is especially important in adolescence because this is a time when youngsters most need their parents' moral counsel to counterbalance the growing influence of their friends, which is so powerful but which can be faulty. You have to protect adolescents from their immaturity and encourage them to use reason in their dealings with the increasingly complicated, stressful world that confronts them – and they are more likely to accept your advice if it is offered in a spirit of love, not criticism.

Using reason and imagination to solve problems shouldn't stop once you've sorted out the family dilemmas. How do you get adolescents to think about the problems of society and the immediate problems they themselves have within society? There's no point in sitting down with a fifteen-year-old who knows absolutely everything about absolutely everything and trying to convince her that she doesn't. Again, what you have to do is to get her to start thinking about things. That is why giving reasons is so important; not just saying 'do it', but explaining why, if she doesn't do it, this or that is likely to happen; that this is why she should do X, and these are the implications if she does or doesn't do it, for herself and for other people, which is just as important.

Things to talk about
Professor Wilson says it's vital to put the emphasis in moral education on to issues that teenagers have some hope of understanding. 'Most of the stuff they do in school is with issues which, firstly, are controversial and, secondly, are adult issues that the kids can't do very much about, like capital punishment or the arms trade. Whereas if they did something like: "Why aren't you nice to your little sister?", something where the answer, if they think about it, is fairly clear, then they can actually deflect the children's behaviour. It's important to start with simple cases and leave the controversial ones till later.'

If you talk to your children about events that involve them they will continue to talk about them even when you're not there, so it's worth hunting out suitable material. You can ask them, for instance, what they would do if they saw a child being bullied: 'Would you intervene? Tell a teacher? Is it wrong or right to tell tales? Which is worse, telling tales or letting a bully go unpunished?'

Watching and talking about television programmes like *Grange Hill*, which deal with the sort of dilemmas children

187

face every day, also gives your children the chance to enter into the lives and problems of people like themselves and consider what they would do if they were in those circumstances, and you can use the chance to talk through the problems with them. Although it is easy to sneer at the Australian soaps, one reason they're so popular with young teenagers is that they continually raise issues adolescents can identify with. They are small-scale family or social issues and they get youngsters thinking and reflecting on what could and should be done. You can encourage them by asking what one of their friends would think of such behaviour, how would they feel if they did such and such, is it wrong or right to act like she did – wrestling with these ideas gives them vital practice in how to think through moral dilemmas and formulate a moral response.

'I'm an addict of *Neighbours* for just that reason,' says Professor Wilson. 'It raises many interesting questions of moral conflict. It is real, and if they can act that out in their own lives in some way it helps. You want a whole range of methods you can use with children, running from straightforward talk about what counts as a good reason for deciding what moral principle to take, through things like *Neighbours* and role-playing and acting, which I think is terribly important, and a bit of literature if you can read it, all facing them with real-life situations in which they actually have to pull their weight.'

The moral tug of war

There is a competition going on for the minds and hearts of children in the moral arena. On one side are those who insist that children learn to toe the line even if it means indoctrination. On the other side are those who insist that defining the moral line should be left entirely up to the children even if it means calling into question all and every moral principle.

Dr Dwight R. Boyd, Associate Professor of Psychology at the University of Massachusetts, likens it to a tug of war: 'On one end of the rope are the fundamentalists, who quite often stop moral discussions by emphatically asserting something like this: "But it's just the principle of the matter! That's just wrong, period. And that's all there is to say." The important thing seems to be the "sticking to" the principle, rather than the quality of the principle itself.

'On the other end of the rope are the free-thinkers. It's hard to identify them in terms of how they use the term "principles", because they would rather not waste their breath talking about something that to them is essentially an object of historical wishful thinking. Principles, for the free-thinkers, are those drab, outmoded relics of simplistic thinking, those escapes from personal existential choice, that we should avoid mentioning in good company. And children of this persuasion tend to think that principles should be locked up in a museum as an interesting oddity of simple people and simple lives.'

The professor quotes as an illustration of how far some teenagers have gone in disowning all moral principles some letters that were sent to a Canadian newspaper after it ran a story about Values Education in schools. One teenager wrote: 'Moral values cannot be taught and people must learn to use what works for them.' In other words, whatever gets you through the night is all right. Another wrote even more bluntly: 'What one person thinks is bad or wrong, another person might think that it is good or right. I don't think morals should be taught because it will cause more conflicts and mess up the student's mind.'

At the risk of messing up our teenagers' minds, let us press on with looking at how you can teach them morals, which remains the parent's role even if we get little encouragement. One of the things you have to do is explain your own moral standpoint to your children. Adults do have a point of view to put over, and the experience to back it up. One of the things this country has done is thrown out the old-fashioned idea of wisdom. I couldn't help reflecting when I lived in East Africa on how pleasant it was to grow older in a society where old age was valued and old people were listened to with respect.

As David Ingram puts it: 'I would argue that many older people are probably more knowledgeable about the nuts and bolts of life, simply because life does have a habit of knocking the corners off. OK, so you prattle on at kids, but I think one has to make these statements and, just as it's the role of young people to kick over the traces, it's part of the job of older people to sit there twittering on at them.'

Staying friends with your teenagers

When we are faced with difficulties, one of the important ways that the social support of your families and friends can help is that you can talk about your worries, concerns and anxieties with them. Children will inevitably want to spend more time with their friends than with their families as they move into adolescence, but you shouldn't see the fact that they like to hang around in groups as threatening. It's just that teenagers are beginning to leave the security of the family unit and find the group reassuring.

It is good to belong and feel there are other people who feel as you do, and teenagers, especially, need someone to talk to. They're going through major changes in body shape and size, sexuality and relationships and these are all things they desperately want to talk to someone about. A recent piece of research on children's friendship reveals that one of the most important things about friendship for adolescents, what they wanted, what they looked for, was someone they could actually talk to about their feelings and go over their worries, anxieties and concerns.

However, their friends don't have the experience or detachment to solve all their problems. Although you may well feel that your adolescents have moved into an alien world peopled by dishevelled creatures with awkward limbs speaking in incomprehensible monosyllables, they still need regular, close contact with grown-ups to help them cope with everything that is going on in their world.

There may be a problem of gender here, because many parents seem to find it much easier to talk to their teenage daughters than their sons. Girls are seen as chatty, often charming and generally non-threatening. Boys, however, often report that they pass through a very lonely time in adolescence because their parents seem to flinch away from them: father, because he is too busy or impatient to cope with stormy teenage ups and downs, and mother because she is disconcerted by the sudden signs of emerging sexuality in her boy, from poorly concealed erections to soiled sheets, and feels uncomfortable with him. Boys say that they suddenly feel shut out and neglected by the people they were closest to, and they find little comfort for their miseries from their male friends either, who are all boast and bombast to hide their own insecurities.

You can see teenage boys casting envious or resentful glances at a gaggle of girls who are chattering away to each other about all and everything, sharing their ideas and problems, finding sympathy, being supported. Boys are handicapped by simply not being as articulate at this age as girls, and by the basic biological drive to seem powerful and strong, and they need special patience and attention so that their needs, too, can be addressed.

Staying in touch with your teenagers means you have to make lots of time available for them. They won't necessarily talk just because you happen to have a few minutes free. There has been a lot of talk of parents putting aside a period of 'quality' time each evening when they will focus on their children's preoccupations, but children are not so easy to organise. Your period of quality time might not be the hour when they feel like chatting; it might clash with their favourite television programme, or they may have been bursting to tell you about something when they first came in from school but have had second thoughts about it since. To sustain a successful relationship, where you really know what is going on in their heads and can convince them that you care and have helpful things to offer, you have to be prepared to set a lot of time aside when you're nearby and accessible, and let them choose the right moment to open up.

Time is the most precious thing you can give your children. When they are little it means spending time playing cards, catching a ball, digging sand castles, collecting shells, feeding ducks and walking the family dog. Later it means dressing-up games, helping them paint and make things. It is boring living life at a six-year-old level at times though it can be fun too – but you have to be prepared to put the hours in if you want to build a solid relationship. You have to spend time with your teenager, too, if you want to stay close to her, which might mean sitting through *Top of the Pops* with her occasionally, even if you're catching up on the day's paper at the same time, so you can get some idea of what she is interested in from music to clothes to attitudes, and what makes her tick. She's not going to tell you, you have to observe it for yourself.

If it all seems too demanding, remember the child did not ask to be born – she has had life thrust upon her willy nilly and it is up to you, who put her into this situation, to make it bearable and, if possible, rewarding.

Unsuitable friends
A friend of mine who teaches drama in Scotland was on the way to a school in a small town to assess their work. With time to spare he dropped into the local magistrate's court to watch some real-life drama. The case involved a group of teenage boys who had been up to mischief. Most of them looked rather scruffy and were being represented by the duty solicitor, but one boy was well dressed and had a lawyer who made an impassioned plea for the lad to be given special status: he came from a good family, had good prospects at school, had never been in trouble before and had been led sadly astray by unsuitable friends.

The judge listened to these moving words and then looked sternly at the boy and said (I cannot reproduce the dour Scottish accent): 'If you stand with the crows, you must expect to be stoned.' It is a wonderfully succinct dismissal of the idea that good children are somehow led into bad deeds by accident and therefore cannot be blamed. The fact is that if you know how to be good, but choose to behave differently, you are not a good person. It is no use parents saying, 'He's a good boy really, he just gets led astray.' If he knows how to behave but doesn't, then he is stupid or bad.

To our dismay, our charming well-brought up children often seek out friends who make us shudder, especially in their teens, but it is a mistake to over-react. Ask yourself what they see in these people – and remember they are looking beneath the veneer, which might seem crude, rude or nasty to you, to some quality underneath that captures their interest. Often the new friends seem glamorous or exciting to them: they may well lead much less supervised lives and can tell your children about clubs and other places they have been to that seem terribly adult and exciting. Good children are just as curious about the adult world as bad, and if you are forbidding them access to it just yet because you think your child isn't ready, they will seek out second-hand experience.

Sometimes the naughty friend allows them to explore an aspect of their own behaviour which has been suppressed. I remember one of my daughters going through a patch at primary school when she suddenly became uncooperative and surly. It seemed to hinge on the example being set by a new girl in the class who was cheeky and aggressive. I realised that my little girl was fascinated by this bad behaviour and was trying it on for size – to see how it felt to be 'bad'. Luckily she soon decided it didn't suit her; being bad was not her way and in a couple of weeks she reverted to her old sweet self. You can't blame a child for trying out something new – that is human nature – and if you've laid the ground well, the experiment won't do any lasting harm.

Not so easily led
The danger parents see of good kids being turned bad by the wrong company can be overstated. Professor Nick Emler, a lecturer in the Department of Experimental Psychology at Oxford, says: 'There's been quite a lot of work recently on peer relationships, especially in early adolescence, looking

into what kind of friends children prefer or are attracted to. And if anything the research suggests not that company determines your conduct and your outlook, but that your outlook tends to influence the company you prefer.

'We talked to young people in Dundee a few years ago, for a study on delinquency, and asked them quite a lot about their friends and what their friends thought about what they did, and what they'd do if their friends suggested they do things that didn't seem to be part of their code of conduct. And, for instance, a child who has a reasonable conduct record would say, "Well, I'd change my friends," or "If I did that my friends would disapprove." '

The research suggests that children are much less susceptible to outside influences than we fear, as long as they have good strong standards of their own. That isn't to say they will immediately shy away from bad company: children are less judgemental than us, more willing to tolerate bad behaviour in other children and endlessly curious, but the fascination won't last.

Professor Emler advises: 'One's instinct is to let them find out for themselves the bad influences are not all they're cracked up to be. If you've done a reasonable job of bringing up your own child – and that's got a lot to do with having clear standards and enforcing them but also putting a lot of emphasis on reward and praise – then you're not that likely to have a child who's going to be susceptible to the first bad influence that comes along. They're as likely to say, "No, I don't like that child. I don't approve of what they do," and have nothing to do with them.' He adds that their old friends will support them in rejecting the bad newcomers because they will almost certainly hold the same views. We all like people who are like ourselves, and well-behaved children tend to have well-behaved friends.

Falling in with a gang
What we all fear, of course, is a situation in which a good child loses control of their decision-making faculties and

starts to fall under the influence of the crowd. This is the basis of the mob, which is a collection of ordinary people, many of them probably decent-hearted, who lose themselves and their good nature in a collective frenzy. It is a surrender of control to the group, which is always bad news and explains why gang attacks or gang rapes are always so particularly violent and horrible. You might expect from the fact that the assault is carried out by the many upon the few that they would not have to use much force, but the very fact that they are a gang leads to a loss of self-control which generates extra violence.

As we have seen, children who are good themselves will prefer the company of other good children, but that works both ways, with bad children seeking out bad. Professor Nick Emler's research revealed that to some degree the willingness, inclination and openness to get up to bad behaviour of some children leads them to prefer the company of others who have a similar inclination, and it's when such children get together that these inclinations towards bad behaviour are likely to be translated into action. The tragedy of the Bulger case began to unfold when Jon Venables met Robert Thomas in a remedial class.

Professor Emler explains: 'Most delinquency is a collective activity. It's not a solitary activity. It doesn't occur with one individual lacking a conscience who feels completely unconstrained about getting up to mischief. It's a group of kids. And you need to ask, "What is the composition of that group?", "What kind of comment or criticism is a child likely to be exposed to in proposing or indulging in mischief?", "What kind of collective decision-making is going on?" ' In other words, we should be asking in what circumstances the usual social controls stop working.

The Citizenship Foundation devised a story to be used in schools which tells of four young people accused of robbery and you could use it at home to help children explore what it means to become involved in a gang and get sucked into crime.

195

Kevin is walking home from a friend's house about ten o'clock one evening across a piece of open land. Halfway across he is stopped, attacked and knocked to the ground. The attackers take his wallet containing £50 and leave him bruised.

The four members of the gang each offer their version of events. Alison says: 'It was stupid what happened. Glynn said it would be easy to stop someone and get some money. He told me to go on ahead and ask him the time. I didn't know he was going to hit the man.'

Sean says: 'I didn't want to get into trouble but the others laughed at me. We stopped this man and Glynn hit him. Then when he was on the ground Glynn and Craig kicked him and Craig grabbed him wallet. I didn't do anything, I just pretended. I didn't want to look scared. Glynn offered me some money, but I wouldn't take it.'

Glynn says: 'We met this man walking along the path. Alison stopped to ask him the time, but he swore at her and pushed past. We couldn't have that, so we bundled him. His wallet fell out of his pocket, Craig picked it up, and we left him.'

Craig says: 'We'd been walking around looking for a laugh. Glynn said it would be easy to stop someone for a bit of money. We saw this man walking by himself. Glynn told Alison to stop and ask him the time. Then we all piled in. I didn't hit him, I just grabbed his jacket and looked for his wallet.'

The pupils are asked who they think is the leader of the group? Why do they think Sean found it difficult to stay out of trouble? What could he have done to keep out of trouble? Then they are asked to consider each member of the gang and say: 'Did the person carry out the robbery? Did they help or encourage anyone to commit the robbery? Should they all be punished equally? If so why? If not, why not? Are there mitigating circumstances which should reduce the sentence of some?' Then they are asked to imagine the conversation that might have taken place between the four members of the gang just before the attack.

The aim of the exercise is to get teenagers to think about the dynamics of the gang and the ways in which the less dominant members could have avoided getting involved. It also teaches the practical facts that it is an offence to aid or abet someone who is committing a crime and that just because you don't actually swing a punch or make off with some of the stolen property doesn't mean you are innocent. As the boy in the Scottish court found, if you are part of a criminal group, you will be found guilty. It is very helpful to teenagers to realise that if they identify with a group, they will be judged alongside that group, and that it pays to choose one's friends with care.

The best protection from unsuitable friends lies in a good relationship at home: it all comes back to the parent-child relationship and what degree of interest the parent takes in the child. Even though teenage children are growing more capable and independent, it is still your job to keep a close eye on their activities. Do you know where your son or daughter is or where they are supposed to be or who their friends are? Do you know the parents of their friends or anything about them? Are you monitoring what your children are up to?

Professor Nick Emler points out: 'When it comes to adolescence there is a striking difference in the number of male and female delinquents. There are various factors which are likely to make a contribution, but one of them is that parents just keep a closer eye on their daughters than their sons. They're more likely to encourage them to socialise at home.'

Unsuitable sportsmen
Don't think that the way to nudge your teenager into good company is to sign them up at the nearest sports club for a character-building course. The latest research shows that sport is not the unmitigated Good Thing that generations of headmasters have cracked it up to be. Dr Dorothy Begg of Otago Medical School in Dunedin, New Zealand found that

the long-held belief that sport builds character was torpedoed by research which showed that some sports appear to encourage delinquent behaviour in teenagers.

She found that involvement in non-team sports encourages aggressiveness and even cheating – because cheating can lead to success in some events. For instance, boys who took part in lots of individual pursuits such as tennis, athletics and wind-surfing at fifteen were almost twice as likely to indulge in car theft, burglary, shoplifting and fighting with a weapon by eighteen as boys who did little or no sport.

The news was even worse for girls, who are generally far less delinquent than boys. Those girls who were heavily involved in individual sports at fifteen were almost three times as likely to be showing deviant behaviour by eighteen as non-sporty girls. It seems that children taking part in things like athletics can actually learn behaviour such as cheating from watching others do it and sometimes getting successful results by lying over whether the ball was in or out, taking drugs or whatever. Sport is not a panacea for delinquent behaviour; 'if anything it may exacerbate the problem,' reports Dr Begg.

Team games, however, did not have this bad effect. Dr Begg found that, 'Conventional sports which incorporate many aspects of the broader society, for example, rules, regulations and authority figures, may appeal to the non-delinquent, but for the delinquent, who by definition violates the rules and norms of society, such activities offer little appeal.' If you want your children to make some sporty friends and avoid the potential delinquent, you are obviously better trying to persuade them to choose a team sport, where they will learn to be responsible to their team-mates, and where there are fewer rewards for the individual who cheats. Or encourage them to try something like an Outward Bound course where the child is only concerned with discovering her own strengths and capabilities and is not in competition with anyone but herself.

Good people, bad behaviour

American psychologists R. Brown and R. Hernstein describe a common puzzle: 'Students of cognitive development studying the development of moral reasoning in young people have found that the great majority attains a conventional law and order morality, which involves obeying the laws and trying to treat people decently. But students of social psychology have discovered that in certain circumstances, respectable young people are capable of deceit, vandalism, indifference to the life-and-death problems of strangers who ask for help and capable even of endangering the lives of others. Yet these are the same young people – therein lies the paradox.'

The problem is that there is always some disharmony between the way people think about moral issues and the way they act, and so it is not enough to teach children the correct answers to moral questions, somehow we have to make them want to do the right thing. This is a much tougher task. We are all liable to forget our abstract moral principles when faced with some real-life dilemma: the NIMBY phenomenon (where people profess to want all sorts of useful things like roads, power stations and prisons, but not in my backyard thank you) shows this in full flower. Self-deception is a powerful human characteristic: you can see it at work in the way that child abusers are unable to relate the act they condemn with what it is they are doing. It takes a lot of therapy to get them to make the link.

Two steps are necessary before someone takes a moral action. The first is making a judgement about what is right. The second is accepting the responsibility to act on that judgement. If you use words like 'ought', they are prescriptive: that is, you are committing yourself to action. It's not like just describing things as 'red' or 'round'. If you say an act is right, you are saying, in effect, that you ought to perform it. This is not just a simple obligation to practise what you preach, but the acceptance that this particular sort of behaviour can clearly be designated as right and therefore has to be carried through.

Some philosophers also like to distinguish between a moral rule and a moral principle. Rules are things like 'don't steal', 'respect property', 'be honest', and rules can conflict. Professor Lawrence Kohlberg used to pose a dilemma to youngsters to illustrate this: Heinz's wife is very ill and need medicine, but he is desperately poor and can't afford to buy it. The chemist refuses to give him the medicine free of charge. Kohlberg asked the youngsters, 'Should Heinz break into the chemist's shop and steal the medicine in order to save his wife's life?' Here the moral rules conflict: 'don't steal' comes right up against Heinz's obligation to save his wife's life. A principle is a way of choosing what to do when the rules collide; here the moral principle says that the value of a human life must always take precedence over the value of property.

In the past couple of decades, psychologists have begun to explore the gap between what people say should be done and what they are actually likely to do. One way to do this has been to give schoolchildren two different sorts of moral dilemma to think about. The first was a 'classical' dilemma such as should poor Heinz rob the chemist for the drugs that will save his dying wife? This is an abstract, hypothetical problem rather than a real-life one and the answer will be a prescriptive 'should': 'Heinz should do this.' The second type of dilemma was a 'practical' one which presented the youngsters with the sort of problem they might face themselves in real life, and the answer to these is a 'would': 'This is what I would do.'

So do children score differently when faced with real, genuine dilemmas? First of all, there is a problem with classical dilemmas, such as the Heinz situation, which are hard for a child to grasp, especially if they have grown up in a society where sick people get any treatment they need free of charge. Also, children are more likely to be concerned with respect for life, which they have, than respect for property (robbing the chemist), since they don't own much in the way of personal property and haven't struggled to acquire it. So the judgement they make is likely to be swift and confident but not necessarily in tune with their current stage of moral development. They will say, 'Heinz ought to steal the medicine to save his wife,' because that seems to them an easy thing to do. However, when they are posed a problem closer to home, their judgement is not so swift or so advanced and the results reflect their true response much more accurately.

Dr J.S. Leming, for instance, tested some classical dilemmas on young teenagers against more practical problems such as would you deceive your parents in order to go to a party, or cheat on a school assignment? When he tested students' responses to these dilemmas against the Heinz and similar classical dilemmas, Dr Leming found that students who scored highly when they were considering classical problems about how you *should* behave got much lower results when they were making practical judgements about how they probably *would* behave in a real situation. Classical moral judgement seems to take the high road, practical judgement the low.

This result is confirmed by experiments carried out by Kohlberg and others in a reform school where they tested classical moral dilemmas against real-life prison dilemmas. They, too, found over and over again, that delinquents who seemed capable of making high moral judgements on the classical dilemmas slipped back into less mature judgements on the practical ones. Kohlberg concluded that moral judgement is not simply a fixed ability of the individual, his or her level of moral competence, but that it is affected by the moral climate in which the individual is making his decisions. The prisoners' low-level response to practical dilemmas was more the result of the prison environment than of the prisoners' personalities. You would never get subtle or unselfish moral principles developing in a reform school where watching out for yourself and disregarding others is the norm.

The moral climate surrounding the child makes all the difference to how the child behaves. Professor Nick Emler asks: 'Is she embedded in a network or society of people who

201

say, "You shouldn't be doing that, that's wrong"? Of course no society relies exclusively on men of good conscience, we rely on locks and other safeguards of our property. But we also rely on a degree of mutual control. We rely on people being willing to say, "no you shouldn't do that", "that's unfair", "that's unreasonable" or "that's someone else's property". If you're in a group where nobody ever says that, then you're not going to behave well.'

Professor Emler's research on delinquents shows that one of the things that set these boys apart was their lack of contact with adults – not just adults in their own family but almost any adults since they were very often playing truant from school. The result was that almost all their social contact revolved around their peers. Non-delinquents also had strong peer relations, but there's good evidence to show that peer relations aren't enough, and that they are no substitute for relations with adults and parents. In so far as the relations with adults and parents go well, the peer relations go well too. So if teenagers seem to be living in a world exclusively inhabited by their peers, we shouldn't assume that everything is going well. They need to inhabit an environment where adult society's rules and sanctions operate and where they can grow into a more mature level of good behaviour.

Who cares about people they don't know?
In their early teens, children become far more aware of the outside world in the form of school, the town they have grown up in, and their own community, but it is still hard for them to feel directly linked to the larger world beyond. This makes it difficult for them to understand or care about the world at large. So one of the things you can do is help them to understand that even people they don't know deserve respect and consideration, just like their friends and neighbours.

John Woods, a consultant psychotherapist who works with groups of troubled teenagers, says: 'I think moral understanding comes at quite an advanced age. You get idealism in adolescence certainly, but you also get adolescent abusers. I see adolescents of fourteen and fifteen and they are very preoccupied with right and wrong and sorting it out with each other but you get very absurd and contradictory statements. For instance, one of the boys in my group said it was all right to kick other children in school, because they were swots and didn't count. But if it was somebody from this group, he would defend them to the hilt!'

It is always easier to relate to people we think of as being rather like ourselves, and easier to attack someone seen as different. So if we want to live in a gentle and harmonious society, we must try not to portray other races, religions or classes of people to our children as alien, because that makes it hard for them to feel a link, to suffer when they suffer, rejoice when they rejoice. It is wrong to jeer indiscriminately either at fat cats or at dole scroungers, to moan about northerners or southerners, set cat lovers against dog owners or whatever. If you want to build a finer world, it is better to stress the things that all the different groups have in common, not the things they don't. If and when you do have a criticism to make, back it up with good and valid reasons, don't simply use the fact that they are different from us.

An interesting survey in 1996 by the British Social Attitudes Report shows how much easier it is for youngsters to empathise with people they know than with faceless strangers. Children from twelve upwards were given a simple moral problem: a man gives a £5 note for goods he is buying in a big store. By mistake he is given change for a £10 note. He notices, but he keeps the change. The youngsters were asked what they thought of his behaviour.

The majority thought it was wrong – 3 per cent said very seriously wrong, 13 per cent seriously wrong and 43 per cent wrong. The others were not so sure: 35 per cent thought it was a bit wrong and 6 per cent saw nothing wrong at all. However, even some of those who condemned the man's behaviour as wrong had lower standards for themselves: when asked if they might keep the change themselves, only 52 said no and 41 admitted they would.

However, when they were presented with the same scenario translated to a corner shop, their attitudes became more moral. The numbers seeing nothing wrong in keeping the change fell from 6 per cent to 5 per cent, while the numbers admitting that to keep the money was wrong rose in every category: 24 per cent thought it was a bit wrong, 48 per cent wrong, 18 per cent seriously wrong and 5 per cent very seriously wrong. When they were asked if they were likely to keep the change in a corner shop, the number saying yes fell from 41 to 28, while the number saying no rose from 52 to 68.

Clearly young people make a distinction between crimes committed against some unknown 'other' and crime being done in one's own backyard against someone you might know or could identify with, which is good news for the people running the corner shop and bad news for banks, supermarkets and other large concerns. None the less, most youngsters seem to think that the concept of finders-keepers is wrong, most of them would not keep ill-gotten change and most would condemn anyone who does so as wrong, so it is good news on the whole.

If we want to move youngsters on to a more mature level of moral behaviour, where they would no more dream of robbing a bank than robbing the man next door, the best place to start is by exploring what standards they have already and trying to persuade them to extend these standards to new categories of people. Moral philosopher Mary Midgley points out that they do have standards: 'One talks of honour among thieves and there's certainly honour among teenagers. They feel very strongly who they admire and who they despise and the things they admire often have a lot to do with conventional morals: courage and honesty and well-known virtues will get high marks from them.'

The trick, she argues, is to move them on from recognising these virtues in their friends to seeing that they can also apply to the institutions around them. Teenagers have to be given time to move from the standards they already do acknowledge towards something that encompasses other people. If they feel they are against the whole of society, Midgley points out, it will take a lot of time and patience to bring them within sight of agreement, but the agreement will come, because there is actually not a lot of difference between the standards that even alienated teenagers have and those of society, once they can be brought to see each other's problems.

'One difficulty, when you're in your teens,' says Mary Midgley, 'is that if you discover one matter on which you disagree with other people it looks as though everything is different, it looks as though there's a great gap between you and everyone else, it gets out of proportion. So you want to look instead at the bits where there is agreement – and there are plenty. The core of it is you must keep on listening to them. And you will keep on forgetting – it's actually very hard not to lay down the law! But if you can focus the child's attention on what they are doing, they won't run away with the idea that thought wouldn't help. Thought helps.'

When we're dealing with teenagers we need to hold fast to the knowledge that although there are the yobbos, the Dutch courage ones, bursting with inferiority and showing off like mad and doing all kinds of awful things, the vast majority of young people are sensible, thoughtful, honest and good and they offer great hope for the future.

Interlude

Boys' morals, girls' morals

Anyone who has raised children knows that boys and girls are different. They behave differently, react differently, play differently. You can see it in action in any playground. American psychologist Janet Lever studied ten- and eleven-year-olds in the school playground and at home and reported that boys play out of doors more than girls, more often in large groups of mixed ages, they play competitive games more often and their games last longer than girls' games.

The reason why boys were able to keep a game going for a long time is because when disputes arose, boys were able to resolve them more effectively than girls. 'Boys were seen quarrelling all the time, but not once was a game terminated because of a quarrel and no game was interrupted for more than seven minutes. In fact it seemed that the boys enjoyed the legal debates as much as they did the game itself,' reported Lever. This confirms Piaget's view that boys become increasingly fascinated with the rules of the games they play, and enjoy drawing up fair procedures for settling any conflicts that occur.

Girls' games are less competitive than boys'. Traditional girls' games like jump rope and hopscotch are turn-taking games where one child's success does not necessarily mean that another child has failed, so there is less likelihood of a dispute requiring adjudication cropping up. By and large, you don't argue if there are no winners and losers. In fact, girls seem to think that their relationships are more important than the need to keep the game going. Piaget noted that girls are more flexible in their attitudes towards rules, more willing to make exceptions, more easily reconciled to innovation. If the rules are causing conflict, girls don't follow the boys in working out elaborate ways to decide who's in the right; instead they will happily change the rules, or even abandon the game and move on to something else rather than have everyone stressed.

Who says boys are more moral?

For a long time, since all the psychologists carrying out the early research into the moral development of children were men, the accepted belief was that boys' morality was superior to girls' morality because it was based on rules and the concept of justice. This attitude was first launched in the 1930s when Piaget argued that children learn the respect for rules that is necessary for moral development by playing rule-bound games. Because girls showed less interest in these, and were willing to bend the rules where they seemed uncomfortable, he felt they were morally immature compared to boys.

Piaget's work was followed up in the 1970s by American psychologist Lawrence Kohlberg who did research into how children learn to distinguish good from bad. Kohlberg saw that children's moral development took place in stages as they gradually became more sophisticated in their way of thinking about right and wrong. Like Piaget, he believed that the evidence showed that boys were more likely to reach a higher moral stage than girls. Kohlberg felt that women tended to get stuck at the lower levels of moral development, where morality is seen in personal terms and goodness is equated with helping and pleasing others. He argued that only if women entered the masculine world would their moral development progress toward what he saw as the higher stages, where relationships are subordinated to rules and, eventually, rules to universal principles of justice such as the Golden Rule.

However, Kohlberg had done all his research in boys' schools, following groups of boys from early adolescence to adulthood. Dr Carol Gilligan, who was working with him, wondered if this was affecting the results, and began to do some work of her own with women. David Ingram, Director of the Norham Foundation which runs projects to further the moral development of young people in Britain, met her at Harvard while he was working with Kohlberg.

'She went about her research in a different way to Larry Kohlberg. He had tested boys with moral dilemmas he thought up when he was a PhD student and said to them, "If you were faced with this, what would you do?" Carol Gilligan asked, "What kind of problems do you have and how do you think about them and how do you deal with them?" So where Kohlberg's dilemmas were moral puzzles that he'd invented, Gilligan's were dilemmas that people had experienced in their own lives. And she found a dimension of morality which Kohlberg was missing, which is compassionate concern for persons.'

Listening to women

Carol Gilligan began by talking to women who had had, or were thinking of having, an abortion. What she found was that the women talked about how the decision would affect their partner, their families or their other children; they worried about how to care for themselves, the baby and the other people to whom they felt obligations. They seldom talked of cut and dried, right and wrong answers, but worried away at all the competing demands on their feelings and responsibilities and tried to strike a balance that would be fair to everyone. Women did not see the dilemma as a conflict of justice between the foetus's right to life and the mother's right not to have an unwanted baby. They saw it as a conflict between caring and responsibility.

Dr Gilligan concluded that women's moral decisions grew out of the idea of relationships, or the connectedness of people; concepts that they valued. They did not decide by balancing individual rights. So she found that there were two different perspectives on moral issues, which she called the justice perspective and the caring perspective. The justice perspective tends to be more concerned with rights and obligations: given some cases, people who take the justice approach will ask: 'Who's in the right here, whose right has been violated?' Those who take the caring perspective tend more to say: 'Well, this is a problem involving several people, is there some way of sorting this out so that nobody loses too much, possibly by talking it through?'

Gilligan argued that her female sample didn't respond so easily to the justice demand, they responded much more to responsibility and caring. The implication of her work is that there are parallel moral stages based on responsibility and caring as well as on justice. Women's alleged moral weakness, which earlier psychologists had said was shown in their apparent confusion of judgement, is really inseparable from women's moral strength, an overriding concern with the continuation of relationships and responsibilities. The woman's reluctance to make judgements is not a flaw but indicates her care and concern for others. She has, says Gilligan, 'a very strong sense of being responsible to the world.'

The porcupine and the moles
You can check which approach to morality and justice your children hold by telling them a fable that psychologists use to test moral attitudes, about the porcupine and the moles. The moles are sensible creatures who plan for their future and they find a nice warm hole for the winter and set up house there. A porcupine comes along who hasn't got anywhere to live and the weather is getting cold so he asks the moles if they will allow him to share their hole. The moles are quite generous and say yes, but they find they keep getting pricked by his spikes. The problem is, what should the moles do about it?

Children who take the justice perspective tend to say the rights are all on the moles' side. They are only giving charity to the porcupine, the porcupine had no actual right to be there in the first place, so the moles have every right to turn him out. Children who take the caring perspective tend to say something like: Well we have a situation here which is a problem, what is the solution? What can we do? Well, we could dig a bigger hole, or we could give the porcupine a blanket to cover up his spikes. By and large, more boys take the justice perspective and more girls the caring perspective, though there is considerable cross-over.

How soon do boys and girls start to look at moral issues from a different standpoint? Jan Newton, who works with the Citizenship Foundation preparing material for schools to use in moral education, says: 'Boys in primary school have a strong sense of retribution, a punishment thing, where girls will link it more to why that person might have done it.'

Dr Helen Haste, a psychologist at the University of Bath who has been researching moral development for over twenty years, says: 'Girls tend to respond to moral problems differently from boys. The latter tend to be more concerned with justice, with who is in the right. Underpinning the concept of justice,' says Dr Haste, 'is the idea that people are autonomous beings in conflict with each other and that you resolve this conflict through justice: by finding rules, laying out rights, making contracts. Girls, or people who are responsible and caring, tend to see people as interwoven, connected to each other. They think that possibly what morality is about is finding ways of negotiating between people to achieve harmony and maintain the relationship. So the focus is on caring and responsibility rather than justice.'

However, Dr Haste points out that while Gilligan found there was a sex difference, with boys tending to think one way, girls another, this is not a hard and fast distinction. 'What everybody finds is that boys tend towards a justice response when you first ask them, but they are quite capable of producing a caring response if you probe them. And for girls it's vice versa. And it's only a tendency anyway.'

Attitudes are also likely to be affected by the culture you

grow up in. In America the majority of people, men and women, lean towards the justice perspective – influenced, perhaps, by all those goodies and baddies in the Westerns – with the result that America has more lawyers per head of population than any other country in the world, and both men and women are swift to use litigation to sort out the ups and downs of everyday life.

The sexual slant

What is it that makes boys lean one way, girls the other? American psychologist Nancy Chodorow puts it down to 'gender identity'. What happens is that the main carer in a baby's life is usually the mother or another female and so girls can identify with her. However, boys, to define themselves as masculine, have to see themselves as individual and separate, cutting the tie to the female. So masculinity is defined through separation, while femininity is defined through attachment and the consequence is that men tend to have difficulties with relationships while women tend to have problems with individuality.

Professor John Wilson, of the Department of Educational Studies at Oxford, agrees that there might well be different bits of behaviour that different sexes are better at. 'I think on the whole women are more observant about people's feelings. Certainly different individuals vary enormously. I mean, I think I'm quite good at treating other people as my equals, but I'm terribly bad at knowing what other people, particularly women, actually feel. So I call up my mother and she says, "Can't you see, John, she's X, Y and Z", where probably a woman would have seen that right away. So I think women are possibly kinder, more sensitive, and more concerned with harmony than to say who's in the right. I think Carol Gilligan's quite good on that.'

John Woods, a London psychotherapist who works with young people in trouble, also sees some degree of sex difference: 'I do group therapy with boys and girls together with a similar age range, similar backgrounds and similar types of behavioural problems so I get an opportunity to compare their characteristic ways of thinking. And there is undoubtedly a way in which the girls are much more aware of people's feelings, their own vulnerabilities, their own needs, and more verbally inclined to communicate. And you can balance that against the boys' desire for action, their more self-centred approach to things.

'I do hear parents sometimes saying to boys, "Think of the other person's feelings," and it's quite clear that the boy is a long way from doing that so you're wasting your breath. It's much easier to say, "That's wrong and if you do it again I will punish you." It's a cruder approach, but nevertheless there are times when that is what's needed.'

It is helpful to find out where your children stand on these issues before you start to discuss morality: check, for instance, if your son is more concerned with justice than caring and then, if you feel he's doing fine on questions of justice but could do with a bit of help on responsibility and concern for others, you can work on that by getting him to think about negotiation, reconciliation and caring.

The best way forward is by provoking him into thinking as widely as possible about any moral dilemma he faces. If he seems stuck on the 'I'm right, he's wrong' level, you could help him to consider other possibilities by saying, for instance: 'Fine, but how about this or that? Let's think about another possibility.' Or: 'Let's think about the consequences of this action, not just for you and your brother but for the family as a whole (or for the other children in the street, school or whatever).'

The best of both worlds

However, to say there seem to be two different approaches to moral questions, the justice and the caring, does not mean there always has to be tension between them, or that you can only hold one perspective or the other: both are crucial. If you care about someone then you will want to avoid oppressing them, being unfair to them yourself or allowing anyone else to be unfair to them. If you care, you will want justice, and if you want justice, it shows you care.

It is easy to see why a justice-based morality with its potential for indifference and unconcern can seem severe and unattractive to women, while a morality of responsibility appears, from a male perspective, inconclusive and woolly-minded. The answer is that we really need both if we want to balance justice with mercy.

From the point of view of society at large, the justice perspective offers a code of conduct that specifies mutual rights and responsibilities and prohibits unsociable acts. This 'male' system of justice, looking for who is in the right, is the morality of the law courts where one's person's innocence must mean another's guilt. At the personal level, the caring perspective is concerned with the individual's helpful and harmonious relationships with other people. This 'female' system of responsibility is the morality of the industrial tribunal or of peace negotiators, where the aim is to see how much ground each side has in common and how they can be brought to an agreement with each other. And both things – rules and negotiation over the rules – are necessary in a fair society.

Chapter Seven
Late teens: standing on the threshold

By their late teens our children are almost ready to be launched on to the world and sometimes things that seemed easy and straightforward in the security and familiarity of their own homes will seem less sure and clear when they are living with new friends in different circumstances. For instance, a young postgraduate psychology student told me how shocked she was when an American colleague described how she had claimed to have five years' funding in order to get a visa to work in Britain. If she had told the authorities the truth, that she had funding for only one year, she would not have been granted a visa.

The student was upset not only to discover that her fellow psychologist had lied, but because the other woman was not ashamed of her dishonesty or attempting to conceal it. She seemed to think it was quite acceptable as a practical way out of a difficulty. Perhaps many people would agree with her. The question is, though, if she could be dishonest to suit one purpose, how easy would she find it to lie for another? Would she be tempted to rewrite her research or to cheat in an exam? Can a decent person be honest just in parts and only when it suits them?

These are the sort of moral dilemmas your children will face as they join the adult world and they need to keep up that interior dialogue that will help them to puzzle out the rights and wrongs of these new situations and disentangle the right thread.

Searching for universal moral laws

As they approach adulthood, children move out of the rather self-centred environment of the young teenager into a world where they start to be more concerned with working out their relationships with their peers and developing their social skills. In the process, they begin to feel respect for the expectations of the other people around them and to pay serious attention to the principles that govern our personal relationships: fair play, equality and retribution.

Now that they are almost grown up, they start to look for moral principles which they can accept as valid in their own right, regardless of the authority of the people holding these principles or their identification with these people. Now they start to believe that certain values are right because they have some sort of universal status and not because Daddy or God says they are.

What is happening is that as children become adults, they start to favour the idea of a social contract and to define morality in terms of the rights of the individual plus a set of standards that have been agreed on by the whole of society. Because they can now see that relying on personal opinions alone could lead to endless confusion and conflict, they also approve of having some sort of procedure laid down by which conflicting parties can reach agreement. They begin to acknowledge the usefulness of having a legal framework for society, though they will be quick to point out that sometimes the law is an ass and needs to be changed. In areas of private life, where the law does not apply, they believe that people are bound by the restraints of reciprocal agreements and contracts freely entered into.

Yet there is still confusion. Just as older teenagers are seeking universal moral principles to frame their lives, they often get themselves into a panic and start to believe that there are no such things as general moral laws, but that everyone must do as they think best.

'Even with students you can get quite a lot of this,' observes moral philosopher Mary Midgley. 'Though they are not completely cut off from society or they wouldn't be at university, they are still cut off from a lot of things that society believes in and very often they have the idea that there aren't any universal standards, there is only your own subjective view.

'But these young people always have very strongly-held moral standards. What they're saying is that "everyone should be free". So underlying their views there are always very strong convictions about the importance of freedom and the wrongness of trying to discipline everybody and make them all the same, and these are perfectly good moral judgements.'

What these young people are doing is confusing the right to liberty with a belief that ethics are relative, not realising that liberty itself is a universal moral principle. The very same people who argue that all morality is a matter of personal opinion, something about which people should make up their own minds, argue in the next breath that there are such things as universal human rights. A teacher who argues that everyone should have his own views would nevertheless feel bad if the class then said they thought that cheating was OK. We tend to have more faith in universal moral principles than we realise.

Rules at the top

One of Lawrence Kohlberg's most influential ideas as he set out a blueprint for children's moral development, is that there is a final stage of moral reasoning to which only a handful of very special people can ever aspire, a level where people are capable of making their own universal moral judgements. Kohlberg gives as examples Jesus Christ, Mahatma Gandhi and Martin Luther King.

Although the rest of us ordinary people are not expected ever to reach this level, the idea that the individual at the pinnacle of moral development is a person wise enough to make his own autonomous rules has been very powerful, and it has resulted in a tendency to be a little contemptuous of those who follow the rules rather than make them. These conformists are sometimes likened to the Good Germans – perfectly decent people in undemanding situations, but liable to turn a blind eye to evil when it is a question of the individual making up his own mind and being prepared to stand up to authority.

Dr Helen Haste, for example, argues that when you are dealing with the moral development of children, the choice is between obedience and independent thinking: 'We can bring them up to be a conformist, a Rotarian, obedient and good,' she says. 'This might not produce people who can stand up and say, "Hey, this is wrong". It might not even enable them to say, "Stop beating up that kid", but they probably won't steal your car.

'Or we can adopt a different approach and teach teenagers to ask questions. Then they are going to be rather a nuisance and question everything, which can be very uncomfortable. But you will, in the end, have people who are capable of changing the system either in the playground or, later, in society.'

What's wrong with conforming?
Is conformity always so bad? Is non-conformity really so wonderful? Psychologists Dr Robert Hogan and Catherine Busch decided to investigate. They began by asking whether our sense of moral standards lies within us or outside and they found that some people are inner-directed and are principally attuned to their own standards of performance: as a result they may seem stubborn, independent, principled and non-conformist. Others are other-directed and are primarily attuned to the demands of their peer group and they can appear to be wishy-washy and conforming.

Hogan and Busch found that there was a problem caused by the long tradition in American psychology 'which holds that persons who conform to group pressure are nervous, indecisive and perhaps cowardly; that people who conform to ordinary social rules are not very bright, well adjusted or moral'. So they examined Kohlberg's view of the evolution of moral reasoning, which says that people who conform to social expectations or moral codes are in a kind of developmental holding pattern, waiting for the time when they will be mature enough to make judgements according to their own personal perceptions of certain abstract principles of justice.

This view meant that autonomous behaviour was seen as the hallmark of maturity – but are non-conformists really autonomous? Hogan and Busch developed the 'reference-group' theory to explain people who were autonomous or inner-directed. According to this, if we are non-conformists we refer our behaviour to a sort of internal review board, a panel of observers who exist inside our heads, whose praise we seek and whose censure we shun. The group may include former teachers, colleagues whose good opinion we value and other adults whom we respect. In other words, we are still motivated to achieve social approval and to avoid social criticism, the only difference is that for the inner-directed, the review panel is in their heads rather than in the world outside.

So even apparently non-conformist, highly-developed moral people conform in their fashion. This is not surprising since we are, above all, group animals who need to fit in with our fellow men without too many rough edges or differences. In fact, most people conform. Criminals, for instance, may appear to be professional non-conformers, but even they care deeply about how they are regarded by their fellow crooks and carefully tailor their public behaviour to fit in with what is expected of them by other criminals. Academics, another group of people who like to parade their idiosyncrasies and indifference to conformity, in fact care deeply about how they are evaluated by other academics, and stay close to the accepted standards of professional conduct.

Hogan and Busch concluded that the emphasis laid on the value of being a non-conformist by psychologists like Kohlberg stems from the fact that this is how most psychologists see themselves: 'When psychologists think that non-conformist is

219

best, this is just because tests show that most psychologists have a non-conformist, creative personality. Although it is comforting to think that people like ourselves are the best and most moral people in the world, such a conclusion is a little self-serving and not entirely credible.'

This might all seem pretty irrelevant and arcane, but it has had an important practical effect. The consequence of putting non-conformity on a pedestal and suggesting that people who observe society's rules and codes are somehow dull and limited is that top-quality morality has come to be seen as a private and personal affair, an individual choice that you make with no reference to others. This undermines the social ties that link us with other people and the need for each individual to consider the well-being of the wider community we live within. If everyone was truly marching to a different tune, there would be much chaos and casual cruelty.

A word from the wise
Since the idea that individualism is king and we should all be independent moral agents has been the height of fashion for the past few decades, the idea of transmitting moral values by telling youngsters about them has also been scorned. For thousands of years people took it for granted that each generation had a moral heritage to pass on to the next generation and felt they would show a lack of virtue if they failed to do so. It is time we took steps to hand on the best of our own moral legacy by telling young people what we value.

Of course adolescents will add to and alter the values we try to pass on to them – that is understandable – but at least if they start with this foundation, something to work from, they will not be adrift on a sea of relativism. You are dodging your responsibility as a parent if you don't stand for anything, never express a position on the great moral issues of the day, fail to react to the moral events in your immediate environment and generally do not talk or act as if morality really matters to you.

This sort of talk is sneered at by some people involved in

moral education, who dismiss it as 'moralising' and say it is no longer valid, does not respect the child as a thinker and won't work anyway. However, Kohlberg, for one, changed his views after working with adolescents in his experiment in the Bronx, where he attempted to run a high school on the principles of a Just Community in which everyone, staff and students, discussed all the issues and talked them through. Though the process proved a success in the long run, the problem he discovered was that the students naturally took years to move on to the next moral stage while in the meantime, stealing from lockers, vandalism and violence were rife in the classrooms every day and had to be stopped right away. So the staff had to start vigorously advocating the need for trust and honesty in the community while they waited for the youngsters to work out the truth of what they were urging for themselves. Telling young people what is acceptable and what is not is sometimes very necessary.

A model to copy
Talking to youngsters about what you value is important but, as we have seen, they are even more strongly influenced by what they see people do. When researchers ask parents and teachers: 'How did your parents influence your moral development?' far and away the most common answer refers to the example a parent set and the effects linger on long after the child has grown up.

D.L. Rosenhan, for instance, studied young civil rights workers who had joined in the marches for de-segregation in the southern states of America in the 1960s, often at considerable personal risk of beatings, arrests and even lynching, for a year or longer. He found that these fully-committed students typically looked up to their parents as people who lived by their moral ideas. Other students, who disliked their parents, remembering them as preaching one thing and practising another, were only partly-committed: they took part in one or two low-risk freedom rides but their commitment was more talk than action.

221

The research shows that the child is influenced not only by how his parent behaves towards him, but by the example the parents provide in their interactions with other people. A survey of 'rescuers' – people who had risked their lives to save Jews from the Nazis during the Second World War – found that they consistently remembered their parents as strong, good people who both preached and practised morality. One man involved in the rescue of over 200 Jews over a four-year period explained: 'You inherit something from the parents, from the grandparents. My mother said to me when we were small, and even when we were bigger, "Regardless of what you do with your life, be honest. When it comes to the day you have to make a decision, make the right one. It could be a hard one. But even the hard ones should be the right ones." '

We create many problems for young men and women just entering society if the culture they see around them sets an example of selfishness and immorality. Fifty years ago Alfred Adler pointed out the dangers of a society that had become corrupt: 'Businessmen have little concern for the welfare of competitors or much interest in social feeling. Some business practices are actually based on the principle that the advantage of one businessman can result only from the disadvantage of another. Everyday business practices that express greed and lack social feeling poison society as a whole.'

It is a message that is as relevant today as it was for Adler: if we want to build a more moral society, we have to start by monitoring and improving our own adult behaviour. However, individual moral decisions are often made in the context of a group, which means that although an individual may have high moral standards, he can easily slip a level or two in the wrong environment.

One of the most notorious examples of this process was the massacre at My Lai during the Vietnam War, where individual American soldiers went into a Vietnamese village and murdered civilian women and children. The soldiers who committed the atrocity did not do so because, as individuals, their moral judgement was so immature that they could not work out that their behaviour was wrong. Nor did they do so because they were sick in some sense and unable to make a moral decision. They did something awful because they were part of a group and followed the rules of the group. Their decisions were dependent on a shared definition of the situation and what should be done about it. The moral atmosphere that prevailed in that place at that time was primitive and uncaring, but it was more powerful than their own individual moral characters.

If we want young people to behave well, we cannot expect them to manage it on their own, untouched by the world around them. We have to do our utmost to see that the environment we surround them with fosters their moral side by showing them that the community they live in puts a high value on caring and responsibility.

Lending a hand

We try to persuade youngsters to help and support others as part of the goal of building society and helping each member to thrive, but research shows that helping others also helps you, because it reduces your feelings of distress. For instance, people who helped a person having an epileptic fit were less upset afterwards than those who did not help.

When you feel distress for someone else's misery, it predisposes you to act and the action will relieve the distress you feel, while doing nothing will not – a lesson children learn with experience. If they don't try to help, they will either continue to feel distress for the person in trouble or else they will have to restructure the situation to justify their failure to act, usually by disparaging the victim or otherwise convincing themselves that the victim wants or deserves what he gets. So the more we can persuade youngsters to take action, the better their motivation will be.

However, human nature being what it is, the helping hand may be withdrawn if circumstances do not seem favourable. A group of Harvard undergraduates studying to enter the

Church were tested to see how they responded to sounds of distress and calls for help. The students were asked to sit an important exam. On the way to the exam hall the psychologist running the experiment arranged for them to come across a man lying on the ground, groaning and begging for help. It was timed so that some of the students risked being late for their exam when they came across the victim.

The psychologist had already assessed the students' current level of moral reasoning and, as might be expected, those with the most advanced level of moral reasoning, who were willing to take responsibility for their own and other's welfare, proved the ones most likely to help the victim – but they only did so if they had enough time and therefore would not meet with disapproval for being late for the exam. Those who were short of time, even if they had overriding moral principles when tested on abstract dilemmas, turned out not to be Good Samaritans in real life. Their ambition to get on with their work reduced their willingness to help: selfishness defeated altruism.

The study reveals once again the gap between what people say and what they do, and children must have been encouraged to help and taught how helping makes you feel good from the earliest days if they are to do the right thing when faced with tough choices.

Sinking and swimming together

As children turn into adults and start to think about their place in society, they see that morality is not just a question of 'How do I behave?' – a way of regulating one's own conduct – but includes the question, 'How should I behave to others?' – a way of regulating the relationships between individuals. Now they see that a person is good or bad according to how he behaves towards the community.

Professor Derek Wright, Emeritus Professor of Psychology at the University of Leicester, explains that the moral domain is founded upon some such principle as that all persons are of equal worth or value, and the notion of equal basic or natural rights. Professor Wright points out that you can only start to see the moral connection between yourself and others as you grow up: 'For small children the notion of lying always remains sort of stuck on, external, because telling the truth can only be understood when you are older, through experience. You must have felt a real desire to exchange your thoughts with other people in order to discover all the mess that a lie can involve.'

For any society to survive, there must be an area of shared values, and another area where everyone accepts that individual differences are not only allowed but are desirable. In time these values will change in emphasis and become blurred, and the line between shared public values and what are considered to be private ones is constantly being redrawn.

Two things have happened lately that have affected our attitudes to morality. First, respect for and obedience to institutionalised authority has faded. This was the inevitable result of a century that saw two world wars where the great majority of ordinary people were victims or witnesses of terrible experiences and lost confidence that their leaders knew what they were doing and could be safely followed. The post-war generation, especially the post-Holocaust generation, felt it had to start making its own decisions about what was right and wrong and not rely on the admonitions of the old authorities.

Second, alongside the increased emphasis on the right of the individual to make his own decisions, has come a weakened sense of our accountability to the community, of everyone being in the same boat. While personal freedom is wonderful when it allows the individual to develop their potential and reach out to new horizons unfettered by unnecessary or damaging restrictions, it is destructive when it leads to a neglect of others, a selfish concentration on the self above all things, and a failure to build and support the community within which we have to live.

So we must foster in adolescents the sort of moral growth that looks beyond the stage of concern for their own rights, and their loyalty to particular people and groups, and encourage them to feel a bond to society at large. It's as well to remember at this point that it isn't just shared interests that bring people together into groups and clubs: adversity bonds people too. You have only to reflect on the close relationships that developed between people who have survived a hostage situation, or a body of workers made redundant at the same time, to see how suffering together creates very strong ties between people.

This is relevant to the way we treat teenagers. We must give them a sense of belonging or we have no sanction of rejection. They do want to feel they belong somewhere and will happily accept the codes of their own clubs and gangs, but if adult society flinches away from them and leaves them to their own company, they will bond only with their peers. If we treat them like outcasts, they will forge strong links with their fellow outcasts.

To build society, we must help young people to see that beyond their immediate circle of friends they belong to a wider community which will also accept them if they obey the rules. It isn't too difficult. The vast majority of teenagers are idealistic and caring: the fact that over half of all the voluntary work done in this country is carried out by young people under twenty-five proves it. The core of morality is respect for the rights, dignity and worth of yourself and others. We just have to help teenagers to see that beyond the friends they care about there are strangers who are not too different from themselves and who deserve to be respected as well.

Just obeying orders

Growing up also means you have to start taking responsibility for your actions. A child can get away with shrugging off or transferring the responsibility for his behaviour to some other authority: teacher told me to do it. An adult has to take responsibility for his own decisions – to 'own' them in the current jargon.

The struggle between deferring to authority and taking

responsibility can be seen in action in the famous Milgram experiment. In this, individual undergraduates were asked if they would help out with a psychological experiment. They were to sit behind a one-way glass observing someone chosen as a guinea pig carrying out a series of tests. If he failed, they were told to administer an electric shock. What happened was that the guinea pig kept on making mistakes and the students were asked to increase the level of shock each time, even though the guinea pig cried out in pain (in fact he was an actor pretending to be hurt and no shock was actually being administered). If the undergraduate was distressed and protested that he didn't want to administer any more shocks to the stooge victim, he was told it was not his responsibility: the experimenter was in charge and knew what he was doing and the subject should let him control the situation.

What emerged from the experiment is that people at a less mature level of moral development, who tended to conform to the expectations of a higher authority, would carry on with the experiment and were at risk of committing gross crimes against a stranger. However, those with greater moral sophistication had such a strong sense of their own personal responsibility for their actions that they quit the experiment rather than continue, regardless of what the authority figure said.

This is the stage that older teenagers are working towards, where they will make independent moral decisions, not swayed by the old authorities of parents or teachers but based on their own sense of responsibility for other people's welfare. Conforming to the rules is a good basis for the growth of decent behaviour, but not the whole of it. When hard decisions have to be made, when you are being asked to do something that makes you feel uneasy, it is time to think the dilemma through for yourself and accept the responsibility for your actions.

'I blame the victim'
Here is a problem that John Gibbs, Professor of Psychology at Ohio State University, uses in his work with juvenile

offenders which gives an insight into how they try to duck out of taking responsibility. Professor Gibbs tells them the story of Gary, who is in the kitchen of his apartment. Gary's girlfriend is angry at him for something he did to hurt her. She yells at him. She pushes him in the shoulder. Gary becomes furious and swears at her. A sharp kitchen knife is nearby. Gary picks it up and stabs her, wounding her seriously.

First of all Professor Gibbs asks the young delinquents to put themselves in Gary's shoes and describe the thoughts they think might have been running through his head. Among the most popular answers they propose are things like: 'Who does she think she is?', 'Nobody hits *me*', 'I wear the pants around here, I do what I want' and 'How dare she touch me!'

Thoughts like this are self-centred and Gary (and the youngsters who think like him) is thinking in a self-centred fashion. He shows no understanding of his girlfriend's point of view. He gets angry because he takes only one perspective: his own. He is entitled to do whatever he wants. If he wants to come home drunk and throw the furniture around, or beat his girlfriend, he's entitled to. He doesn't consider how he would feel if he were treated the way he has treated her, so it doesn't occur to him that she has a right to be angry.

Nor is he fair: in so far as he thinks of his girlfriend at all, he thinks she has no right to object to anything he has done. Gary comes first, and what is 'unfair' is any attempt by his girlfriend to object to, protest against or interfere with anything he has done or wants to do. His self-centred thinking means that not only is he unfair to her, he doesn't empathise with her suffering and hurt, even though he caused it.

Gary's self-centredness resembles that of a small child and, in fact, he is immature, or developmentally delayed. He isn't trying to correct his self-centredness, in fact he may be rather content with it. His bias towards himself makes him think that, 'because I want to do it, that means I am entitled to' or 'because I desire something, that makes it mine'.

Gary's moral judgement (and that of youngsters like him)

is equally immature: he thinks might makes right, especially that his might makes him right. He's stuck at the level which misinterprets the Golden Rule as 'Do unto others if they've done for you lately' or 'Do unto others if you figure they'll do for you later' – or, in the spirit of some juvenile delinquents, 'Do unto others *before* they do it to you'.

A youngster like Gary needs to be challenged so his moral judgement can catch up to a more mature level. Part of moral education is to provide developmentally-delayed individuals like him with opportunities, for example in group discussion, to take the perspective of others. Most delinquents like Gary have been at the receiving end of harsh and arbitrary discipline: 'Don't ever let me catch you doing that again, or you won't be able to sit down for a week!' So the child's attention is directed to the threatening, rejecting parent and not the behaviour that prompted the outburst and this is more likely to stimulate the emotions of fear and anger than empathy.

Yet even youngsters brought up in an atmosphere of coercion and physical abuse will feel a little potential empathy for the people they hurt, which is uncomfortable for them. So you can see them trying to rationalise away that empathy so they don't have to feel bad about themselves or what they've done. When Professor Gibbs asks young delinquents what went through Gary's head when he attacked his girlfriend, they suggest that Gary didn't think stabbing her was so bad: maybe this way she 'learned a lesson' she needed to learn so that she would 'know her place' in the future.

One youngster, who stole a lady's handbag as it dangled from the supermarket trolley, told Gibbs he remembered thinking, 'I bet she won't do *that* again.' In his mind he didn't harm her, in fact he provided an educational service to her, which in the long run was beneficial to her. This rationalisation is called minimisation and mislabelling. By minimising the harm done, and mislabelling it as 'help', the young thief can neutralise or pre-empt any incipient feelings of empathy or guilt.

Another common answer is something like, 'It's her fault she got stabbed, she was asking for it.' Along this same line is the comment that if she were a better housekeeper, she would have seen to it that the kitchen knife got put away and then Gary couldn't have grabbed it! These delinquents are busy wrongly attributing their own blameworthiness to others.

It's pretty easy to see that putting the responsibility on to other people is a good strategy for suppressing or neutralising empathy. Just as you don't have to feel bad if you haven't really hurt somebody, you also don't have to feel bad if it's their own fault they got hurt. You can see this at work in the report of a seventeen-year-old concerning his recent break-ins: 'If I started feeling bad, I'd say to myself: "Tough luck on him. He should have had his house locked better and the alarm on." ' He's saying, in effect: 'Upon experiencing empathy-based guilt for causing innocent people to suffer, I would neutralise my empathy by blaming the suffering on the victim.'

Dumping the responsibility for your bad behaviour on to someone else is a childish level of behaviour and not something we should allow young people to get away with. It's easy for them to talk in euphemisms about 'liberating' something from a department store, as if someone had wickedly imprisoned a pile of innocent goods, but we should not be squeamish about calling it stealing or shoplifting. It no doubt makes them feel better to say the State is oppressing them when it tows their buses off someone's field during a rave, or refuses to pay out endless benefits, but the truth is that it is often the people who cry victim who are oppressing the citizens who make up the State by their self-centred behaviour. Being decent means accepting responsibility.

Four steps to a moral decision
Trying to make the right moral decision can seem a pretty daunting task, but Professor John Wilson of Oxford argues that making moral decisions involves skills which people can easily acquire, such as the ability to translate one's principle into action, to have insight into other people's feelings and to identify with others in such a way that their interests count as equal to one's own.

230

Professor Wilson believes youngsters should be taught these skills in school: 'I think that teaching morality is analogous to teaching Science or History, where you try to make the pupils into embryonic scientists or historians. For instance, in Maths we don't just give them the right answers on a plate but make them work them out for themselves. You show them how to operate in that department, how to evaluate the facts and reach conclusions. The whole weight would be on showing them not what to think but how to think.

'I actually had a kid who said, "They teach you how to do Maths and History here, but they don't show you how to make up your mind about morals. I would like to be educated in how to think." '

Professor Wilson identifies four components that are involved in coming to a moral decision. First, he says, you need to think about the person and have feelings or a sense of duty which supports action that is orientated towards them. Second, you need empathy, the ability to put a name to the emotions you feel and to identify these emotions in other people. Third, you need to know the hard facts relevant to the moral decision you are about to make, facts relating to health, safety, the law and social conventions, for instance, and facts about individuals or groups in need: the existence of old people, starving people, the handicapped and so on. The fourth skill is the ability to bring all the previous components to bear, thinking things through, making an overriding, prescriptive and universalised decision to act in the other's interests, and being sufficiently wholehearted to carry out the decision in practice.

This is an important move away from the sloppy view that morality is a sort of gut reaction to circumstances where you can always trust your first instincts. Moral decisions need thought and reflection. Morality is about making choices when moral rules conflict, feeling sympathy for others and wanting to do what is best for the community. You can ask your children to obey you when they are little, but when they are about to leave the nest, you have to encourage them to reason things through. As moral philosopher Mary Midgley says, 'Thought helps.'

Sex and drugs and rock and roll

One of the most important areas for emerging adults to apply their brain power is in the fraught arena of sex and drugs. It is hard, if not impossible, to influence young people's sexual behaviour directly. First, because the sexual drive is so very powerful they have to cope with it themselves; secondly, because they are listening to their friends and thinking they know best; and third, because most parents find talking to their grown up children about sex intrusive and embarrassing.

If ever there was a case where the brain should be engaged in decision-making as well as other parts of the anatomy, it is in sexual matters and the best thing you can do is to encourage your children to keep up that internal dialogue that helps them to think through a situation clearly.

You cannot lay down the law about what they should do or not do, or when. It is too late for that sort of approach because, rightly or wrongly, they won't listen. That doesn't mean you wash your hands of their behaviour. What you have to do is suggest the sort of dialogues they should be having with themselves such as, Could anyone else be hurt by my behaviour? If so, how does this make me feel? Would I want someone else to behave to me in this fashion? What is the point of waiting till I'm older to have sex? What are the advantages likely to be? Are there any disadvantages? Am I mature enough to cope with the emotional repercussions of sex – which can range unpredictably from passionate love at one end of the spectrum to a desperate feeling of loneliness at the other? What if the result was a pregnancy – could I cope with looking after a baby? If not, what should I do? Whose responsibility is it? Mine? His or hers? Who is going to care for the baby – me, the family, the State? Why? Why should they?

Getting your almost-adult children to think about these issues will help to balance the mass of information they have been inundated with from the media of the how-to physical aspect of sex. You will probably notice a difference in the attitude of your sons and your daughters. A sex education teacher says that when she asked a class to write down the words that first sprang to mind about sex, all the boys' words were about doing – screw, shag, pull and so on – while the girls' words described feelings – warm, love, cherish and the like. It shows the gulf between the sexes and the way that misunderstandings can so easily arise as each interprets the other's reactions in line with their own instincts. If you can explain to your sons that girls tend to have an emotional attitude to sex as well as a physical one, which has to be allowed for, and make your daughters understand that however romantic young men are, there is usually a physical undertone to their intentions too, you will help them both to think a little more clearly and sensibly.

The detail of young people's sexual behaviour is a matter for the people most concerned to resolve. You may not mind a teenage child bringing their boyfriend or girlfriend home for the night, or you may feel uncomfortable about it. Whichever it is, say so. If there are younger children in the house, their reactions and feelings must be taken into account too. My own instinct is if someone is old enough to have sex, they should be old enough to provide their own accommodation in which to pursue it – but you may just call me old-fashioned.

Drugs are a more serious – because more damaging – problem: we all get hurt in love at some point, but for most of us the good outweighs the bad and the game is worth the candle. Drugs can destroy a life as well as seeming to enrich it, and need a great deal of thought.

We have to start by accepting that today's youngsters are all exposed to drugs in a way that was unimaginable a few decades ago. They have friends who take drugs, enjoy them and appear to suffer no ill effects. They are offered drugs regularly, not occasionally, and they know a lot about them. They may believe that some drugs should be legalised and that society is hypocritical in banning 'their' drugs while

233

allowing dangerously addictive drugs like nicotine to be freely available. They may be right.

Again, just lecturing on the dangers of drugs doesn't work as any decent parent of a drug-addicted child has been forced to realise. Children don't turn to drugs because their parents forgot to tell them not to. Most have had an anti-drug message repeated at very regular intervals, they just haven't accepted it. What you can do is get them to think through the facts. The first fact is that drugs are still illegal and whatever they think about the rights and wrongs of that, they are breaking the law. So they should be asking themselves, is it all right to break the law? How would I feel if I was caught? Would it be right for society to punish me as a law-breaker?

One of the most thoughtful moral comments on the right of the individual to break a law he sees as unjust was made by Dr Martin Luther King in 1965 in his 'Letter from a Birmingham Jail'. Asked how he, a Christian minister, could advocate breaking the law he replied, 'One has not only a legal but a moral responsibility to obey just laws. One has a moral responsibility to disobey unjust laws, though one must do so openly, lovingly and with a willingness to accept the penalty . . . A law that uplifts human personality is just; one which degrades human personality is unjust.' It is good for young people contemplating taking drugs to ask themselves, does the law forbidding me to do this actually degrade human personality? And if I were caught, would I accept my sentence 'openly, lovingly and with a willingness to accept the penalty'? Or would I whinge? If so, why?

Many young people believe that drugs, or some drugs, should be legalised and, again, you can help them to clarify their thoughts with questions. Does this mean drugs could be sold in shops and advertised? Could they be sold to youngsters, like alcopops? If not, why not? Misuse of legal drugs like tobacco and alcohol already leads to a huge amount of ill health, and alcoholism fuels most domestic violence and public aggression. If legalising other drugs had similar consequences, would this be acceptable? Since drugs can be abused, if they become legal should the non-drug takers have to pay for the hospital bills the drug takers run up in rehabilitation? Or should drug takers have to take out insurance, like car insurance, to cover themselves against any damaging effects? Or should drugs be taxed to pay for it? Is it right for the government to take money from an addictive substance? If it turned out in twenty years time that their drug of choice was life-threatening, as tobacco turned out to be, would they blame the manufacturers or themselves?

You can also encourage young people to think clearly about just what it is that drugs offer. Is it really a special experience, or is it just a chemical change in the brain that makes them feel they're having an experience? Is the food or the wine or the sex or the film really more magical when you have taken a drug, or is the food, wine, sex and film just as it always was and you just think there's been an improvement? Would it be better to go out into the world and really do something amazing than to sit around feeling you're doing something amazing? Is it better to work at caring and loving people because that's an integral part of the person you are, or to take a tablet that makes you feel soppy about everyone and anyone for a few hours and then wears off?

Finding room for compassion

Young people's morality, as we have seen, is very strong – they see absolutely no problem in saving the whale and abolishing landmines – but it can also be very fierce and uncompromising, a matter of black and white. The final task for parents is to draw on their own experience to point out that life will almost never be simple and uncomplicated. There may be some easy moral decisions – whether to return the wallet you find on the pavement, for instance – but most moral issues are not black and white. They are grey, blurry and confused. A woman's right to abortion conflicts horribly with the child's right to life. An Orangeman's right to march peacefully in a free country conflicts with his Nationalist neighbour's feeling that such an action is an affront. Whichever side you stand on seems to be wholly in the right.

So, it is important, before your children leave home, to help them understand that morality also involves mercy and forgiveness. Justice is the necessary cornerstone of a just society: the belief that everyone should be rewarded equally according to their desserts and punished even-handedly according to their sins, regardless of wealth, position, looks, sex, nationality or any other attribute, is at the core of our beliefs.

However, although justice is crucial, it isn't always enough. Whether we side with Portia pleading for mercy for her client rather than the cold justice of Shylock's knife, or with a pressure group pleading with the government to provide the poor with not just enough to keep body and soul on the breadline, but a little more, we are asking for the little extra that makes us human. We may call it compassion or generosity, but we all have a yearning to be granted more than merely our just desserts, and we admire the person who is generous and condemn the one who is mean – for meanness is always seen as a sin, not as a virtue. We should also help our fierce young adults to see that people are seldom perfect, that situations are mostly very complicated, and that moral decisions involve taking all these different facts into account, reflecting on the various possibilities and implications, and making a thoughtful and generous decision.

What you want to do is encourage them to soften up, think it through, pause for thought, hold back from rushing to judgement and, when they are making any moral decision, to temper reason with imagination, compassion and human kindness. After all, the first people they are going to judge in their new-found independent moral status is their parents.

Interlude
Black sheep

If your instinct when you see children going wrong is to think, *I blame the parents*, the black sheep poses a problem. How is it that some parents have clearly done a splendid job with some of their children yet have one child who is a torment? How can the same parents produce both Richard the Lionheart and Bad King John? Why was it that hard-working, focused men like Presidents Jimmy Carter or Mikhail Gorbachev had a ne'er do well brother hovering in the background to embarrass them? Can the parents who raised a president also be held responsible for the drunk?

Dr David Weeks, a clinical psychologist in Edinburgh, contacted over a hundred people who said they were the black sheep of their family to see what might have caused them to turn out that way. The first surprising discovery was the speed at which the black sheep had been identified. Parents, it seems, do not wait for the adult conman to emerge, or even the teenage layabout, before deciding that one member of the family is an outcast. Over half the black sheep already felt ostracised by their families by the time they were eleven; three-quarters by their teens.

Nor were they mostly men. Dr Weeks found that women were just as likely as men to feel they had been cast out, and none of them took the label as a joke or a compliment. 'They felt very embarrassed and felt the stigma had endured and extended outside the parental home,' reports Dr Weeks.

'One thing they had in common was feeling, when they were children, that the family was stricter and harsher with them than with their brothers and sisters. Most of them had been bullied and intimidated at home and over half were chronically and severely punished, if not abused,' says Dr Weeks.

The headmaster's son

Duncan, for instance, was the youngest son of a Scottish headmaster. While his three elder brothers went to university and into professions, Duncan left home at seventeen to become a farm labourer. 'I felt different from about the age of nine,' Duncan says. 'That was when my mother died and I was accused of causing it. When I was born she had massive haemorrhaging and was left in ill health and my father and brothers would say, "If you hadn't been born she wouldn't have died." '

Duncan was forbidden to go to her funeral and found he was being treated differently in all kinds of ways. For instance, after his mother's death, various domestic duties were divided out: one week one of the boys would have to wash the dishes, one week go to the local farm to get the milk, but if Duncan's brothers didn't want to do their bit they would tell him to do it. If he protested they would threaten to tell their father that Duncan had broken something. 'And he would believe them, oh yes.'

Duncan also found that he was treated more strictly by his father, who was a powerful figure. 'My father was the headmaster, the local minister and my father. He was very influential.' He was a lay preacher, so there was no reading papers or watching television on Sunday. The brother next to Duncan was allowed to go out on a Saturday night and get blind drunk and get up to all kinds of mischief, but would not have to go to Church, whereas Duncan was made to go three times on a Sunday.

'There's load of stories about what my brother used to get up to and basically a blind eye was turned. But there was one occasion, when I was about eleven, when I and four others broke a window. And I got thirty-six of the good old Scottish tawse on the bare backside. And then next morning I got another twelve in front of the entire school; the other boys got three or four.'

At seventeen, when his father expected him to try for university like his brothers, Duncan left home and spent five years labouring and doing odd jobs. Then he married a nurse who encouraged him to study and he became a psychiatric nurse, and then an author and lecturer. The misery did not stop, however, even after these achievements, and when, years later, the two middle brothers were still accusing him of his mother's death, he finally told his eldest brother over a bottle of whisky how sorry he was for all the trouble he had caused everybody.

'He was flabbergasted. He'd been away at university and didn't know what they'd been saying. And he told me that between myself and the brother above me my mother had had three or four miscarriages; she wanted a girl you see. He said, "It's nothing to do with you. It's as much father's fault as anybody's." '

Duncan is still struggling to overcome the feelings of worthlessness he was brainwashed with in his childhood. He has been through heavy drinking bouts and depressive suicidal attempts. Even with all his present insight and understanding, he explains that he cannot wipe out thirty years of being made to feel guilty and rejected. He can't make life happy at a stroke.

The girl no one wanted

André, however, is repairing her life after being thrown out by her family. A New Zealander, she was one of five children whose mother died of a brain haemorrhage one night when André was thirteen. 'I went a bit off the rails because my father then discovered he had a brain tumour and was given six months to live.' After her father's death André was sent off to live with one of her father's brothers, who seemed to take an instinctive dislike to her and his attitude was shared by his mother. 'All us children would go and visit my grandmother and she just didn't like me at all. She'd talk to everybody else but not to me, she would look right through me. When a family that is really strong ousts you, you really are cast off on your own.

'I tried to commit suicide and ended up in hospital and uncle said, "She's a dead loss this girl," to the social welfare, and the State Department just took me away from hospital one day and put me in a remand home. From there I went into various foster homes and back out again. My uncle always used to say I'd fail.

'The children at school totally cut me off because I lived in foster homes or remand homes. None of the so-called "nice" girls wanted to know me at all. I had one friend but they threatened not to talk to her unless she stopped talking to me so I was effectively cut off. And living in a remand home outside school, I went from bad to worse, but then those are the people who accept you. I had a baby at sixteen.'

At twenty André inherited some money and set off for the Far East and the hippie life, but eventually she arrived in Britain, settled down, went to university as a mature student and now has a successful career as a graphic designer.

'Here I've slowly become used to society, but for a long time I found it very difficult. I had terrible social skills, because I had never been invited into a group before and feared rejection. It took me many years to stop every time I thought of this uncle because I felt the most incredible bitterness, it was a real body reaction, the sort of anger you get. He was so mean and cruel and said terrible things that really turned a lot of people against me.

'For a while I wanted to go back to New Zealand and say, "Look what I've done, aren't I successful?" But now I think that if you can rise above the group, it makes you a better person.'

Picking on one child

It is hard for most of us to understand the cruelty of adults who can behave to a child the way Duncan and André were treated, but in fact they are following a very common pattern. Over and over again it is clear that it is not the behaviour of the black sheep that causes them to be cast out, but rather it is the act of being ostracised by the family that turns a child into a tearaway. They are singled out by the families for criticism and rejection from an early age and the experience turns them sour.

Why do parents or guardians pick on one child this way? It is because all families suffer a certain amount of stress and conflict – some of it external and some of it the inevitable clash of different people living together day in, day out. It can't always be perfect. Most families handle the stresses in fairly normal ways – they shout, sulk and argue and then they make up, apologise, rub along and acknowledge that the good things about family life far outnumber the bad.

However, some families handle it differently. 'They allow themselves, unconsciously, to distance themselves from anxiety, threat and conflict by displacing it on to one individual,' explains Dr Weeks. 'He or she is then held responsible for all the family's problems.' It is so easy for the parent to say, 'If only John wasn't such a nuisance, or Joan such a trial, we'd have no problems.' This makes life more comfortable for the rest of the family, who escape the tension, but it is rough on the scapegoat. So how does one particular child come to be chosen for this role?

Why one child is rejected
Emilia Dowling, a consultant psychologist in the children and family department of the Tavistock Clinic in London says there are many reasons why one child is singled out for disapproval, but the process isn't always rational. 'The parent may explain it by saying that "He looks different" or "She is more difficult" than the rest, but there are also unconscious reasons why this badness or difference is located in one child.'

She says it can happen because possibly the child looks different – he or she might embody ethnic characteristics the family is trying to distance itself from, so the child's looks are an embarrassment. Sometimes the child is a disappointment to their parents because they wanted a boy and the child is a girl or vice versa, or the child may have been conceived as a replacement child after a bereavement and be cast out because it isn't the same as the child who died. Some parents have very particular beliefs and expectations about what personal qualities count and for them nothing else counts. For instance, some families believe that beauty is the most important thing, for other people it might be the capacity to get on and be popular; then if a particular child is plain, or withdrawn and shy, they are scapegoated.

The parents' rejection of the child also ruins that child's relationship with brothers and sisters. Often they are thrust into a kind of rivalry with another child and the one who is scapegoated is made to live up to the other one's standards: the favourite becomes a yardstick and if the black sheep isn't the same, physically or emotionally, they are labelled bad. Sadly, the other children in the family do not rally to the defence of the sibling under attack but are sucked into joining in the rejection. This is partly out of a natural sense of loyalty to the parents, and also because they want to side with the stronger camp: it won't make a child very popular to side with the scapegoat.

David Weeks found that being cast out by your family affects the victims deeply and for life. They suffer from overriding low esteem and are unable to think of themselves as lovable or worthwhile. Some become withdrawn children, expecting little from relationships because they anticipate being rejected. Other outcast children become demanding and attention seeking, which is unfortunate because it is unpopular both with other children and with adults and so results in even more rejection, which adds to the hurt. Some get into relationships as adults where they are victims of abuse because they think they are not worth very much.

So, although the popular image of the black sheep is of a carefree, selfish person concerned only with having a good time, the reality is sadder and lonelier. 'The proportion who are single and living alone is the highest I've ever encountered,'

reports Dr Weeks. More than half are single, another quarter
are divorced and only 20 per cent are married.

'I think they have great difficulties in forming attachments
because they are always expecting rejection,' he says. 'So they
have few children of their own. But the handful who do have
children tend to be very faithful and loyal to them and treat
them very well, almost as a way of undoing what they
suffered in childhood.'

Could it be you?

Could you, quite unwittingly of course, be in danger of
singling out one child for special treatment? If you have a
'problem' child, are you absolutely certain the problem lies in
the child and not in the way you treat him or her? Do you
ever feel a secret sense of satisfaction when this child does
something wrong, confirming your bad opinion of him or
her? Try Dr Weeks's questionnaire to see if you are raising a
black sheep without realising it.

Does your child:
- hold grudges for long periods?
- always seem to be the culprit when something is amiss?
- befriend other children with obvious problems?
- argue back seemingly unnecessarily?
- seem not to respect authority of any sort?
- complain about other children being treated more favour-
  ably?

Do you find:
- your child's bad behaviour especially wilful?
- you have much recourse to physical discipline?
- yourself baffled by changes in your child's personality?
- it difficult to reconcile your child's needs with the rest of
  the family's?

If you answer yes to six questions or more, you should think
about the stance you are taking with your child. Consider

243

your behaviour, talk to the child about what he or she wants, listen carefully to the replies, and strive not to diminish the child's self-respect. Try to start every morning afresh by pretending your child has just done something wonderful and treat them with praise and delight. It might sound phoney and it will certainly surprise the child, but it can trigger a wonderful change of atmosphere and bring your child back into the family fold.

Chapter Eight
Turning youngsters round

It is a sad but inevitable aspect of our imperfect world that some families will fail their children and these children will then become a menace to society, the juvenile delinquents who threaten our homes and peace of mind. However, it is important to keep the issue in proportion. While there is more robbery on the streets than in the past, and most of it is committed by young people, this is not so much because more children are turning to crime but because the minority who are delinquent are committing more and more crimes due to the failure or slowness of the judicial system to detect and deter them. Figures show that 67 per cent of juvenile crime is committed by only 5 per cent of offenders, so it is the few who are giving a bad image to the many. The majority of young law-breakers quit pretty fast as one experience of being caught is enough: according to John Harding, chief probation officer of the Inner London Probation Service, seven out of ten young offenders cautioned by the police do not get into trouble again.

What makes a delinquent?
The factors which indicate that a particular child is at risk of growing up to be an offender are sometimes visible from an early age and an experienced headteacher can often spot a delinquent in the making in a scruffy, inarticulate, neglected or belligerent small child starting primary school. The chief

245

risk factor is gender – boys are far more likely to offend than girls. The next risk factor is inadequate parenting which leads to aggressive and hyperactive behaviour in early childhood and then to truancy and expulsion from school as the child gets older. Finally, in the teenage years, the risk factors are peer group pressure to offend, unstable living conditions, lack of training and employment, and drug and alcohol abuse.

Professor Nick Emler, a social psychologist at Oxford who studies young offenders, says, 'You have to look at what's going on at home and at school. At home, what kind of regime are they subjected to? Do they have parents who make consistent demands, who make it clear what their standards are and are consistent about enforcing them and who praise them as well as criticise? And at school, how are they performing academically? Do they actually have anything to feel some sense of satisfaction about?'

Emler points out that a lot of children who end up in delinquency really don't have anything else in their lives they can take any satisfaction from, so delinquency becomes a way of demonstrating their abilities. It may seem perverse to want to be admired for being a nifty shoplifter, or being able to write graffiti in outrageous places, but there is a degree of risk and excitement involved and also a degree of achievement which will win approval from at least some other children.

It is hard for ordinary people to shake off the feeling that these young louts have chosen their intimidating way of life out of laziness, selfishness and greed, but reality does not support our instincts. The inescapable truth is that many young offenders have had miserable lives and never been loved or taught how to care. Many have not even had a home: a third of juvenile offenders have been in care. In other words, they were taken away from their families by us, the State, because we decided that their homes were intolerable and we could offer better, and then treated so poorly in our care that they ended up in court. It is not an achievement for us to be proud of.

The worst offenders have often had the worst start in life. A recent study, by Dr Gwyneth Boswell for the Prince's Trust of 200 juveniles sentenced to long-term detention for serious offences, found that almost three-quarters had suffered emotional, sexual, physical or organised abuse, and over half had been traumatised by the loss of someone dear to them. The factors which can lead a handful of children to commit the dreadful crime of homicide include physical and sexual abuse, traumatic loss, exposure to repetitive or extreme violence, parents who are mentally ill, parental rejection, drug abuse and sometimes their own mental illness.

A probation worker in Southwark, South London, working with teenagers explains: 'They look very arrogant and cocky, but they're not inside. I sometimes think, "He looks mean," but once you break through that bravado, inside is a little child. They have to put up this facade so as not to be picked on, to survive. The young men will tell you that when they go into a young offenders' institution, they more or less have to be the one attacking first, to be the one shouting loudest, putting on the most mean appearance. It's defensive. It gets results. They put on an armour to keep people off. Gangs of black youths look threatening, but when you come into this line of work you see they're little boys, they need cuddling and caring. They should be at home, not on the streets knocking people down, taking things.'

I'm bored, I'm bored

Another major risk for producing criminals and one that seems likely to increase is that too many youngsters have absolutely nothing to do. Gangs of young boys roaming the streets are almost begging to get into trouble, yet there are more of them about as schools have become quick to exclude or expel any pupils who are giving them hassle and threatening their exam ratings, while cash-strapped local authorities have fewer facilities where disturbed and potentially delinquent youngsters can be helped, and steered away from trouble.

A report from Sherbourne House Probation Centre in Southwark, London, in 1996 noted that many delinquents 'are youths excluded from school, or who have absented themselves because they are unlikely to be entered for exams. These youths are often not picked up by the education system. Those excluded are not immediately offered alternatives; those who truant remain on the school roll but are not pursued vigorously.' Black boys are particularly at risk in this respect since they are five times more likely to be excluded than white boys, and from as young as eight or nine. If you tell a child at eight that he is not worth educating, what future has that child got? At twelve they are on the streets in a gang and the life of crime begins.

Elisabeth Boyle, a London probation officer explains: 'With little to do and no money, groups of aimless youngsters are starting to form in inner city areas. These gangs provide an identity and purpose which is missing because of no school and poor parenting. In the gangs there is a hierarchy, with some of the older ones prepared to break the law to pick up what they want. And in this environment the younger, newer members are often required to commit robberies as an initiation into the gang. So you now get more first offenders involved in serious offences like robbery where in the past it might have been minor shoplifting. You have to wrap your children up a bit to stop them being drawn into these gangs.'

Keeping them out of trouble

So what keeps most young people safely on the straight and narrow? Professor David Smith of the department of criminology at Edinburgh University says the crucial thing is: 'The fear of incurring the disapproval of people who are important to you. Those with whom we have reciprocal relationships exert a powerful restraint.' These relationships with people whose approval we seek are usually formed in the family or the workplace, so a strong, supportive family will help to keep a child out of trouble in the first place, while a successful career at school followed by full-time employment is the second crucial support.

However, if the family breaks down for some reason, the consequences for the child can be serious. 'A typical case is a boy who at fourteen was doing well, had started college and got four GCSEs,' explains Elisabeth Boyle. 'Then his Nan died and he started selling drugs and became dependent on drugs himself: suddenly everything started to go wrong. There is something like a death in quite a few cases. I don't know if people realise how death affects children. Often it will be a grandparent, because that is frequently an important, sustaining relationship: they're often closer to their grandparents than their parents.'

Even if a youngster has started to wander, you can sometimes bring him back on to the right path by playing on his feelings for others. One probation officer reports: 'We use brothers and sisters a lot. We're forever challenging them on that, saying things like, "What example do you think you're setting your brother?" And that does hit home. Or in Parenting classes (because a lot of teenage offenders already have children of their own) we will say, "Do you want your child to go through what you went through?" and the answer's always "no". So we ask them how they are going to prevent it and then they really have to start thinking about that.'

Dealing with the disaffected

David Rowse runs a centre for disadvantaged and disaffected pupils called Values Education for Life at the University of Central England in Birmingham, which aims to turn around children who look as though they are headed straight for trouble. The children are at that difficult age from fourteen to eighteen. The majority are boys and most of them are finding it very difficult to make out in mainstream society for a variety of reasons. Some just don't fit comfortably into the routine at school – the 9 to 5 regime does not suit every child; a lot of them are on the edge of crime or into crime or drugs;

and there are quite a few who are homeless – all things which don't exactly make life easy.

The children come on courses in groups of ten: that's the maximum the centre can cope with, and they enjoy the individual attention and rate it very highly. The course lasts nearly a year and it is voluntary: any youngster has the option of going if they so choose.

One of the key features of the course is that, following Kohlberg's principles, there is a weekly group meeting where the youngsters themselves have some clout and are given a say in the things that are happening to them. 'We try to develop a sense of responsibility by allowing them to use it,' says Rowse, 'because I think morality is one of those things like art that you don't learn from a book. You learn by doing it and getting it wrong and getting it right.'

Each course starts with an induction period and after that the pupils sort out the rules for the group through the weekly meeting. Rowse finds that the youngsters usually come up with the same rules, which are punctuality, attendance, and respect for self and others and others' property which always figures highly. 'Then I plonk in a few rules like, "if you do the course you've got to do all of it and not pick and choose", otherwise they'd come some days and not others. If they don't want to come on the course, they don't have to, but if they do decide to come, they have to attend regularly. One of the things we've found interesting from working with these youngsters is that they like an environment which has a lot of order, with more mature people knocking around.'

Once the group has decided on the rules, they are asked to sort out a series of rewards and also of sanctions for anybody who does not conform to what the majority have decided on. It is worked out democratically, so if somebody is going to be excluded from the course because of bad behaviour, for example, then the youngsters themselves will have worked out what the procedure will be and the community group meeting will decide whether that pupil stays or goes. 'So it's their peer group that's making the most important decision,' says Rowse, 'and they realise the community at large has to be taken into account, that you have to fit in, or discuss things with them.'

The basic aim of the course is to try to get the pupils to start thinking in a moral way about themselves and their families and their communities and society, rather than disregarding them. 'We get them to look again at their values and do a reappraisal, so they're not still just carrying the values of somebody else, but thinking about what's really valuable to them.'

The centre also holds a weekly session where staff and pupils look together at issues that have arisen during the course of the week. 'One of the problems for many of the youngsters who come here is that they have no realisation that they can have some control over their lives, that in a democracy they can have some say in what goes on. They don't recognise the different degrees of freedom and they don't recognise the responsibility that freedom brings with it. They tend to hedge towards licence if they possibly can: don't we all? And at the community group meetings we keep bringing them back to the fact that things have consequences, that if we do this, it's likely to lead to that. So it's all about practical experience, taking the issues that arise while they're still fresh in people's minds and dealing with them. Sometimes successfully. If not, we come back the following week and have another go.'

Because so many problems can be traced back to the parents and the home life that they provided, it seems obvious that turning these troubled youngsters around can't all be left to their teachers. David Rowse has tried to involve parents in the work of the school by inviting them to take the course that is provided for the school's social advisers.

'We got one or two to come but unfortunately a high proportion of the youngsters who come along are homeless in the sense that they don't know who their parents are or they've been taken away from their parents into care, so that can pose problems. But where we can, we do try to get parents to join the course so they know what we're trying to do and how we're doing it. Then they can reinforce it, so we're all talking with one voice.'

Rowse's system of giving the youngsters a lot of responsibility for running their lives, listening to what they have to say, and showing them how to listen and take account of each other helps them to get a less hopeless and more positive view of themselves and their futures. 'I wouldn't pretend for one minute that we have a 100 per cent success rate because we don't,' says Rowse, 'but we do get them into jobs or further training at the end of the course, which means they've got a little bit of hope for the future, they're looking further than the ends of their noses.'

Youngsters in trouble

Children under fourteen who come into conflict with the police are dealt with by the Youth Justice Departments of their local authority. On the whole, staff find that young girls tend to get more involved with assault or stealing from an individual – you don't get many girls charged with burglary, which involves breaking into premises – but young boys cover the whole range of offences from burglary through to rape and murder. Anything adults do, they do.

The good news is that 70 per cent of the children dealt with by Youth Justice Departments grow out of crime by their twenties and settle down. In the meantime, the local authority has to deal with the problem. Jackie, a Youth Justice worker in Brent, North London, explains the challenge that faces them. 'Often a family will have had enough and say, "We don't want to deal with them any more." So a lot of our job is to try and keep them with their families because then they're more likely to grow out of whatever it is they've got into than if they were put into care. And we try to divert them from custody because, again, once they've been to prison they're more likely to keep going into prison.'

There is no single, clear-cut way of getting through to these young delinquents, she explains: 'You use different techniques.

I favour the behavioural approach whereby you just keep going over and over what they've done until it finally sinks in.' Her colleague, Josh, says: 'Lots of people use the profit and loss system. All young people tend to think that offending is quite profitable – you'll find someone saying, "I got £500, I'm in profit." So then we make them work out how much the offending behaviour actually cost and ask, "What is the profit?" A lot of young people have the impression that burglary is profitable, so you go through the cost to them in terms of their time in court, the family conflict, the involvement of social workers, time spent in custody and detention and so on. If they look at the time they might have to spend inside and add up the loss of earnings of, say, £100 a week if they had a job, they see it wasn't a practical approach after all.'

The hard nuts
Elisabeth Boyle works at the toughest end of the scale, in Sherbourne House Probation Centre in Southwark, London, run by the Inner London Probation Service. There she and her colleagues deal with young men aged sixteen to twenty who have either committed a very serious offence or are persistent offenders running the risk of going into custody. Their sentence is either a probation order or a supervision order and they go on a special ten-week course before they start on the supervision period. There are no courses for girls because very few young women offend in comparison to young men, though when young women do offend they tend to be dealt with more harshly by the courts. However, by their late teens, most female delinquents are growing out of crime and making a home for themselves and there are not enough to make a group worthwhile.

'We start with about twelve to sixteen, in a group,' explains Elisabeth Boyle, 'and they go through the whole course together so a group culture builds up and you can use peer pressure. At the beginning of the programme we'll do something like climbing – it's quite good activity to start with to get people to gel as a group and find status within the group.

Sometimes you'll get someone who is very extrovert or can be a bit of a bully and often he's the one who's frightened of climbing and that's quite good. And there's the trust element too, if you're on the end of someone else's rope.'

The core of the ten-week programme, however, is to get the delinquents to look at their offending behaviour. 'The first thing the young men have to do is to draw a picture of the offence that brought them here,' explains Elisabeth Boyle. 'They all have to do this, however good or bad they are at drawing. Once they've drawn their offence they have to talk about it in the group.' It may seem an odd way to start tackling young hoodlums, but it gives the staff a very good avenue into exploring their offences.

Elisabeth Boyle pulls out a board with a strip cartoon sketched on it and explains that this is the work of someone involved in a series of sophisticated burglaries. He had broken into an office block and stolen computer chips, which he put in a padded, stamped addressed envelope he carried with him and posted as soon as he got outside: clearly he was being briefed and used by an adult criminal. While he talked to the group about what he'd drawn, the probation officer prompted him, saying things like, 'What were you thinking then?' and 'What were you feeling then?' The young man replied that he was thinking: 'Skint, office – I could smell the office [the cleaners had just left and it smelled of disinfectant] – computers, great, money, money, money. But feeling nervous, a buzz, hide, then [when the red alarm lights go on] fear, regret, mother in tears, then [out of court] relief, home.'

Elisabeth Boyle says, 'I think it is very good, because he's standing in front of everyone else in the group saying "not scared there", but then they see that he actually was scared later because he knew he was going to be caught. Then he admits feeling bad when his mother is crying in court. Some of them will even say, "that hurt". Some will even admit to the fact that they cried when they were in the police cells.'

Another cartoon strip shows a boy and two friends robbing a shop. It starts with them wandering along with 'skint', 'broke' and 'want some crack' in bubbles over the three heads. Then they go to an off-licence near where they live, smash the window and go in. 'I'll get the booze', 'I'll get the fags', 'I'll get the scratch cards'. Then the policeman and his dog catch them, and finally they are shown in court.

'The thing about this sort of offence,' says Elisabeth Boyle, 'is the effect of peer pressure. You could say that if the three of them hadn't met up that night, or if all three hadn't been broke, or if one of them had gone out on his own, he's unlikely to have committed that sort of offence, because they don't do that on their own.'

Thinking about the victims

Once they have drawn the offence, the probation officer can start to draw their attention to the victim. 'You've got someone now. "Who was the person who was in that shop? Was it a woman? Was it an elderly person?" If they're here in the group they've got to say who that person is, and they have to tell the truth because we know what the offence was so there's no getting away from it. If they were inside in custody they're not going to say, "I hit a woman" – at least, not in the context of offending. You can say you've slapped your girl-friend, it's all right to say that, but they don't like to say that they've attacked a woman in the context of offending.'

The probation officer will insist on hearing the truth and force the young criminal to admit that he attacked the elderly woman running the off-licence – and that, suddenly, doesn't look very heroic. The probation officers also find that if the offence involved intimidation and bullying, the youths some-times draw themselves as the same height as the victim, but the probation officer can't be fooled since he or she knows the victim was, say, a twelve-year-old boy and the offender is eighteen, so they're told, 'No, that's wrong.'

'Again, if they're in custody they won't tell that to anyone,' explains Elisabeth Boyle. 'But here there's an element of shame, of having to face up to the reality of what they've done. There *is* a victim. And whether that victim was hurt or not, psychologically they were affected by it and it's important to get them to admit it: "This is what I did and I own it." But that's just what you can't do if you're committing offences, you can't think about the victim. As one young offender commented: "If I thought about the victims, I'd never do anything." And so we go through this procedure. And in some cases young offenders are made to confront the victims of their crimes and apologise and this can be enormously effective in bringing home to them the hurt and fright they have caused. But not all victims want or are able to handle this sort of confrontation, and some offenders are unable to apologise.'

At Southwark, they introduce them to victims by indirect means. 'We have a video of a woman talking who's been a victim of an armed robbery and they can't bear to watch that. They try to say it's her fault for working in a bank. What they can't stand is the fact that she's a woman, she's articulate and she's saying how she felt. It's quite interesting getting them to face up to it. We also have a video about racist attacks and we use that in a group with young white men. We've got one violent young man on the course at the moment and he can't watch the victims talking. He actually turns his chair away and looks out the window and we say, "No, look." And he can't. He can do it, but he can't confront it.'

Probation workers also get the offenders to sit down and write a letter to their victim. The victim is more easily identifiable if it's a burglary than a street mugging, nonetheless the offenders do try to avoid writing and say things like, 'Well I don't know whose house it was,' and 'They've got insurance anyway.' Then the probation officer will push them to think hard about the victim: 'What did the house look like? Who do you think lived there? Were there photographs of the people?' The aim is to personalise it all the time, because for the offender to say it doesn't matter because the people they stole from had insurance, or it was a company, is a cop-out.

Here for the first time they get an alternative view put forward and learn to see themselves and their behaviour in another and less flattering light. 'One of the probation officers here has been burgled three times and she says, "Why should I work with you, tell me why am I not thinking, lock them up and throw the key away?" It's good for them to hear that. And though they very often put up a barrier because it's too painful for them to look at, we know it has an impact. You might not see it straightaway, but we know that they change.'

Making connections
The group is also encouraged to think about how their lives have been affected by their offending and very often discover elements in their own lives where they have been victims. The probation officers encourage them to talk about their lives and to link things up so they can start to understand why they behave the way they do.

'We had one young black man who had been excluded and when his mother appealed, the school admitted there had been a racist element in his exclusion and apologised and took him back. But he couldn't fit in after that and felt very uncomfortable and his mother finally moved him to another school, but he never did as well there. He used to hang around a college near where he lived, go there every day though he wasn't attending the college. And his offence was robbing a young white man at the college of his mobile telephone. He beat him up quite badly. At least he was able to talk about it when he was here, and make the links and realise what he'd been doing. He was very open about saying that it was a horrible offence. Yet you could link it back.'

The evidence shows that young black men do better on the programme than white youths, a bizarre side-effect of the fact that there is a racist element to their arrests. Black youths are stopped more readily by the police than similar white youths, and sentenced by the courts after committing a lower level of offence. So they are seen by the probation service at the beginning of their career, after only a few offences, with the result that they respond better to going on the course and

many of them move on into further education or training.
White youths, who are not picked up so readily, are older and
harder and tougher to treat, so they have a lower success rate.
All of which reinforces the finding that the time to tackle a
young person's offending behaviour is as soon as it is noticed,
before it becomes so ingrained it is hard to eradicate.

Violent lives

You cannot change the young offender without addressing
the environment he grows up in. Some of the young men the
probation workers see come from violent estates where gang
fights and murders are commonplace, and it is difficult to get
them to show remorse for violence or to see anything wrong
with it because it's been bred into them almost from when
they were born. They have grown up in a violent environment: their families are violent and the estates on which they
live are violent.

'But we've seen changes in them over the ten weeks,' says
Elisabeth Boyle. 'There's one boy, what he did was to stamp
on somebody's head. It's upsetting to hear that someone's
been stabbed and they stamped on his head while he was on
the floor. That's the gang frenzy. But it's good that they're
here and being challenged about that. And they're not going
to be challenged anywhere else: if they were in prison they
would get status for that behaviour. They don't go away from
this course thinking it's the norm.'

Sometimes the home lives of the young offenders make a
descent into crime almost inevitable. The sessions on Parenting are very difficult, raising all sorts of questions in the
minds of these young troublemakers about the sort of parenting they had themselves.

'We get them to brainstorm first what sort of things parents
should do and that reveals a lot about how they've been
treated,' says another probation officer. 'You can't give what
you've never had. For instance, it came out that one young
man had been sexually abused. It was the first time he'd told
anyone. Another young man revealed that his father's in

prison for drug dealing. What does that say to the boy?'

She cites another case of the sort of accumulated misery some children face. 'His mother's partner is in custody for murder. The murder squad raided the house when he was there and I think that's had a very bad effect on him and a lot of his offences have happened since. And his mother has a drink problem, though he doesn't admit it. He also saw his father die of a heart attack – he lived with his father after his parents separated and he witnessed that. So we're talking of a young man who's had a lot of stress. And this is the only way they can cope. They get involved with a gang, have a gang identity and the gang brings out all this violence.'

However, if you try to replace the gang in a youngster's life with something more constructive, you have to think about what are you going to put in its place. A youngster who has committed offences has all the friends that he committed the offences with and he will not be weaned off their companion-ship unless their place is filled with something that absorbs his attention and fills up his time as the gang used to do.

Professor Nick Emler explains: 'The so-called adventure holidays have been a cheap target for politicians when they fail, but the same politicians seldom ask how often does this kind of approach work? It works rather well compared with the politician's favourite alternative, which is bang them up in an institution, which is an incredibly expensive disaster. A tough prison regime actually suits many of these characters because it allows them to show how hard they are. All prison does is produce fit, disciplined delinquents.'

Delinquents who are carers

Even young men from homes where there is no crime or violence in the background have often had to shoulder adult-sized responsibilities, which has confused their sense of values. Often the parent has a drink problem or a drug problem, or suffers from some disability and the youngster has to take responsibility because the parent is dependent on him and that stops him going into training or into employment. Or the parents are simply so overwhelmed with their own problems they haven't got time to give the child attention. Elisabeth Boyle quotes one young man on the programme who was playing truant at the age of fourteen and hanging around the King's Cross area collecting money for pimps, earning up to £40 a day.

'The mother's got younger children and the father had left them and he took on a lot of responsibility for the family. He said, "It's very hard to see your younger brother not have shoes on his feet."

'We point out that it's not his responsibility to provide that, but obviously he felt it was. But he's now seen that he can't help his family if he's in custody. And he's not helping his younger brother, not setting a very good role model, being in trouble with the law, the police coming to the house. He's setting that pattern for the younger ones and, looking back on it, he realises it wasn't right.'

What contributes enormously to the success of courses like this is that all the questioning and challenging takes place within the group. It is not a case of some know-all adult professional telling them what is what, to which they would pay no attention, but other youngsters like themselves, puzzling and arguing and offering their views, and that makes what they say much more powerful. 'It's using peer pressure in a positive way, whereas in gangs and in institutions it's used in a negative way.'

Control and respect

One of the proven techniques for turning around difficult young people is to treat them consistently and fairly. 'We have boundaries,' explains one of the Southwark probation workers, 'we give them care and control. You show that you care for them, you listen to them, but you don't let them walk all over you: we have sanctions if they're rude. Another big thing is respect. At the beginning of the programme we ask them what they want and the word that normally comes up is respect. So we say, we will respect you but you have to respect us, and this building. And if you give children a reason why they can't do something they'll usually accept it.'

David Rowse argues that: 'It's more important to be respected than to be liked. I think an awful lot of parents want to be liked by their children and therefore when they draw the line, they vacillate endlessly. I think it's more important to be respected, and that liking will come anyway as a result of that because every child values security and structure.'

From the viewpoint of people like Elisabeth Boyle who are charged by society with setting difficult young men back on the moral track, the characteristics they most wish the average parent would display include, 'Praise, respect, giving explanations for what you want. Set clear boundaries – be consistent. Avoid domestic violence: when parents argue in front of children, the conflict that causes affects the children. And love. You see these very needy young men and you just want to give them a hug. You can't, but they've missed out on that. You know that if someone along the way had given them a little cuddle they wouldn't be so angry, so aggressive.'

It is no part of the work of the probation service to tackle the family who have produced the delinquent, yet you can't help thinking that the child might have a much better chance of reform if its parents were sent on a parenting course. Professor Nick Emler says that: 'If you asked somebody in the psychology service rather than the prison service what to do about young offenders, they might be more likely to raise that as one of their preferred options. We are not born with parenting skills.'

Now the Home Office has floated the proposal that parents of delinquents might one day be obliged to attend courses. In some ways, parenting courses seem perfectly unexceptional. If we decide to learn to drive, or to take up golf or line-dancing, we normally sign up for a few lessons from a professional first. So before embarking on the infinitely more complicated activity of raising a child, why not take a few classes in parenting? There are excellent courses and workshops for parents who want a little help run by organisations such as Exploring Parenthood.

However, these courses succeed because they are chosen by the parents, they are not imposed and, rightly or wrongly, most of us flinch from the idea of being taught how to be a good mother or father by a stranger, no matter how professional they are. And should such classes be made compulsory for the parents of delinquents, other parents will feel even more sniffy about them. We prefer to pick up the ideas we need from the example set by our own parents, by talking things over with friends in the same boat, by watching other parents with their children in real life, in books and on television – and agreeing or disagreeing with what we see. We instinctively make a note of what seems right and sensible and reject what seems wrong.

In any case, there is no weekend course that will provide a quick fix of moral education: morality grows slowly and needs daily reinforcement and as parents we just have to keep on trying. We are never going to get it completely right and our children are always going to have minds of their own. As long as we get them thinking, and thinking kindly, we are more or less winning. Love is the first and most important quality required of parents and most parents do try hard to do the right thing by their children. After love comes discipline and with it the need for consistency and fairness, and later we have to be willing to offer reasons and explanations for what we propose. We have to watch what we are doing, for our children are watching us, and we have to be prepared to argue our case if we want them to accept it. If we can do this with a little imagination and some good humour, we'll succeed. After all, the children are on our side, they are not our enemies.

Schools also have an important role, but society at large must also face up to its responsibilities and make a contribution. Good children don't emerge easily from brutal and desolate environments. Moral principles are not fostered by a culture of selfishness. The close attention children need so that their learning can flourish is not possible if working practices force their parents out of their lives. Though families are in the front line, what we have to do as a society is give them our full support and stop pushing children to the margins. Raising a decent child is a job for all of us.

Bibliography

Adler, Alfred *What Life Should Mean to You*, George Allen & Unwin, 1980.

— *Understanding Human Nature*, Oneworld Publishers, Oxford, 1992.

Boyd, Dwight R. 'The Principle of Principles' in *Morality, Moral Behaviour and Moral Development* (ed. William M. Kurtines and Jacob L. Gewirtz), John Wiley & Sons, New York, 1984.

Burton, Roger 'A Paradox in Theories and Research in Moral Development' in *Morality, Moral Behaviour and Moral Development* (ed. William M. Kurtines and Jacob L. Gewirtz), John Wiley & Sons, New York, 1984.

Damon, William *Greater Expectations*, Free Press, 1995.

— 'Self-understanding and Moral Development from Childhood to Adolescence' in *Morality, Moral Behaviour and Moral Development* (ed. William M. Kurtines and Jacob L. Gewirtz), John Wiley & Sons, New York, 1984.

— with **Selman, Robert** 'The Necessity (but Insufficiency) of Social Perspective Taking for Conceptions of Justice at Three Early Levels' in *Moral Development – Current Theory and Research* (ed. David J. DePalma and Jeanne M. Foley of Loyola University of Chicago), Lawrence Erlbaum Associates, New Jersey, 1975.

Eisenberg, Nancy and Murphy, Bridget 'Parenting and Children's Moral Development' in *Handbook of Parenting*, vol 3, Lawrence Erlbaum Associates, New Jersey, 1995.

Erikson, Erik H. *Childhood and Society*, Penguin, 1965.

Gibbs, John C. 'Inductive Discipline's Contribution to Moral Motivation', paper presented at the meeting of the Society for Research in Child Development, New Orleans, 1993.

— 'Fairness and Empathy as the Foundation for Universal Moral Education', paper presented at the Symposium on Moral Development, Rijksuniversiteit Leiden, Netherlands, 1993.

Gilligan, Carol *In a Different Voice*, Harvard University Press, 1982.

Higgins, Ann, Power, Clark and Kohlberg, Lawrence 'The Relationship of Moral Atmosphere to Judgments of Responsibility' in *Morality, Moral Behaviour and Moral Development* (ed. William M. Kurtines and Jacob L. Gewirtz), John Wiley & Sons, New York, 1984.

Hoffman, Martin L. *Emotions, Cognition and Behaviour*, Cambridge University Press, 1984.

— 'Empathy, its Limitations and its Role in a Comprehensive Moral Theory' in *Morality, Moral Behaviour and Moral Development* (ed. William M. Kurtines and Jacob L. Gewirtz), John Wiley & Sons, New York, 1984.

— 'The Development of Altruistic Motivation' in *Moral Development – Current Theory and Research* (ed. David J. DePalma and Jeanne M. Foley of Loyola University of Chicago), Lawrence Erlbaum Associates, New Jersey, 1975.

— with **Busch, Catherine** 'Moral Action as Autointerpretation' in *Morality, Moral Behaviour and Moral Development* (ed. William M. Kurtines and Jacob L. Gewirtz), John Wiley & Sons, New York, 1984.

Kant, Immanuel *Metaphysics of Morals*, Cambridge University Press, 1992.

Keasey, Charles Blake 'Implicators of Cognitive Development for Moral Reasoning' in *Moral Development – Current Theory and Research* (ed. David J. DePalma and Jeanne M. Foley of Loyola University of Chicago), Lawrence Erlbaum Associates, New Jersey, 1975.

Keller, Monika 'Resolving Conflicts in Friendship: The Development of Moral Understanding in Everyday Life' in *Morality, Moral Behaviour and Moral Development*, (ed. William M. Kurtines and Jacob L. Gewirtz), John Wiley & Sons, New York, 1984.

Kohlberg, Lawrence *The Philosophy of Moral Development*, Harper & Row, New York, 1981.

— *Moral Stages: A Current Formulation and a Response to Critics*, Karger, 1983.

— *The Psychology of Moral Development*, Harper & Row, New York, 1984.

Krevans, Julia and Gibbs, John C. 'Parents' Use of Inductive Discipline: Relations to Children's Empathy and Prosocial Behaviour', Ohio State University, 1996.

Lickona, Thomas 'Parents as Moral Educators' in *Moral Education: Theory and Application* (ed. Marvin W. Berkowitz and Fritz Oser), Chapter 5, Lawrence Erlbaum Associates, New Jersey, 1985.

Liebert, Robert M. 'What Develops in Moral Development?' in *Morality, Moral Behaviour and Moral Development* (ed. William M. Kurtines and Jacob L. Gerwitz), John Wiley & Sons, New York, 1984.

Midgley, Mary *Wickedness: A Philosophical Essay*, Routledge & Kegan Paul, 1984.

Myron-Wilson, Rowan and Smith, Peter K. *Perceived Parental Style and Bullying*, Department of Psychology, Goldsmith's College, University of London, 1996.

Neill, A.S. *Summerhill*, Penguin, 1968.

Nicholson, John *Seven Ages*, Fontana, 1980.

Piaget, Jean *The Moral Judgment of the Child*, Routledge & Kegan Paul Ltd, 1932.

Plato *The Republic*, Cambridge University Press, 1966.

Pringle, Mia Kellmer *The Needs of Children*, Hutchinson, 1974.

Smith, Peter K. and Myron-Wilson, Rowan *Parenting and School Bullying*, Department of Psychology, Goldsmith's College, University of London, 1996.

Smith, Peter K., Sutton, Jon and Myron-Wilson, Rowan *Bullying: Perspectives from Social Cognition and Attachment Theory*, Department of Psychology, Goldsmith's College, University of London, 1996.

Staub, Erwin 'Steps Towards a Comprehensive Theory of Moral Conduct: Goal Orientation, Social Behaviour, Kindness, and Cruelty' in *Morality, Moral Behaviour and Moral Development* (ed. William M. Kurtines and Jacob L. Gewirtz), John Wiley & Sons, New York, 1984.

— 'To Rear a Prosocial Child' in *Moral Development – Current Theory and Research* (ed. David J. dePalma and Jeanne M. Foley of Loyola University of Chicago), Lawrence Erlbaum Associates, New Jersey, 1975.

Straughan, Roger *Can We Teach Children to be Good?* Open University Press, 1988.

Tizard, Barbara and Hughes, Martin *Young Children Learning: Talking and Thinking at Home and at School*, Fontana, 1984.

Turiel, Elliot 'The Development of Social Concepts: Mores, Customs and Conventions' in *Moral Development – Current Theory and Research* (ed. by David J. DePalma and Jeanne M. Foley of Loloya University of Chicago), Lawrence Erlbaum Associates, New Jersey, 1975.

Wilson, John *A New Introduction to Moral Education*, Cassell, 1990.

Winnicott, D.W. *The Child, the Family and the Outside World*, Pelican, 1964.

Wright, Derek *The Psychology of Moral Behaviour*, Penguin, 1971.

— *Fairness in the Classroom*, Values, 1986.

— 'Discipline: a Psychological Perspective' in *Progress and Problems in Moral Education* (ed. Monica Taylor), NFER Pub. Co., 1975.

Yapp, Nick *My Problem Child*, Penguin, 1991.

Index